*To Nathan and Mary-Phillip who encouraged me to tell
another story, to Keith for listening to a whisper and finding me,
and to Pam who lives her life with the courage of a
fierce warrior and the compassion of a saint.*

CONTENTS

Prologue   vii

Part One: 1941 – 1946   1
Early Katherine   3
Her Two Worlds   13
Meeting Murphy McGregor   17
Pixie Gifts   22
One War Ends   29
Murphy's Inheritance   34

Part Two: 1966 – 1975   37
Trouble at Beechwood   39
Fire   55
After   60
Romance   72
Party of Three   89
Beauty Shop   95
Doc and Baxter   102

Part Three: 1977 – 2014   107
Savannah   109
Leaving   125
Proposal   131
Journey   136
Sam   141
Murphy   151
Hollis' Secret   159
Delivery   163

Settle In	177
Baby Jesus	182
The Revealing	192
Do Unto Others	218
Katherine	223
Reading of the Will	225
Postlude	237
About the Author	239

PROLOGUE

None of them had any idea how their lives would be connected by the reading of the will. Having been summoned by her attorney, they gathered to hear what Katherine had bequeathed to each of them.

The walnut furniture and the paste wax had grown old together, permeating the room with a distinct aroma, inviting to the nostrils, stirring memories of the days when furniture was crafted from real wood and the polish required muscle to apply. The books added another layer to the smell. A good smell. One that beckoned you to lose yourself in their pages. But they were not there to read. They were there to listen, to absorb her wisdom one last time.

Waiting for him to enter, they shared in somber tones the details of their sorrow during the last few days since the burial. They saw it in each other's eyes. Her love was their anchor, their unifying bond.

Each one straightened a bit as he entered the room, carrying a large calendar atop a cumbersome stack of files. He paused in front of each of them, regarding them directly before extending a warm, strong handshake. He knew. He knew their pain and sorrow. He feared his own grief from losing her would reside permanently in a portion of his heart, but today he would fulfill one of the most important tasks of her life, and he was proud to be her messenger.

Arranging the folders at the end of the long table, he gave a nod of dismissal to the two young clerks. One exited through the north door and closed it securely while the other exited through the south door, leaving it slightly ajar. Not wide enough for one to enter or exit, but plenty wide enough for someone to sit clandestinely in the adjacent room and absorb all the words soon to be spoken.

"Within minutes, your lives are going to change, and I want us all to remember this time, this place, this collective group." Holding the calendar in midair for all to see, he used a felt tip pen to draw a thick red circle around the date, making sure they understood the enormity of the moment.

"Katherine specifically requested that you read your letter aloud, one by one. What you're going to find is each of these four letters is a sum part of a whole." And although it was something they already knew, he reminded them as he distributed the envelopes, "Katherine loved you very much, no doubt. She kept each of you in her heart as if you were her own."

Holding their envelopes gave each a sense that she was with them still. One raised the envelope to his nose to see if it smelled of her; one held it cockeyed to the light to see if she could decipher the contents; one held it in his lap and traced her handwriting with his finger; and one clutched it to his heart and closed his eyes.

Never taking his eyes off the assembled, the attorney magnified his voice and dropped a bombshell, "And if all goes as planned, we'll be joined by one other."

He then took a long sip of his iced tea and said, "I have been instructed to read Sam's letter aloud after he opens it, so I think it's time for us to begin." Realizing he might be rushing the man, which Katherine would have adamantly opposed, he corrected himself and said, "That is," nodding as he continued, "whenever you're ready, Sam."

And it was then that Sam clumsily and wordlessly ripped open his sealed envelope and handed it over to be read aloud.

PART ONE

1941 – 1946

Early Katherine

One morning mid-May in 1941, Martin Engstrom planted a goodbye kiss on his wife's forehead and playfully tugged his daughter Katherine's long blonde ponytail just as she was sitting down to a plate of scrambled eggs. He walked out the door headed to Burke, the next town just twelve miles east. And like the morning dew, he disappeared.

The sheriff's department launched an official search. Seems the entire town of Kingston banded together to find him and bring him home, wearing out the road between the two towns, and letting the hounds rip through the countryside. They did everything they knew to do.

Sheriff Sullivan stopped by the Engstrom's house about dusk each day to relay to Emeline the dismal absence of any fresh leads in her husband's case. Paunchy and disheveled, he walked with an arrogant swagger, giving people reason to think they'd elected the wrong man, but no one seemed to know how to go about correcting that kind of wrong.

Hesitant to invite him inside, Emeline always stood braced against the oak post on the front porch listening to the sheriff's obvious inadequacies. All the while, young Katherine stood soldier-still just on the other side of the door, eavesdropping on those ugly conversations between her mother and the lawman.

Almost two weeks into the investigation, Katherine listened as her mother courageously, but completely out of character, questioned him. "It's been twelve days now, and your men haven't found a single clue, so are we sure they're looking in the right place? It just seems maybe…" Emeline stopped abruptly when her eyes shifted from the floor up to Sheriff Sullivan's reddened face.

Katherine saw it too as she cocked her head around the corner. His anger was evident, looking as though he might detonate.

Ready to pounce, he used words meant to frighten as he tore into Katherine's mother, "How dare you try to tell me how to do my job? Don't you know my men have been workin' this case day and night since your husband *left* you?" His sour breath was hot on her face. Nothing was going to stop him now. "Martin would've been ashamed to know 'bout you talkin' to me like that. By God, you better get that stupid idea out of your head and don't even think about gettin' no state authorities comin' in here. Ain't nobody gonna tell me how to investigate *anything*. You hear me now?"

As Emeline back-stepped he stomped his muddy boots toward her until he had her pinned against the screen door. He raised his hand above her but then stopped suddenly when he saw movement out of the corner of his eye. Katherine had deliberately stepped onto the porch, and she fixed him with a fearless stare, which he was not expecting.

Bounding off the porch, he slammed the door to his patrol car with such force it's a wonder the window didn't crack and then left tire tracks on the tarred driveway all the way onto Central Avenue.

She was only seven, but Katherine's brain registered the fact that the sheriff had just referred to her father as if he were never going to return. *Would have been.* And if she heard it, she was sure her mother heard it, too.

It would be seven years prior to Katherine's own death when she'd learn the indisputable details. Her father's disappearance and then learning the truth surrounding that terrible event would serve as the bookends of her life story.

Nothing in Martin Engstrom's lifestyle predicted any type of trouble. He lived a simple life, a carpenter by trade, widely reputed to be the finest woodworking craftsman in the area. Meticulous and slow as a turtle, anyone who hired him knew they'd chosen wisely. His sense of design guaranteed him an extensive list of clients and job security but an ulcer at the same time. But now he was simply gone. Obliterated from existence but not from memory.

Katherine's mother had always been the quiet one of the three Engstroms, content to spend hours piddling around the house without much talk. When one of her dark moods crept in, Emeline did a poor job hiding her frustration with her daughter's steady stream of chatter. Frequently, she took her dinner plate on a metal tray and sat alone in the bedroom, exhausted from fighting the onslaught of depression. Her husband's and daughter's endless talking, talking, talking agitated her nerves. She resented the noise, knowing their conversations were as predictable as clockwork, beginning the second her husband walked through the door each evening and ending when Katherine finally closed her eyes each night.

But then, without warning, like the snap of a finger, like the clang of a bell, she would emerge from the darkness and then happily spend weeks at a time enjoying the presence and commotion of her family. No one understood it—Emeline least of all. And now she faced the cataclysm that her husband would probably never return, and she feared she did not have the strength to endure life without him.

Katherine's childhood ended abruptly as May turned into June. She and her mother traded places as Katherine became the caretaker when Emeline could simply no longer will herself out of bed. Each morning she brought her mother dry toast to soothe her upset stomach. She sat dutifully at her bedside as her mother lay motionless, staring into space, tears dripping like a slow faucet in need of repair. Her mother ate very little, and as the heat of the summer days arrived, she spoke less and less.

The good people of Kingston rallied together to encourage and support the remnants of what used to be a family of three. There was money in the bank to pay the house note, but their only transportation vanished with Martin.

Doc Bishop was a man of integrity, and he knew a tragedy when he saw one. He did more than supply pills. He stopped by twice a day to check on both mother and daughter, keeping the pill box replenished and instructing Katherine to make sure her mother took one each morning and one each evening.

He tossed around several ideas, with his wife, Mary Nell, who helped him navigate these rough waters. "I thought I'd seen it all, but this scenario just about breaks my heart."

"Emeline has a pantry full of blue ribbons from the Davidson County Fair. No one makes better pies. Could she make a living doing something like that?"

Doc shook his head as he listened and emitted a quiet but pained sigh. "She's so fragile. I'm not sure she's able to get out of bed, much less bake pies."

"What are your worst fears?"

"The worst-case would be institutionalization." He studied Mary Nell's face to make sure she fully grasped what he meant and added gravely, "Perhaps for years."

She knew Doc might not be able to save Emeline, but she was sure her husband would do everything within his power to give Katherine back her childhood—with or without her mother. "What can I do to help?"

He must have been pondering the answer before she asked the question. "I don't care what it is or what it costs; I want you to find me something I can take that child each and every day. Not food, of course. Kingston has given them enough food to feed Washington's army. I want something that's just the perfect fit for a seven-year-old girl. Something Martin would have wanted her to have. Something to give her respite from the sadness around her and rescue her from the tragedy that's strangling the life right out of her childhood." He was obviously filled with a combination of fatigue and worry. "Most importantly, whatever it is, it needs to be something I can deliver seven days a week, without fail."

So it was that summer that Katherine became a nursemaid and a bookworm, thanks to the bundle of books Doc delivered daily.

Like a hungry dog with a bone, she devoured each one, zealously reading through all the Nancy Drews, all the Hardy Boys, all twelve of the Five Little Peppers series, and every other title Doc's wife acquired from the library.

Doc found time each day to listen as she recounted the details of what she'd read the day before. Stretching out his long legs, hands cupped behind his head and glasses propped on top of his salt and pepper hair, he convinced her that nothing in his life was more important. "So, how'd she know the missing portrait was buried in the bungalow's basement?" And that was all it took. Katherine would tell the story, sometimes stopping to show him a word she didn't understand. The next day would replicate the day prior. The only deviation would be the way he'd frame his leading question, based on the book's title.

Doc laughed hard when the plot turned comical. He pounded his fist when things went awry. He moped when a character met misfortune. He vigorously rubbed his graying temples when danger lurked. He was her entire audience, and he took it all in, never missing a beat. It was during Doc's visits with Katherine that her heart began to love him.

But Doc and Mary Nell Bishop did much more than supply medicine and books. They gathered a handful of steadfast Kingston families—the kind of men and women who needed no reminder of what was expected of them, to care for widows and orphans. While the country was beginning to emerge from the great financial depression, Katherine's mother was mired in the other kind.

This small army put together a rescue plan for Martin's survivors. Nick Baldwin, president of First Bank of Kingston, arranged to sell the house while there was still time for Emeline to make a profit. He was certain there would eventually be a life insurance payout, and he would oversee the investment. Ted Graham had only recently reopened his diner on Jefferson Street, and he offered a two-for-one deal. Katherine and her mother could live without charge in the efficiency apartment above the diner if Emeline would supply them with four pies six days a week and clean the diner from top to bottom on Sundays.

This same band of friends, under Doc and Mary Nell's supervision, gathered on an appointed Saturday to move Emeline and Katherine to their new place above the diner. The color of the walls of their meager room reminded the two new tenants of a dirty version of canned lima beans. The room shrank drastically each time they carried a piece of furniture up the narrow staircase, causing one to walk sideways navigating from one end of the room to the other. Most of the furniture was taken right back down the creaky staircase and reloaded into the back of the truck. There simply was not room for anything more than two twin beds, a chest of drawers, a bookcase, and two straight-backed chairs to accompany their now perpetually closed drop-leaf table.

What was left of Martin's family, his pitiful wife and one precious child, stood and watched as the reloaded truck, looking like a pirate ship full of plundered treasures, drove down the street and slipped over the horizon.

The stark reality of what their lives had become hit them both at the same moment, like the sting of a hard slap on wet skin. Katherine watched silently as her fully-clothed mother slipped off her shoes, climbed into one of the twin beds and cocooned herself underneath the covers, completely oblivious to Katherine's needs. This neglect of her daughter would become Emeline's pattern for the next nine years.

Katherine found the thick layer of sadness suffocating, and she hungered for the fresh air outside. Low hanging tree branches from a massive pin oak beckoned her out the back door of the diner and after a quick shimmy upward, she roosted in a secluded spot.

Only a minute or two passed when Katherine realized someone was standing directly below her, looking upward into the tree, straight at her, as if she had expected to find a girl perched high among the magnificent limbs. Katherine found herself peering at an abundance of brown. A dark-skinned lady with a nice smile.

The smile seemed to start in the lady's eyes and continue straight through her smooth lips. She had a good face. A dark brown face with skin that reminded Katherine of her father's coffee after he added a drop or two of fresh cream. That kind face had big brown eyes and a brown hat that Katherine supposed might be covering a big bun of dark hair. She was carrying a couple of brown paper packages and a pocketbook. Brown on brown.

The lady was the first to smile, but Katherine was the first to speak.

"Hey."

"Well, hey yourself."

They both waited to see who would speak next. The tree's shade offered a welcome respite from the August sun.

"How'd you climb yourself in that big ole tree?" Her voice was calm, relaxed. Katherine liked the sound.

"Easy." Katherine's voice had an eagerness about it. She wanted to say more. "I've been climbing trees my whole life."

"And just how long that's been?"

"I've been climbing a long time. I'm seven now, but my birthday's next month and I started climbing trees probably when I was about three."

Gently resting her packages on the bench under the massive tree, the lady nodded as she listened to Katherine's answer, agreeing as if she already knew the answer. "You say you're seven now? And you been climbing since you were 'bout three? So how long would that be, you reckon?"

"Four." Katherine displayed four splayed fingers, eager to show off her mathematical aptitude.

Her enthusiasm brought a look of surprise to the brown lady's face. "So, you're an expert at climbing trees *and* at arithmetic? You might just be the smartest seven-year-old I know. I bet you're what some folks call a nat-ur-al." She drew the word out as she spoke, enunciating each syllable precisely.

Katherine cocked her head and studied the lady's face before she answered. She was taken back to hear her say that word. "People used to say that about my daddy and the things he built, but I've never heard anybody say that about me. I like it though." Emulating the lady's pronunciation, she asked, "Are you a nat-ur-al about anything?"

"Let me think on that." She studied Katherine's face hard like the answer could be found written somewhere across her forehead. "Folks tell me I'm a natural at some things, especially cooking. I do think my chicken's good. You like crispy chicken?"

Katherine's ponytail bobbed as she answered, "Oh, I wish you'd teach me so I could make my momma chicken every day." Then she added, "She might like it enough to want to get out of bed."

"Your momma sick?"

"My momma's sad. Just real, real sad."

Katherine watched as the lady seemed to study her own brown shoes temporarily, eyeing them carefully like she was seeing them for the first time in her life. Without intending Katherine to hear, she muttered softly, "*Lord, help my words be few but seasoned up with Your grace.*" A deep sigh escaped as she looked back up at Katherine with understanding. "Tell you what. Let's trade smarts sometime. I'll teach you how to fry chicken, and you can teach me something I don't already know."

A look of hope spread across Katherine's face. "Oh, I'd like that. Do you live around here?"

She pointed in a direction across from the diner. "Down the road a long walk from here. I get off the bus right here just about every day, and then I walk home." Seeming to lose a little energy anticipating the long walk ahead she sighed and asked, "Where do you live?"

"Here." The solitary word from Katherine's lips seemed to erase the hope that had been shining in her blue eyes.

Trying hard to coax back the smile, the lady said with a bit of sass, "Now, pretty girl, I know you don't live up there in that tree."

Katherine solemnly motioned with her head, pointing to

the second floor of the diner. "We moved *there* today. Just my mama and me." She searched the lady's face, curious to see if she indicated any surprise that someone lived above a diner. Or surprised that she belonged to a family of only two. They were difficult words to put together in her head and even more grueling to hear how they sounded when spoken aloud, especially by her own voice.

The lady pulled the cotton hanky that had been peeking from her belt and captured the beads of sweat multiplying rapidly on her brow. She didn't seem a bit surprised, almost as if in some way she already knew the words would be hard ones to say. "Well then, seems like I should be welcoming you to your new home *and* your new climbin' tree. That tree's mighty lucky to have you." And then she added, "I bet it's been standing there all these long years just waitin' for you to come along."

With courage, Katherine looked right at the lady and asked, "You want to be my friend? I don't think any kids live around here. You could be my first new friend."

Sticking her brown hand right up into the tree, the lady said, "I'd sure like that. A lot. I'm Lily Mae Warren."

"I'm Katherine Engstrom," she said as she reached for Lily Mae's hand. And then she added, "And sometimes my daddy used to call me Katie Mae just for fun. That's sort of like your name when you think about it."

"Well, how do you like that? I think Katherine's a beautiful name; it fits you and those lovely blue eyes. The second I laid eyes on you I saw the kind of beauty fit for a queen. Anyone ever call you Queen Katherine?"

"Course not! I'm not a queen. Why would you say that?"

"I think I'm going to call you Queenie."

"Queenie?" The thought enchanted Katherine.

"Something tells me you'll one day be the queen of something, and I like knowing I'll be able to tell folks I was the first to call you that."

"Queenie," Katherine whispered her new name aloud and nodded eagerly. "I like that."

"I'm going to get on now. About time you climbed on down and went inside. I'll be by about this time most days, and I'll look for you up in your tree. Tomorrow's Sunday so I won't see you 'til Monday."

Katherine remembered the lady had a long walk home, but she hated to see her go, knowing now she had to go back inside the smothering room. "You promise you'll come back and see me? Promise?"

Guiding her down from the tree, Lily Mae rested her hands on Katherine's small shoulders, locked her brown eyes on Katherine's and said, "I do promise you that. One thing you'll learn about me, Queenie, is I always, always keep my promises."

Like a moth drawn to the porch light, Katherine fell under Lily Mae's spell from the very beginning of what would become a friendship that would cross all barriers of age, color, and family relations.

HER TWO WORLDS

On the first day of September, Katherine's six-days-a-week routine began in keeping the promise to supply the diner with a variety of homemade pies. She roused her mother out of bed when the alarm rattled at 5:00 a.m., and together they made four pies. Her mother made the rich crusts and supervised while Katherine mixed the ingredients for the fillings. It was a new beginning, the fresh start they craved. But slowly, as the newness wore off, the reality of the poverty of their lives covered her mother in a thick fog that drove her even farther into the downward spiral that worsened when Martin disappeared.

There were usually a few good days each week, but the rest teetered on a tightrope between hope and despair. On the good days, her mother made the crusts for the day plus several more to add to the icebox. On dark days, she sat on the stool with clouded, despondent eyes and watched Katherine thaw the crusts and prepare the fillings. Emeline was paralyzed by depression and fear, dependent on her young daughter to keep their world spinning in the right orbit.

On those days when the light in Emeline's eyes was extinguished and her movements were clumsy and labored, Doc was known to throw on an apron and pitch in with the pie production during his crack-of-dawn visits.

Staying ahead of all the extra pie orders that first Thanksgiving was quite a chore. Many Kingston families wanted at least a couple of pies for their holiday meals, requiring the bakers to work early morning and late evening. Lily Mae stopped in each evening to check on the progress of the orders. She never really knew who or what to expect. Occasionally it was Katherine and her mother, well under way with the magical smells of holiday baking. But usually it was just Katherine, sitting alone and waiting. Waiting for normalcy to reclaim her life. Those were the evenings Lily Mae had to forget how her tired feet dreaded the long walk home or how her fingers ached after working hard all day at Tenenbaum's Finer Wear altering expensive garments to make other women look glamorous.

But how Lily Mae could bring life to that industrial kitchen. Sometimes singing, sometimes telling a story about her own people, and sometimes just listening to music on the old radio. It didn't matter. Her being filled up the whole room. She was the vitamin that brought energy to Katherine's life.

Sometimes bossing before she was completely in the door, she'd announce, "Queenie, you best get that radio turned up loud as it'll go. I got singing all stored up in me, and tonight you and me'll be singing us some of the Lord's music." Squealing with excitement, Katherine would race across the kitchen, eager to turn the knob. And just that quick, Katherine's world would come alive.

Other nights Lily Mae might come through the door quiet and fatigued after a long day of watching wealthy women squeeze into gowns much too small, expecting, even demanding, that she work her magic with a needle and thread. Those were the nights Katherine would meet Lily Mae at the door with cotton house slippers and help remove the laced shoes from her tired feet.

"Want me to read to you tonight while we bake, Lily Mae?"

"How'd you know, Queenie? Lily Mae's pretty tuckered out tonight. Start up right where you left off last time. I'm hungry for your stories." And on those nights Katherine would pull her stool as close as possible to Lily Mae and read far into the night, watching as Lily Mae masterfully turned out the holiday pies.

By the time they took down the calendar and removed the December page, it was evident to all that Emeline was not climbing out of her deep, dark well. And so, the pattern was set. Doc became Katherine's morning beacon, and Lily Mae assumed the role in the evening. Katherine was delighted when she first realized the two knew each other but never once wondered about the logistics that brought them together. As children do, she just took for granted that all good people somehow knew each other.

Not that the entire town of Kingston wasn't aware of the tragedy that cursed the Engstrom family, but everyone eventually got busy living their own lives, putting out their own fires, and managing their own catastrophes. And so, for the rest of her childhood, Katherine walked in two different worlds. Doc Bishop oversaw all the decisions regarding Katherine and her distraught mother, while Lily Mae was charged with carrying them out. For long stretches at a time Emeline was hospitalized in Richmond, undergoing electric shock therapy to curb her depression and weaken her desire to end her life. During those times, Katherine and Lily Mae lived above the diner during the week and spent weekends together at Lily Mae's house, which Katherine greatly favored.

Lily Mae's became her favorite place to be. It was a busy, comfortable place, one that beckoned neighbors to stop in and share their day. Their voices and laughter stuffed the small rooms with vibrant energy, making Katherine sometimes wonder if the front door would fling itself open, just trying to consume more air. She often fell asleep at night, snug in the lap that held her so safe, falling under Lily Mae's spell as she told the friends who had congregated the stories of her people years before, in the days before freedom came. All the neighbors had skin somewhere close to matching Lily Mae's, and no one seemed to notice Katherine's was different, as though it didn't matter. Lily Mae's people became Katherine's people, always making her feel she belonged right there, among them. She mattered something fiercely to all of them, and Katherine was hungry for that.

Sunday was a day of ritual for them. They dressed in their best and walked the three blocks north to Bethel African Methodist Episcopal Church and listened to the Reverend Rodney Morris preach the good gospel to remind them what they had been commanded. They sat hipbone to hipbone on the second pew.

Occasionally, as they walked hand in hand down the aisle, Katherine would overhear someone refer to her as "Lily's girl." She was more than fine with that.

There was shouting and excitement and a great sense of community during the full day's services at Bethel AME. The preacher's voice bellowed with unbridled energy, as he thumped his worn leather Bible, reminding them the Lord promised to walk among them again one day. Katherine's little body found it impossible to sit still as she swayed and tapped and bounced, letting the spirit move her, joining those around her.

Sometimes Emeline was well enough to come home to her daughter and stay months at a time. It was during those Sundays Katherine attended St. Thomas Episcopal Church, sitting with her mother on one side and Doc and his wife Mary Nell, on the other. She loved St. Thomas too, especially the beautifully hand-carved altar statue of Jesus with his hands outstretched to welcome all. The church had been built at a time when America's boundaries were moving westward, and Kingston was large enough to attract several devoted, wealthy Episcopalians who were willing to plant St. Thomas' cornerstone in 1840. The century-old pipe organ bellowed regal music, and the choir and congregation sang the hymns reverently. They stood when they sang, sat when they listened, and knelt on tapestry cushions when they prayed, immersing her in a calming reverence that soaked through her pores and flowed in her veins.

She learned at an early age that Kingston was the most segregated on Sunday mornings which made no sense to her, but no one seemed able to explain it, and she stopped asking questions.

If people in town had opinions about her divided life, no one ever revealed them to Katherine. Doc and Lily Mae found daily opportunities to communicate, and they magically kept the town's wagging tongues out of Katherine's earshot. By then she was rooted in two worlds, and both of them felt like home.

MEETING MURPHY McGREGOR

E xcept for Doc and Lily Mae, the only others who were fully aware of the details of Katherine's splintered life were Conor and Helene McGregor of the renowned McGregor fortune.

Kingston might have turned out to be nothing more than just a speck on the map if not for the immense wealth of this single family. The McGregor clan settled in the area well before the patriots declared their independence from the crown. In 1740, Donovan Colin McGregor made his fortune by marrying the only child of another Irish immigrant, a wealthy one. Over the course of the early years of America's development and through the shrewd business decisions of several generations of Donovan's descendants, the Irish family aggressively purchased large quantities of thick woodland until they owned over 586,000 acres rich in timber, securing their status as one of the most powerful timber moguls in the country.

Until the invention of the automobile, it took four solid days traveling by horse to cover the McGregor's massive land holdings which spread across three county lines. The land was divided into north, south, east, and west quadrants, and each had the look of a miniature village—several massive barns and stables, a sawmill, a blacksmith's operation, a dining hall, a superintendent's cottage, a groundskeeper's cottage, many rows of housing, a bunkhouse expansive enough to house fifty or sixty men, at least two carriage houses, a fruit tree orchard and bountiful harvest garden, a recreation hall, a general store, a school and a church, and a herd of cattle and sheep raised for dairy, protein and hide. Hiring on at one of the McGregor quadrants was more than a job and housing; it was a community and a way of life.

Almost a full century after Donovan McGregor acquired the family's first fortune, his descendants built Beechwood Manor in 1837, a palatial estate just a short drive from Kingston.

Then, just a decade after Beechwood's completion, the McGregors parlayed their timber resources into a third fortune, making them the principal owners of Central Pacific Intercontinental Railroad, connecting America's boundaries from the Atlantic to the Pacific.

Beechwood, the 96-room Greek Revival mansion built on the northwest corner of the McGregor's fourth quadrant, took almost 900 workers and four years to complete. Surrounded by massive beech, pecan, and oak trees, the grand manor house outdid herself each season of the year. It was designed for entertaining, and the McGregors did so handsomely. A summer invitation to lunch at Beechwood often included swimming or boating, then dinner, followed by late evening cocktails on the Great Lawn. A fall invitation included a quail or dove hunt deep in the acreage or a duck hunt on one of the large lakes using McGregor hunting dogs bred, trained, and groomed just for the autumn hunts. A winter invitation might involve a two- or three-night stay in one of the guesthouses and a sleigh ride under the bright moonlight reflecting majestically off the snow. Beechwood had a way of making guests linger longer than they should. It was a difficult place to depart, and guests hungered to return.

To Murphy Egan McGregor, Beechwood Manor was simply his home, and Colin and Helene were simply his parents. To the rest of America, the McGregor family's estate represented a powerful dynasty that only a small handful in the entire country could equal.

Now home on a forty-eight hour leave after earning his wings to fly a B-24, Murphy would soon join the Allied forces to fight the ugliness of the enemy on the other side of the world.

Helene McGregor updated her son on the mysterious disappearance of Martin Engstrom, the missing man who only months before had completed his unrivaled handcrafted woodwork in Beechwood's newest addition, a modern guesthouse situated just south of the big house. Helene recounted to Murphy the dismal update on the wife and young daughter's relocation to the apartment above Graham's Diner.

She handed Murphy the front page of the *Kingston Daily News* she had saved for his visit, and he read the headline aloud, "Exhaustive Search for Engstrom Ceases."

Helene saw his bewildered look and said, "Read on, it only gets worse."

As she stood over his shoulder, he continued, "Thanks to the good men in my department, every single lead has been ruled out and dismissed. Martin Engstrom has now been classified as a missing person, and the case is closed unless new evidence comes up."

Confusion clouded Murphy's face. "The sheriff had the audacity to close a missing person's case after just a matter of weeks?"

"Your father and I are just as baffled. And so is Doc, who's quite concerned about the situation. He's entirely immersed in trying to help them put their lives back together. He's become their bulwark."

"I'm sure you and Dad have offered to help in a variety of ways. Will Doc let you?"

"Yes, he and your father have created a plan that will begin next week. We've purchased a car with Lily Mae Warren's name on the title, and we're providing the startup money for her own storefront, an alterations shop, just a block away from the diner."

"Do I know Lily Mae Warren?"

"Probably not. Doc says she's the best prescription he has for the little girl. She's a seamstress in town and takes care of the young daughter when the mother has to go away for treatment. I'm sure Doc has a number of other helpful ideas he just hasn't proposed yet to your father, but he will when the time is right."

Murphy wasn't surprised by his parents' actions because it was what his father and mother did best. *To whom much is given, much will be required* was an expectation rooted in their core.

Helene glanced at her watch and gasped at the time. Handing him a copy of the order she had placed for Thanksgiving pies, she shooed him out the door. "Now hurry! The diner closes at 6:00 tonight since tomorrow's Thanksgiving. You absolutely cannot pick them up late so skedaddle!"

The list of pies would feed the inevitable crowd of family and friends expected to gather the next day at Beechwood: five pumpkins, four pecans, two pecans with bourbon sauce, and one lemon chess. His mother hadn't forgotten his favorite. He was planning on eating that one all by himself.

He pondered the unfortunate Engstrom saga as he drove the fifteen-minute route and wondered what would have caused the sheriff to end the search so early. Surely in a town the size of Kingston, someone must know something. A man doesn't just disappear off the face of the earth, and for that matter, a sheriff doesn't simply stop looking. Or does he?

By the time Murphy arrived at quarter past six, the diner's overhead lights were off, and the CLOSED sign was dangling on the door. It appeared the McGregors' Thanksgiving would be without pie until Murphy's eyes caught an unexpected sight as he began making a U-turn in the diner's parking lot.

A young girl, not more than seven or eight, stood just inside the screen door, as if she'd been expecting him. She opened the screen door and waited for him to enter.

"Did Mrs. McGregor send you after her pies?" she asked with innocence, not knowing he was the heir of the McGregor fortune.

"She sure did, and I hope I'm not too late. I'll be cooked just like the turkey if I mess this up," he said as he gave her a wink.

Her ponytail danced with her laughter. She began handing him pie boxes, each labeled in the top right-hand corner with a red grease pencil and tied neatly with string.

"You must be the famous pie queen. How'd I get so lucky?"

Another laugh. Murphy realized those blue eyes and blonde hair were what you'd perhaps expect to see in Sweden. Strikingly beautiful.

As he began placing the pie boxes in his mother's car, he realized the problem at hand. "Let me give you a ride. It's too dark and cold for you to walk alone. Where do you live?"

"*Here,*" she said, pointing above the diner.

Murphy felt a surge of guilt, as he realized whom he was talking to and the unfair hand she'd been dealt. Ashamed of his own ignorance and trying to hide any sympathy in his voice, he stuck out his hand and said, "Well, Happy Thanksgiving. I'm Murphy."

She reached up, grabbed his outstretched hand and with a strong grip said, "Happy Thanksgiving. I'm Katherine. Do you live in Kingston?"

"I grew up here, but I've been away for several years. I'm headed across the world in another day or so, but after the war I plan to move back home. Maybe I'll become your best pie customer if your lemon chess pie is as good as I hear."

Katherine responded with an impish grin and gave him a little curtsy. He responded with a bow fit for royalty and extended his arm. "May I escort your Highness back to your door, my lady?"

She linked her arm in his, and they strode the few short steps back to the diner, laughing together. He opened the door with a grand gesture and watched as she shut and locked it behind her.

It wasn't until he was almost back on the grounds of Beechwood that something deep within his gut reminded him of the irony of Katherine's childhood. What a far cry from his in which an entire staff of salaried people created grocery lists. And did the shopping. And the cooking. And the cleaning. To be fair, even the child raising.

The image of the young girl and the sound of her laughter would linger in the back of his mind throughout Thanksgiving. But soon his leave ended, and his thoughts focused entirely on returning to his base and the many flying missions that lay ahead of him.

Murphy would have scoffed if someone prophesied the little pony-tailed blonde would one day help him find his way home.

PIXIE GIFTS

Katherine referred to them her entire life as her "pixie gifts." They began arriving soon after she moved above the diner, at a time when her mother was walking and breathing but not really much alive.

The first gift was a piece of blue satin ribbon, mirroring the cornflower hue of Katherine's eyes. She discovered it one morning at the diner's back entrance tied loosely to the latch of the screen door. Remembering all the bedtime stories her father used to tell about the pixies who fell in love with her the moment they saw her lying in her cradle, Katherine's heart settled on the notion that the pixies had somehow found her again.

And so it came to be during the days and months ahead that the blue ribbon was constantly in Katherine's possession. In her hair, around her neck, stuffed in a pocket, it was her talisman, always within easy reach. Katherine decided those pixies were quite cunning. They knew she needed to hold something that reminded her of her father. Remembering his strength gave her the endurance she needed while her heart remembered the days of her life before he left them.

The next pixie gift arrived just a couple of days after the first. A pile of the reddest, sweetest pears she'd ever seen, stacked in a small mound on the concrete bench next to the screen door.

And then a short time later there arrived a little carved wooden puppet—a rabbit on a string sitting ever so cleverly upright on the short sycamore stump just beyond the bench out back.

They never arrived daily but often enough, and each gift was just as delightful as the one before.

Her mother seemed to brighten a little when Katherine displayed the latest addition to her collection of pixie gifts. Doc not only seemed intrigued, he was curious to know where she found each one. But the person who enjoyed them almost as much as Katherine was Lily Mae.

"Are you telling me you just walked outside, and you looked over and saw this wooden rabbit sitting on the stump? Think he was sitting there hoping you'd be the one to notice him?" Her voice was leery, but she couldn't hide her playful eyes from Katherine.

"He's more than a wooden rabbit, Lily Mae. He's a puppet! And I love him. I wonder if the pixies know how much I love him."

"Child, believe me, those pixies surely know. Why, I think they're all pleasured up knowing their gifts make you so happy. Think they might already be working on your next surprise?" Then, without waiting for Katherine to answer, she continued, "Those pixies will be there for you as long as you need them. Don't expect them, but don't be surprised by them either."

Occasionally a pixie gift was clearly intended for her mother and those always seemed to coincide with the days Emeline was feeling well. A bushel of peaches, which were immediately turned into fried pies and sold faster than Katherine could peel. Maybe a couple of dressed quail ready for frying. And each fall the pixies left a bulging crinkled paper sack full of shelled pecans, which were stored for the eventual endless list of Thanksgiving and Christmas pie orders.

Katherine never lacked for friends. Her magnetism seemed to work on everyone. She could gather a crowd faster than a six-week-old puppy. The teachers knew about her father's disappearance and her mother's declining health. They also knew to alert Doc Bishop if she had needs of any kind. Physical, emotional, financial, it didn't matter. Doc wanted to know, and he took care of whatever came up.

Each morning on her way to Garfield Elementary, Katherine was forced to walk past a small gang of older girls who lurked in front of the junior high next door. They seemed to relish insulting the younger ones who passed, and Wanda Sullivan was the self-appointed leader.

Like a volcano spewing hot lava, they showered Katherine with vicious words as she walked past. Their taunts zinged and stung day after day, but Katherine was determined not to let the girls see the injury they inflicted on her spirit.

She saved her questions for the evening when she was at home and alone with Lily Mae. "What's a looney bin?"

"Where on earth did you hear that?"

"That mean Wanda girl said that's where Mama lives and Daddy ran off to get away from us."

Lily Mae turned Katherine's face to hers and took a deep, sorrowful breath. "Queenie, that Wanda girl is full of meanness. She's pure trouble. The whole family is. Something evil has crawled up in her heart and turned into some kind of poison in her."

"But why does she have to be so full of mean to *me*? I've never said a mean thing to her ever. I promise, Lily Mae. I didn't even know who she was until she started picking on me one day about Daddy."

Lily Mae studied Katherine's face reflected through the mirror. "So, she's that kind of mean, huh, talking about your daddy? She's mean as a snake doctor, and can't give away kindness 'cause she doesn't know kindness herself. You can't give what you don't know. It's the evil ones who hate the light. But you know what? You're going to have to do something that most people can't. You're going to have to learn to forgive her, Queenie. Not just Wanda, but *especially* Wanda."

Katherine buried her face in the crook of her arm. "I can't do it, Lily Mae. How can you ask me to forgive her? She's probably thinking right now how she can be even meaner to me tomorrow than she was today. I can't do it. I hate her. I hate everything about her."

Lily Mae turned Katherine towards her again, lifting her chin so they could see eye to eye. "Child, we've got to figure out why she does those things. It isn't really Katherine Engstrom she hates. She has hate for her own self, but she sees you as someone she wants to battle. Wants to torment you like the way she's tormented inside her own self."

It pained Katherine to think Lily Mae didn't understand the impossibility of what she was asking her to do. "That kind of meanness doesn't deserve to be forgiven, Lily Mae."

Lily Mae put the brush on the dresser and motioned for Katherine to climb in her lap. "If you don't forgive her, she'll win. She'll win this battle because she'll one day move on to try to break someone else into a million pieces with her wicked tongue, but you'll be the one stuck in the prison of the past."

Katherine knew she couldn't argue with that. "Will she change if I forgive her?"

"Might not, can't promise you that. But you will change if you can't forgive her, that I know. Her poison will seep into you. It'll lock your heart up cold and make you bitter. The Lord says to get rid of that bitterness. You're already as strong a gal as I've ever seen, and now she's making you even stronger. You're too good to be bitter. And I'm never going to let you forget that."

Lily Mae reflected on her own words and decided maybe Katherine needed to hear one more thing. "Besides, child, there'll come a day when someone will pay her back for that ugliness she flaunts around. When she's least expecting it. Don't know who or when or how, but it'll happen. Always does. Seems like the Lord makes sure of it."

Lily Mae's words provided the armor Katherine needed to prevent Wanda's poison from penetrating her own heart. She wasn't wise enough to see it coming, but Katherine's ability to disregard their very existence caused the girls to channel their energy into a cyclone bent for annihilation, aimed right for her.

The first cold winter day of her tenth year she wore the same winter coat to school she had worn for two years. Her sudden growth spurt by summer's end prevented the coat from buttoning across her chest. When the cool weather arrived, Emeline had been home for a few weeks, and she was well enough to plainly see Katherine was in need of a new coat before the bitterly cold winter winds arrived. But the pixies were watching, and within three days of that first cold snap, they left a package for her on the bench by the diner's back door. When Katherine unwrapped the brown paper, she uncovered the most beautiful coat she'd ever seen. It was pale blue winter wool with a rabbit fur collar and a matching fur hand muff. The blue did not surprise her for it seemed almost everything made of fabric the pixies brought her had a bit of blue. But the fur collar and muff were beyond anything she had ever seen. She laid it out carefully the night before, eager for the new day to arrive so she could wear it to school.

If Katherine could have somehow predicted her new coat and muff ensemble would have provoked such trauma, she probably never would have worn it. Just a mere glimpse of the beautiful rabbit fur muff was more than the wicked minds of the covetous older girls could stand. They immediately devised a diabolical plan, improved it each time they had a stolen moment to connive, and carried it out just as that school day ended.

Wanda Sullivan snuck into the janitor's storeroom and found an old rag tied to a stick immersed in a can of thick tar. Holding that stick, strong with stench, she waited until Katherine came down the steps of Garfield Elementary, then she smeared it across the front of the rabbit muff, instantly ruining the one frivolous, beautiful possession Katherine had received since her father's disappearance.

No matter how hard her shoes pounded the pavement as she ran, the sound of the girls' malicious laughter chased her long and hard all the way back to the diner.

There were no words Emeline or Lily Mae could say to console her, and they knew there was no remedy for removing the tar from what just moments before had been beautiful and pristine.

Katherine wept as she watched Lily Mae wrap her tar-stained muff in old newspaper and then placed it in the bottom of the trash barrel, ready to burn in the morning with the rest of the unwanted rubbish.

"Child, I don't know the source of the evil that grows in Wanda Sullivan's heart, but I do know she's seen this kind of thing all around her. Has to. She wouldn't be so cruel if cruel weren't living in her own house." Lily Mae was trying to wrestle the anger in her voice, and it took all the strength she had to keep it in. "This I know to be true. You'll never forget what happened today for as long as you live. What you got to do now is decide where this memory will live. Is it going to live right up front in your heart like it's what you want to think about all the time, or is it going to be just a memory mixed in with all the others? If you can do that, not let it be the most important thing, you're telling that bad deed what kind of strength you have deep inside of you. One day when you're telling your own girl what it means to treat people right, you might pull up this memory and tell what it felt like to be wronged by someone evil. And remember what we are all asked to do...forgive those who trespass against us."

Together, Emeline and Lily Mae put Katherine to bed and sat beside her, one on each side, until she slept, exhausted from the agony and the tears. And then Lily Mae seemed to be in some kind of a mighty hurry, said she had some things that needed her attention and rushed right out the door.

When morning did arrive, Katherine knew she had no choice. There was nothing to be done but return to school and endure the haughty laughter and the smug looks coming from Wanda and her spiteful gang.

Or, at least that was her plan. Evidently, the pixies had another.

It was the first and only time she found a pixie gift anywhere other than the screen door, the bench, or the stump. The next morning, a package sat on her school desk gently wrapped in worn tissue and tied with a piece of thin string. Attached were the words "do unto others" penned boldly on a small scrap of paper, penned by a hand that had already seen a lot of life, an old hand.

Inside the worn tissue was an exact replica of her prized rabbit fur muff. Tar-free and just as beautiful as the original once was, she turned it over and over in her hands, inspecting it with wonderment. Oh, so slowly, a smile emerged on her face as it dawned on her that the pixies had found her school, her classroom, and her desk. This meant they also knew her path to and from school, and they knew of the wickedness and evil in the hearts of those girls. The mean ones.

Katherine never really understood all that took place that day, but she knew her teacher had tears in her eyes when she heard the painful details of what happened the afternoon before. Sometime before the morning recess Katherine looked out the classroom window and saw a car identical to Doc's parked in front of the school. Before lunchtime, she was summoned to the principal's office to once again tell the ugly story, and by the end of the day Wanda and her gang would be forced to apologize. And for the next four weeks the girls were not waiting for her to pass in front of the school each morning and each afternoon. They were too busy scrubbing the desks and the bathroom floors throughout the school.

But Wanda remained like a piece of gravel in Katherine's shoe, which would become more and more irritating throughout each stage of her life. She would one day have to confront again that poisonous spirit and then it would be over something else Wanda coveted that belonged to Katherine—the love of her life.

ONE WAR ENDS

The town of Kingston lost only two of her sons in the first World War, but regardless how many, the town grieved. World War II was a different story, when she saw many of her bravest fight on foreign soil. Some of them came home whole and others returned with injuries, both seen and unseen. Only the dog tags returned home for those who laid their lives on the altar of freedom. And then there were the ones who were listed as missing, leaving nothing for the families to wrap their arms around to grieve.

The entire town of Kingston felt the loss when a family received tragic news. The bell in the belfry of St. Thomas Episcopal Church, located just a block off the town square, tolled three times when horrible news arrived. Some said it was a reminder to pray to the Father, Son, and Holy Ghost. Others thought the three chimes were to remind the townsfolk to pray "Send them home" or "God Bless America." Later, some of the mothers admitted they secretly and selfishly uttered, "Please, not mine."

Katherine was exactly eleven years and one month old the day the *Kingston Daily's* headline read "War Ends – Japanese Surrender," and by day's end every light pole down Main Street was decorated in long red, white, and blue crepe paper streamers dancing in the breeze. Within weeks, Kingston's soldiers and sailors began arriving home to a hero's welcome. The railroad depot had a huge banner hanging alongside the largest American flag the town had ever seen. The banner read, "God Bless America and Kingston's Bravest." The American Legion Drum and Bugle Corps gathered each day for the arrival of the 7:00 p.m. train, playing their small repertoire of patriotic music and igniting the crowd into jubilant hysteria.

Night after night after night, Katherine was there among all the townspeople anxiously gathered to welcome them home. Whistles, cheers, and horns erupted as they stepped onto the platform and embraced his sweetheart or wife or family, grabbing hold like there would be no tomorrow. Those boys had spent years fighting for tomorrow, and now they were home. No question, Kingston was proud of her boys.

Katherine recognized the man the second he stepped off the train, the one who had arrived late one Thanksgiving Eve to pick up the McGregor pie order a few years earlier. She'd secretly been watching for him every night, hoping he would be one of the lucky ones who came home. The crowd roared a thunderous cheer when he stepped off the train, and Katherine was surprised by the energy of the crowd. She wasn't at all sure why he evoked such a frenzied reaction, more hysteric than most, but she enjoyed feeling the pulse of the crowd as it warmed her body. The man removed his military cap and waved to the crowd, which intensified the roar. Immediately his mother and father were at his side, engulfing him in cries of relief, and the crowd seemed to lasso the cluster into an even tighter embrace. Katherine wove her way through the thick crowd, anxious for a closer look just to be sure he was who she thought he was. Angling her body this way and that, she finally made it to the perimeter of the huddled three. He turned and saw her and searched her face, asking himself if she was anyone he recognized. And when he bent low to bow, keeping his eyes steadfast on hers just as he had a few years before, she knew he remembered her. Then the crowd engulfed him and she never caught another glimpse, but she was satisfied in knowing, unlike her father, this man left and came back home.

It wasn't just Murphy McGregor's parents and friends who welcomed him when he stepped foot on the depot platform. Standing in the crowd was Marianne Winter, one of Kingston's most beautiful debutantes. She was also Murphy's on-again, off-again girl through high school and college before he left for war. They never dated each other exclusively, but by the time they arrived on the campus of Cooper-Lee University, they were an item at many of the biggest social events. Not the prettiest or the smartest of the six or seven ingenues Murphy dated in college, but Marianne was the most loyal of all his special girls while he was away. She sent him a letter each week and even sent an occasional letter to his crew members who didn't have girls back home. Unbeknownst to him, while he was away fighting the enemy, their mothers were already planning the wedding and numbering the grandchildren they were hoping for one day soon. Murphy and Marianne became betrothed five months after his return.

Doc Bishop had known the soon-to-be bride and groom since they took their first breaths of life. He doctored them through the typical childhood illnesses, broken bones, and minor accidents.

He had suspected for years the bride had a tendency to feign injuries or illnesses. She was inclined to maintain an on-going ailment of one type or another that needed his attention, even as a girl in her single digits of life. Over the years, he conversed with her parents in hopes they would reflect on her frequent visits to the clinic, but no matter how blunt his approach, he failed. The direct and undivided attention she received from him during her innumerable visits filled her heart like a hand pump on a bicycle tire. Her chart was as thick as an old family Bible, and he made certain her parents saw the stark difference between the size of her chart and those of other patients her age. They barely noticed, and they didn't care. Her visits to Doc made her happy, and that was exactly how her parents liked her. No matter the cost.

Doc watched her need for attention slowly convert to her need for a stash of pills. With only one physician in town, she was limited to the number of illnesses and accidents she could feign. And besides, Doc seemed to begin to question her more and more and prescribe less and less.

A day before her departure for college, she made an appointment and asked Doc to give her a bottle of something to settle her nerves. She was anxious about leaving home and was sure he could help her.

Doc tapped his pen on his desk pad. "I don't have anything to prescribe, Marianne, other than plenty of rest and exercise. Both of those will ease your anxiousness, and they are much better remedies than anything the pharmacist can compound for you."

"You don't understand." There was pleading in her voice and eyes. "I'll get plenty of rest and exercise, but I need something else, something to calm my nerves while I'm adjusting to a new place." There were certain medicines she favored because she liked the way they made her feel. Just a slight buzz, not sloppy and loud like when she drank too much. Her penchant for pills gave her no hangover and no calorie consumption. She kept a stash hidden in a half dozen places at home, and no one seemed to notice.

Doc responded with a look of refusal, which ignited her brashness. She was not at all accustomed to being denied. She attempted to smother it with admonishment; "I only want you to give me enough until I return at Thanksgiving, not for the entire semester."

Firmly, he said, "Not anymore, Marianne. Not now, not later, not if your mother or your father ask for you. The answer will still be no. Pills are not the panacea for your unhappiness."

The anger in her voice was heard by everyone in the clinic. "Why are you so difficult? My parents will have your license revoked because of your incompetence, and we'll make sure the entire town knows it, too."

Doc calmly closed her chart, folded his eyeglasses and dropped them into the breast pocket of his lab coat. "My job is to understand the human body and how it responds to the treatments I prescribe. It is not in your best interest for me to prescribe anything for you. I know you're angry with me, but I'll be angry with myself if I continue to placate your need for prescriptions. You have an opportunity to leave Kingston and attend one of the finest universities in the country. Use this time to discover who you can become and…"

Doc stopped when she slammed the door in his face. But he knew she wouldn't do it, and he also knew if he tried again to raise his concerns with her parents they would ignore him, so he refrained.

But, as addicts are, she was resourceful. Once she established herself and her wealth on the campus of Cooper-Lee, she often went home with friends for the weekend and finagled a way to search their medicine cabinets. She learned to befriend the girls whose fathers practiced medicine, knowing their bathrooms would be bulging with the divine little round pills that helped her get through each day.

And now the ugly war had ended, and she was betrothed. Her days of having to pretend she was doing well in college were over, and she assumed her life as Mrs. Murphy McGregor would be grander than anyone had ever dreamed for her.

MURPHY'S INHERITANCE

=================================

SOUTHERN EXPRESS TELEGRAM

SEPTEMBER 1, 1945

MR MURPHY MCGREGOR
THE BLANSETT BUILDING
DALLAS, TEXAS

FATHER DIED IN HEAD ON COLLISION I NEED YOU HOME
PLEASE ARRANGE TO RETURN TO BEECHWOOD ON
EARLIEST TRAIN OUR WORLD HAS CRUMBLED
MOTHER

=================================

Murphy returned from the war just two weeks prior and was visiting a fellow B-24 crew member in Dallas when he received the telegram. The luxury of a slow transition from father to son of the family's timber dynasty ceased upon Conor McGregor's instant death.

The task of trying to fill his father's shoes was daunting for Murphy. The brokenness he saw in his mother gave him more reason to prove his worthiness of managing all that the McGregors before him had built and nurtured. And he did it well. He brought renewed vigor, insight, and expertise to the business and immediately increased productivity and profits.

But Helene didn't notice anything Murphy did with the timber business because that sort of thing brought her no joy. The only thing that seemed to bring light to his mother's heartbroken eyes was the flurry of bridal activities leading up to his wedding and the anticipation of another generation of McGregors underfoot at Beechwood.

He wanted to tell her, he tried to, several times actually, but his mother wouldn't hear of it. She convinced him that all grooms were susceptible to cold feet and brushed it off as a case of wedding jitters.

"But how do I know?" He looked at her with pleading eyes, reminding her of the young boy he was not so many years before. She was unaccustomed to seeing him so serious, so frightened. He tried to explain, "I think I know jitters from my time in the Air Corps. This isn't jitters. This is me wondering how on earth this all happened so fast."

Hoping the laugh in her voice would mask how unsettling it was for her to see Murphy's agitation, she said, "Sweetheart, you have too much on you. First the war, and then your father, and trying to step into his shoes so quickly. You've had no time to rest and relax. Stop pushing yourself so hard. Just enjoy this time. Marianne certainly is."

He wasn't buying it. "Did you ever question yourself when you and Father were about to marry?"

Patting the space next to her on the sofa, she motioned for him to sit near her. In a hushed tone, she haltingly revealed a secret. "I've never told this to a single soul, but your father got cold feet a week before we were to marry. I had to remind him he could travel the world and back, but he would never find a woman who loved him more. We both knew that if he decided to go, I would wait as long as it took for his return."

Murphy had never before heard any mention of the story. He marveled at his mother's poise, her insistence, her patience in knowing she would wait as long as she had to for his father's feet to thaw.

"And from a son's eyes, you and Father had the kind of marriage anyone would envy. You really did, didn't you?"

"We hid nothing from you, Murphy. Some days were easier than others, and I did little things that drove him a little batty and Lord knows he did the same to me. But in the end neither of us would have changed a single minute of any day we had together."

Murphy turned away and allowed his eyes to focus on nothing but the thin air. He sighed deeply, searching for the courage to tell her he was going to postpone the wedding, knowing it would be a second blow that would cause her tremendous pain.

Helene reached for him and rested her hands on his cheeks. She whispered, "Let's stop all this. We have three parties this week and a wedding in six weeks. No more talk of cold feet! I know if your father were here he would know just the right words to erase that fear in your eyes."

And he knew then he was not going to disappoint her.

It was the most glamorous wedding Kingston had ever seen and for decades to come it held its rank, but not every guest saw the glamour and magic. There were two men at the Winter-McGregor wedding who had to work hard to at least appear they were enjoying themselves. The doctor and the groom.

PART TWO

1966 – 1975

TROUBLE AT BEECHWOOD

Katherine was two months shy of her thirty-second birthday when she walked into Doc's private office to find him sitting, shoulders sagging, one hand still holding the telephone receiver and the other one limp in his lap. In the eleven years since becoming his registered nurse, she'd witnessed this pained look in his eyes many times. It was a look he kept hidden from most, but he knew he didn't have to shield her from life's tragedies because she could speak of them in first person.

"I'm expecting Murphy McGregor to bring his wife, Marianne, through the back entrance. Listen for them and do what you can to help him get her inside without any fanfare and put them in Room 3. I'll continue seeing patients until they arrive. They're headed our way now so it should be about another fifteen minutes from Beechwood. But I'm sure he will be driving like a bat out of hell, so look for him in about eight."

"Should I stay in the room once we get her settled?"

"Not sure. You'll know how to handle it. Just use that level head of yours." Doc trusted Katherine's intuition more than he trusted his own these days. "I think this is going to be rough. Prepare yourself."

Doc was frequently called to Beechwood Manor. He often headed there after a long day's work, always with his medical bag in tow. Katherine scanned Mrs. McGregor's chart. Marianne had seen Doc a total of eighteen times in the past fourteen months alone. Eleven of those entries were prefaced with an underscored capital H, Doc's code for a home visit. It was not unusual for Doc to visit some of his patients in their homes, but the frequency for this patient was baffling. The Roman Numeral IV beside Mrs. McGregor's name on the chart's tab was another flag. A red one. No one else in his practice had ever seen Doc enough times to warrant four charts.

Hearing a vehicle approaching the clinic's private entrance, Katherine stepped out on the small back stoop to open the screen door. Murphy struggled to support his wife upright as she attempted to walk. He gently picked up her limp body, just as he would a napping child, and carried her up the steps, following Katherine into Room 3.

Together they laid her on the examining table. While Katherine began taking her vitals, Murphy removed her house slippers and covered his wife with a soft blanket. Katherine's face never conveyed what her mind had already determined. Mrs. McGregor had overdosed and was barely alive.

Doc came in immediately and began prodding her stomach. While Katherine recited the vitals, she also began preparing for what she knew would happen next. Without saying a word, they prepped Marianne McGregor and began forcing her to swallow a massive dose of a charcoal solution to absorb the poison she had ingested. Katherine knew the liver and kidneys could possibly shut down. She could only assume what the other two in the room were thinking: one was probably incredulous his wife had found more pills, and the other was probably wondering if they could do enough to save her.

The first words spoken by Doc came twenty-seven minutes from the time Murphy McGregor pulled his wife out of the passenger side of his car. "She's going to make it," Doc uttered. And then he added, "This time."

Doc's addendum was powerful. Katherine glanced at Murphy McGregor, realizing Doc's words hit him like a punch in the gut. Wrapping his arms around his stomach with his back against the wall, he crumbled when he hit his haunches, trying to conceal his pain by cradling his face with both hands.

"Murph, I don't know what else to do. She's on a spiral and

neither of us is powerful enough to quell it. I've exhausted my list of medical experts and then some. You've tried the best clinics in the country for this sort of thing. Your only other choice is to hire someone to watch over her twenty-four hours a day and to get her set up with regular appointments with the new psychiatrist I mentioned over in Sulphur Springs."

Murphy cleared his throat before speaking. The pulsing of Marianne's monitor seemed to silence its own rattle as if waiting to hear his thoughts.

"I thought she had it licked this time. She sure knows how to play me though. She had the back door open this morning to let in some fresh air and was even humming while she put on a pot of coffee. She'd gone so far as to cut a handful of flowers from the east garden and was arranging those when I came into the kitchen." He closed his eyes and shook his head from side to side. With a voice drenched in sadness, he asked, "How? How does she find the stuff?"

"I don't even know what it was she used this time, son. But this I do know, she started this path as a young woman, and it had nothing to do with you. Every time I've driven away from Beechwood after one of these episodes, I've beaten myself up for not telling you I knew she had this propensity before you married her."

Murphy was riled. "Propensity? Really, Doc?" His voice was thick with hurt and betrayal, "Just say it the way it's written in your medical journals. *Addiction.* She loves pills and booze more than she loves life itself. She's addicted. My love, my attention, my name, my forgiveness – none of that is what she lives for now. She lives for something round and something wet to chase it with. I've fought it every single day of every single year we've been married. My God, I'm glad we couldn't have children. I knew there was a reason, and I guess now I know what it is." And then tears began again.

Doc held out his hand to pull Murphy from the floor and held him in an embrace for as long as the tears flowed. Katherine stood almost invisible, taking vitals and listening. She was holding back tears, realizing again how fragile life could be for some, while others seem to burst through life with the speed and vigor that would almost make the earth tremble.

The next time Katherine saw Murphy McGregor was two weeks later when he stopped by the clinic with a dog and a rick of wood in the back of his pickup. She and Doc were turning on lights and preparing for the start of their day. He stuck his head in the back door and yelled with a booming voice, "I'm taking a rick of wood to your house, Doc. Want it in the same place as usual?"

"Step in for a minute and have a quick cup of coffee with us, Murph." Doc's tone was more telling than asking.

"You've never known me to turn down a good cup of coffee." Murphy stepped inside, doffing his cap as he crossed the threshold. Good manners.

"Join us, Murph." Doc sat holding his coffee cup with a quarterback's grasp. "Katherine and I started this ritual about eleven years ago. We begin our workday enjoying our first cups of coffee facing east and watching the birds bathe outside the window. Now we've become such creatures of habit we're afraid we might jinx ourselves if we tried to start our day any other way."

Katherine handed Mr. McGregor a cup of hot black coffee while Doc moved her chair over to make room for a third.

"Cream and sugar, Mr. McGregor?"

"Just black. Thank you." He studied her face and enjoyed it.

She turned away, feeling her cheeks reddening, realizing she caught him looking intently into her eyes. *That's only fair*, thought Katherine, knowing she had often done the same to him, inconspicuously, on the many occasions he'd brought his wife through the back door.

They sat in silence for the first few sips, transfixed by the activity in the birdbath. Life was peaceful in this spot. Quiet. Calming. No conflict. No quagmire.

"You spoil me, son, with the wood you bring me, and I know I'm not the only one you surprise with a fresh cord of hardwood just as soon as the woodpile begins to look slim. I bet I could name at least a half-dozen who tell me you spoil them the same way. No telling how many others you do for, ones I don't even know about."

"It feels good to give, Doc. You do it every day. Let me have the pleasure of knowing what that feels like."

More silence.

"Katherine, I didn't bring you any firewood, but I do have something in my truck I'd like to give you." He paused and then added, "That is if you want it. A sack of shelled pecans. This year's crop?"

Katherine searched his face to see if he had any idea what that could possibly mean to her. A sack of shelled pecans had been anonymously delivered to her back door every year she lived above Graham's Diner. A pixie gift.

"I'd like that very much, Mr. McGregor," was all she said, but Doc read her face and knew exactly what she was thinking.

"But, please, only on the condition you stop being so formal and begin calling me Murphy. That's what all my friends call me. I insist."

"Well," she paused, and then with a genuine smile added, "Murphy it is."

Doc said with complete authority, "Okay, as long as we're tossing around conditions, I have one to add. New rule." Moving to the window and pointing outside to Murphy's truck, he said, "Your morning coffee comes with a caveat. Bring that beautiful dog of yours inside during our morning coffee time. Doesn't seem right we're in here solving all the world's problems and he's out there watching your every move."

And so the coffee trio, plus a large, clumsy half Golden Retriever/half Heinz 57 mutt named Baxter, began and continued for several years. Katherine and Doc never knew when Murphy would join them but she always set out a third cup just in case, and a nibble of a leftover for Baxter, and when she remembered someone's favorite pie was lemon chess, there was usually a slice or two on hand. Murphy's ability to join them for coffee depended on the level of calmness at Beechwood. Many mornings Marianne slept until almost noon, but there were plenty of nights she never slept, never laid down and never stopped moving. Murphy knew she was a walking time bomb when she worked herself into that kind of manic state, and he stayed close to home on those days.

There was an unwritten rule on the early mornings when Murphy and Baxter were able to join them for coffee and it was never broken. Marianne's situation was never discussed.

Running out of topics was never a problem for the triad of coffee drinkers; politics, religion, war, travel, literature, Hollywood, life in Kingston, ecology, baits, and lures. They communicated life's experiences without reservation and agreed on almost every issue, at least the important ones, for sure.

It was through these casual conversations Katherine grew to understand the real Murphy McGregor. In her mind, age lost its hierarchy, and she eventually stopped focusing on the twelve-year difference between them. She saw past what most people didn't. He was the only philanthropist Katherine had ever known and she found him fascinating, especially knowing he preferred his philanthropy be anonymous. But he was so much more than just a man of great wealth and prominence. It was his intelligence and humanitarianism that propelled him. He was a man who stood valiantly for social justice, protecting Earth's lands and waters and sustaining all that had been handed to him. And his wit could light up the room like a box of Roman candles on a hot July evening. He had one of those strong laughs that made it impossible for you not to join him. A contagious laugh. One that made her eyes dance. His trim build kept him looking much younger than many comrades his own age, especially the ones who allowed gravity to grab hold of their waistlines. It was more than his dark eyes set against his flawless complexion and russet hair that made him so strikingly debonair. The crow's feet around his eyes were proof his face had been accustomed to smiling his entire life. His appearance, his dress, and his confidence made women of all ages take long second looks hoping to fix his image permanently in their minds.

Murphy enjoyed all the early morning stories, whether he was the storyteller or the listener. He eloquently told stories about the countless places where he'd journeyed as a boy and then later visited as a pilot and as a man trying to be a good steward of all that his ancestors had acquired. His stories took them to so many different places around the world that Doc eventually tacked a large world map on the wall so they could track the locations of Murphy's exploration.

Katherine was surrounded by two men who were equals in intelligence and humor. The time shared by the threesome in the early hours grew to become the greatest delight in this stage of her life. She did not allow herself to wonder how it might change if Murphy's wife became healthy again.

It was obvious to Murphy how profoundly connected the other two were to each other. He enjoyed watching them, the doc and the nurse, taking care of one another.

"I love her like she's my own. Easiest thing I've ever done in this world is to love this gal," Doc said innumerable times. Murphy was always struck by the simplicity of their friendship. And the tenderness.

He was curious to know more details of the disappearance of Katherine's father, but she never spoke of it and Murphy was much too genteel to ask. He knew it was the one unsolved mystery in Kingston's history and wondered if he was in a position to find some answers. Perhaps he could do that for her. She certainly deserved to know. It was a thought he often contemplated on the drive to and from Beechwood. It wasn't just the mystery of her father's disappearance he pondered. Thoughts of Katherine often lingered in his mind.

In time he learned through their morning ritual that her mother died of a massive stroke when Katherine was a senior in high school, and it was then that she moved in with Doc and Mary Nell before heading to nursing school in Gentry. He made the assumption Doc must have paid for nursing school, but, almost as though she'd read his mind, she said, "I was the Kingston High School Class of '52 recipient of the McGregor Fellowship."

"My grandfather started that endowment, and I'm sure no one has or will deserve it more than you." He then forced himself to take his eyes off Katherine, once again struck by how drastically different their childhoods had been. His was one continuous adventure, and hers was unjustly raw. She could have turned into a woman quite different from the one he saw before him. She was an enigma to him. And why she had never married completely baffled him.

Doc had a lighthearted way of teasing Katherine about so many things, and Murphy enjoyed watching their banter. Doc was especially pleased with himself the time he explained to Murphy about the highly contagious airborne disease that had for years mysteriously contaminated the entire town of Kingston. The one he officially labeled the "K Syndrome."

"Now don't you dare start that up again!" Katherine pleaded, but the laughter in her voice only enticed Doc to embellish it further.

Doc rubbed his temples, disturbing the hair that over the years had turned the color of his lab coat. He expounded as if presenting new research to his peers at a medical conference. "I call it a virus, but it technically seems to be more like some type of unexplained magnetic attraction. Appears to strike predominantly in the male species and young children, but mind you, females are quite vulnerable also. Unsuspecting folks go about their normal day, and then certain circumstances arise that put them in the company of my sweet nurse, and they go…" Doc looked at the ceiling, pretending to search his mind for the precise medical term. "Well, for lack of a better word… *goo goo*." They all laughed long and hard at his exaggerated expression of shock and bewilderment. He continued, "Grown men stumble and stutter and can't seem to get their tongues to fit their mouths. Young children just want to climb in her lap or hold her hand. For that matter, so do a few of those men!" Doc laughed merrily at his own joke, and Murphy eagerly joined him.

"Now, just stop all this malarkey," Katherine insisted, standing with her hands on her hips in hopes of stealing the authority, but Doc was undaunted.

"It's been so serious a couple of times, I've had to tap on a man's wedding ring to remind him he was married and try to help him stop slobbering!"

"Oh, for Pete's sake, Doc!"

Murphy played right along with it, as though he and Doc had rehearsed their lines. "You say even young children are highly susceptible?"

"Yes, indeed! I've seen it happen time and time again. If a child gets lost in a big crowd in town, they seem to seek her out as if she is a lighthouse of sorts. I've seen it happen at least a dozen times over the years at the Christmas parade, and you know how big a crowd that draws, the whole town turns out for it. It's also potent in the clinic. I've had kids screaming at the top of their lungs in my examining room, but all she has to do is enter the room, and it's like someone pulled their plug. They reach for her like she's their own mama and that's when I know she has them under her spell. It's frightening, I tell you!"

"If you don't stop all this nonsense, I'm going to start telling a few on *you*!"

But Doc had more he wanted to share. "It's a wonder she made it out of nursing school. Legend says she had many a resident and a gaggle of attending physicians walking around the hospital all spellbound. Seems like I remember something about the hospital's chief of staff having the worst case of the K Syndrome. I hear the only remedy is to move clear across the country because once you've been exposed, you rarely recover."

Katherine stood in the middle of the room with her arms across her chest, giving her best stern look, which only made Doc and Murphy bellow even harder.

They didn't have to say it aloud. These two men shared apparent knowledge. They knew if you tucked a woman's blonde hair under her nurse's cap and then dressed her in a starched white uniform, complete with thick white stockings and rubber-soled shoes, you would hide a great deal of the femininity in most women but it was impossible to douse Katherine's. She radiated beauty, no matter what she wore.

There was one topic that remained off limits during their morning conversations. Doc's private office was the place for Murphy and Doc to talk of Marianne's fragile condition. The two men often retreated there after their coffee ritual as Katherine began pulling files, organizing medical instruments, pulling up the window shades, and turning on the lamps in the waiting room. Honoring doctor-patient confidentiality, Doc always kept the door to his private office closed while talking to those patients needing to disclose personal information. It was different with Murphy though. Doc kept the door slightly ajar, allowing their conversation to drift through the clinic like cigar smoke snaking its way through a room. The men could hear her tinkering as she went about preparing for the day, and she could hear most, if not all, of their conversation. What Murphy would not know for years to come was that Katherine was the source of several ideas Doc presented to ease the heavy burden Murphy dealt with at Beechwood.

Early one November morning Katherine heard the heaviness in Murphy's voice, thick enough to cut with a knife. "My marriage has been loveless for almost its entire existence, and now it seems it's becoming lifeless. If I could just think of something that would make her want to get out of bed in the morning. I don't know what else to try. She no longer cares how she looks or what she wears. Nor do her friends call for bridge or to gossip. On good days, it's as though someone vacuumed out her soul and left her skeleton to rattle around the house. Other days she's a demon with the strength of you and me combined, and she regrets she's ever drawn a breath of life."

Doc's tone was gentle. "You've dutifully tried every clinic and hospital that could help her. I mentioned this idea some time back and I'm going to say it again. I think you might need to add another person to your staff. Not someone else to maintain the house and gardens or the timber, but maybe Marianne needs someone whose only responsibility is to care for her in ways you no longer can."

"What are you saying, Doc? Fish or cut bait?"

"Find someone who will love her on the good days and boss her on the ugly ones. Marianne extinguished your love years ago, and you have none left to give. What you have for her now is your loyalty. She's lucky to have married a man who's still willing to provide that."

"I learned years ago I wasn't going to make her happy. I just thought I could make her healthy again. She resents me when I leave, hates me more when I return, and screams at me when I try to stay."

"I know just the woman, have known her for years, who could handle Marianne. I never mentioned her before because I knew you still had hope and I was saving this idea until all your hope was gone."

"Tell me more."

"It's Katherine's Lily Mae you've heard us talk so much about. She's the one who has called Katherine "Queenie" since the summer her father disappeared. Lily Mae Warren has been a widow most of her adult life. She's big. Big in many ways. A big, buxom woman with a big set of lungs and a big dose of determination. She's available to start now, you just give the word. I can have her here this afternoon to meet you. She owned her own alterations business, with start-up money your folks gifted her when Katherine was young, and only recently sold it for a nice profit. I knew she wouldn't stay still for long; she's already looking for something else to occupy her time. You'll like her immediately, guaranteed." Doc intuitively knew what Murphy was thinking, and he added, "and Murphy, it's important for you to know she's loyal. All she sees and hears will be kept confidential."

Katherine could tell by the lull in conversation someone had rested his head in his hands. Perhaps Murphy. Perhaps Doc. Probably both.

"I guess I need her. I'm tired, Doc. I need something or someone big to come in and take over."

"I'll call you later in the day. Son, trust me. Life's going to get better. I promise. And one more thing. I want you to go by and meet the new rector at St. Thomas, Father Drew Keller. We Episcopalians can be proud of him. He's a gentle sort, and when you meet him, you'll know exactly what I mean. One can't help but be drawn to him."

"I'll do it." His voice searched his soul for optimism but found none.

Katherine stepped inside Doc's office the second she heard the back door close. With his back to her, Doc studied the photo of Mary Nell, his beloved departed wife. He turned slowly and with the slightest hint of satisfaction asked, "How quickly can you get Lily Mae here?"

"The only thing that would stop her from answering the second you beckoned would be a pie she just put in the oven."

They locked eyes and smiled. This was a plan Katherine suggested to Doc months ago, but Doc had to wait until Marianne McGregor hit rock bottom before he brought it up again to Murphy. And now the bottom had been hit.

"Well, go on and call her. I hope you're right. This could be our lucky day. Tell her to take her time, and we won't turn down anything warm she pulls out of the oven."

"You know she's going to ask me what this is all about. I'd like to tell her from my perspective, and then you can tell her from yours. Might be good to hear it from both of us before she decides."

"A young woman with an old soul. How'd you become so wise? And never mind answering, we both know. Just get Lily Mae here by two o'clock."

Katherine was halfway down the hall when she heard Doc call out, "I'm hoping for apple with a double crust."

As the clock in the reception area chimed two, Lily Mae Warren walked in carrying a round dish covered with a tea towel. Dressed in a plaid wool jacket and a crocheted beret, she looked as if she were all business and no fun, which made Katherine giggle.

"What brings that smile to your beautiful face, Queenie?" Setting her aromatic bundle on the desktop, Lily Mae stretched out both arms to welcome Katherine into her embrace. Katherine inhaled deeply. She had loved that smell for most of her entire life. Lily Mae still smelled the same as she did the very first time Katherine met her. A little of strong soap. A bit of whatever fiber she was wearing, sometimes cotton, sometimes wool. Always a hint of something she had recently cooked. And in the summer, there was always a touch of fresh peppermint on her breath.

Doc emerged from Room 2, already rubbing his belly. "Is that Lily Mae I hear making all that commotion? Lord, I swear I can smell apple pie on her."

"Something just told me today needed to be a double-crust-apple-pie day." Doc saw the wink she shot to Katherine and he chuckled.

With taste buds popping, Doc addressed both women, "Well, let's get in here and sample this apple pie before I explain our proposal. You might turn me down on this one, and I wouldn't blame you. Understand?"

Lily Mae observed the seriousness in his eyes and nodded. So, they talked over pie and tea, and Doc told Lily Mae the ugly truth of what went on at Beechwood. But she already knew. Katherine's version was almost verbatim.

The last time Lily Mae saw Doc talk with such sadness was when he told her of the seriousness of his wife's cancer and asked if she would stay with them over the next several months and help provide palliative relief from her pain until the end. And Doc never forgot the peace Lily Mae brought with her. It seemed to fill up their home from corner to corner and seep into the walls. His wife took her last breath with one hand in his and the other in Lily Mae's. Of all the deaths he had attended during his more than fifty years of practice, he'd never witnessed a death so full of hope and promise.

Forming a circle of three, Lily Mae asked the Lord to take His good and faithful servant. And it was then that Doc's wife spoke her final word, "Home," and just that quickly she was gone. Doc had revisited that memory at least a thousand times since Mary Nell's death, and he never ceased to feel the peace of it all.

When Murphy arrived just minutes later, he carried a heaviness about him. Katherine stepped out to give them privacy because she could tell with just a glance that the day had been difficult for him. Listening from across the hall Katherine heard the thickness in Murphy's voice as he told it like it was to Lily Mae, every bit of the ugliness and nastiness.

"I guess it sounds like I'm looking for a miracle, and I'll understand if you decline my offer."

"Here are my conditions, Mr. McGregor. I'll work hard and I'll work long and I'll even stay the night if you need me to now and then. You can trust me. I won't share with anyone what goes on. Your business is none of anybody else's business. But I'd prefer not to stay past 5:00 on Wednesday nights, and I won't work Sundays. Those are times I need to be in church. I do believe in miracles, and I've seen one or two in my life, but I'm no miracle worker. No, sir. Only the Lord works that way. If all that suits you just fine, I'll take the job. If not, I trust you'll find the right person."

And there they stood. A huddle of three. An old doc, a beaten down husband, and a wise woman who was willing to wrestle the devil. Katherine knew the magnitude of the moment. This mighty woman had rescued her once, and she was convinced Lily Mae could do it again for the McGregors. God willing.

Murphy didn't know if he should hug Lily Mae or genuflect. Instead, he gently shook her hand and warmly said, "Welcome to my world, Lily Mae. It will be an honor to have you at Beechwood." And so their journey began.

From then on, as the months rolled on, Murphy was able to join Doc and Katherine for coffee most mornings each week. He shared delightful stories of how Lily Mae set up camp and barked orders to all of them, himself included. He then reported back to Lily Mae any comments from Doc and Katherine, which elicited her distinct chuckle, a rumble that started deep down in her gut. He felt progress was being made in his household. A layer of heaviness lifted from within the walls of Beechwood.

One morning, about six months after her arrival, Lily Mae approached Murphy with an idea. "I've been sitting on this for a while, but it feels right so I'd like you to consider it. Don't know if you've ever heard of Clarence Daniels around Kingston. I was fifteen when he was born, and I've been bossing him ever since."

Murphy was intrigued. "Tell me more."

"He might just be the strongest man in these parts, even now, as he's getting on up in age. I think you could use him around here. We both could use him. Don't know exactly if he'd accept the job, but I think I could convince him."

"What kind of job is he looking for?"

"Well, that's just it. He's not looking for any job." Lily Mae laughed aloud, tickled with herself. "He just retired from thirty years with the railroad. He thinks he's going to like being retired, but I know good and well he's not. Ask Katherine about him, she's known him since she was seven. He's a mountain of a man, about as tall as that doorframe. Makes the word "big" look little, if you know what I mean. Skin's the color of a smooth hazelnut, and it made some folks call him Nut when he was young. When he grew to his big size, he cut out that foolish nonsense name. Our people paid attention."

"I'd like to meet him. Think you could arrange that?"

So, she did and he was hired immediately. Clarence's head was as bald as a freshly laid egg and the shine on it seemed to intensify the sparkle in his eyes. He had the strength of several men his size, but it was his laugh for which he was best known. It started deep down within and left his mouth in a full-throttle boom. Lily Mae could sometimes hear the laughter from far away and see the gathered heads bobbing in the distance, enjoying the lightheartedness

Clarence brought to Beechwood and the surrounding area. He looked like a lumberjack among the trees and he could eat anyone under the table, as long as Lily Mae had cooked the meal.

With Lily Mae's presence, along with Clarence's insistence, Murphy had time to fulfill more of his philanthropic responsibilities. Serving on the national boards for the American Red Cross and the National Forestry Commission required frequent travel, and for the first time in a long time, he was able to keep his commitments of time, energy, and expertise.

Murphy was always eager to see the next day's dawn after returning from one of his trips, anxious to walk the land of his ancestors and then be in the company of his two treasured companions, the coffee drinkers, the ones who brought balance to his life. The ones who had never judged his worthiness based on wealth or heritage. And they didn't let his miserable life at home count against him. In their eyes, he was just a man with a faithful dog.

FIRE

By the time Murphy and Baxter reached the turnoff to Beechwood's long and winding driveway, he already knew there would be death. He felt it deep within, as though all the McGregors who had cultivated the land before his time collectively sent the message, and he heard it clearly spoken in his head. Death he was certain of, but not sure how many. The one thing he knew for certain when he left that morning was the two living beings inside were Marianne and Lily Mae.

The smoke was thick and black and seemed to cover every inch of what had been a blue sky just moments before. He saw cataclysmic flames shooting upward from the back half of the house, and he knew they would devour the entire majestic structure. The flames strengthened as they taunted the limbs of the magnificent trees outlining the back lawn and gave off such unbearable heat that the windows began shattering one by one.

He raced to the back of the house, getting as close as he could manage, and saw the woman kneeling on the ground. Her arms were outstretched as if intending to catch something that might be falling through the air. A torrent of deafening wails rose from deep within her. She rocked back and forth in uncontrolled hysteria. When Murphy heard her wail, he knew who she was.

Pulling her away from the intense heat and smoke, Murphy saw her eyes were almost swollen shut, and her lips and ears were already blistered from the heat. She must have been using her hands to claw her way in or out of the house because they were bloody and already oozing. She didn't resist when he pulled her away. She knew. She already knew the only other person in the house would not get out alive.

When Lily Mae looked into Murphy's eyes through her own, now no more than thin slits, she could tell he knew the enormity of this tragedy on his family's hallowed ground. And she was right. Murphy knew Marianne was either already dead or was taking her last breath, and he would not be able to rescue her this time. This very last time. Her death wish had come true.

As the urgent news frantically passed from quadrant to quadrant, employees began arriving, and many daringly dashed into the bottom floor trying to retrieve any belongings they could carry. The flames seemed predestined to destroy anything of importance to Murphy, as though Marianne had instructed the diabolical inferno what to devour and what to leave behind smoke-ridden and ruined.

There was no hope of anything else surviving by the time the fire trucks arrived from town. At Murphy's request, the firemen spent their adrenaline wetting down the trees encircling the house, trying to prevent the loss of the last remaining glorious reminder of Beechwood Manor. The crowd, growing by the minute, watched as the grand old house began to disintegrate before their very eyes.

Doc and Katherine arrived soon after the first fire truck. Jumping from his car, Doc ran directly for Murphy and took him squarely by the shoulders, shouting, "Are you hurt, son, are you hurt?"

"Find Lily Mae, she's hurt bad, Doc. Her hands and face are…"

Both men turned simultaneously and saw Clarence cradling Lily Mae's head with his enormous lumberjack hands as she lay outstretched on a quilt. Katherine squatted beside her, and a small crowd was hovering at the perimeter of the quilt. Baxter lay whimpering at her feet. Katherine had Doc's medical bag beside her, pulling out bandages. Murphy recognized the familiar bag and knew this time it didn't contain a single thing capable of saving his wife.

Doc ran over, and together he and Katherine began the triage needed to get Lily Mae stable enough to withstand the car ride to Doc's clinic. Clarence drove while Doc and Katherine squeezed in beside her in the back seat trying to cushion some of the bumps and bounces along the route back into town. It would be hours later before Murphy would see any of those four again.

The night sky was full of stars by the time he and Baxter left the smoldering ashes and drove into town, the same sky that had played a trick on him just hours before. When he departed Beechwood earlier, he was struck by the clouds' swirls of white nestled here and there in the morning's blue sky. The next time he fully noticed the sky it had turned black with a wicked smoke that overpowered anything white against the blue. And now the night sky was majestically beautiful again, a reminder that there is light to be found after darkness. But Murphy wasn't ready to ponder that thought.

He drove to Doc's clinic without realizing where he was headed. His mind was numb, he was exhausted and in shock, but his heart knew where to take him.

He saw the clinic lights and entered through the back, following the trail of hushed whispers. Lily Mae was sitting upright in Doc's favorite old slipcovered chair. The lamplight cast a glow on all four of them, side by side, lined up like turtles sunning on a log. Her arms were covered in gauze from her armpits to her fingers. Her face was improved but with blisters still apparent. Eyes closed, her head was resting on the back of the chair, and she was humming. Doc's, Katherine's, and Clarence's eyes fell on Murphy as he took in all that was before him in that small room. Lily Mae felt his presence and with blistered lips tried to form a smile. Even the attempt brought her pain.

It was more than Murphy could handle. He'd been stoic throughout the day, answering the endless questions from the sheriff and obediently thanking the friends and neighbors and Beechwood staff who'd arrived by car and truckload throughout the day. For the first time since he had spotted the smoke, he allowed the intensity of the tragedy to hit him. He knelt in front of Lily Mae and wept.

Lily Mae struggled to speak. "You told me you needed a miracle when you asked me to come work for you, and I told you I didn't do miracles, but I prayed hard for one as I was trying to bust that door down to get Mrs. McGregor out of the fire." Her voice faltered, but she knew there was more he needed to hear, "but the Lord must not have thought the same way I did. He sure didn't perform any miracle today."

Murphy looked into her reddened eyes and tried to speak. His bottom jaw quivered, making it difficult to utter a response. "You're right. I told you I needed a miracle, and I know you don't believe one was performed today, but I disagree. It's a miracle you made it out of that house alive. No one should have made it out of the top floor with all the heat and smoke and angry flames and busted glass, but you did. God could have taken you today just as quickly as he took Marianne."

Saying aloud his dead wife's name shot a bolt of sadness through Murphy's entire body. A reminder of a life that would be no more. A wife who was miserable living the life she'd been given and wanted no part of it any longer.

It would take Murphy time to grieve. He had lost not only his wife, but his home and all the possessions passed down through generations of McGregors. It was the home in which he grew up, and, as he was often reminded during his childhood, he was the fifth generation of the McGregor clan to live within the walls of Beechwood Manor. He felt responsible for the death of the house. The sense of loss he bore on his shoulders was heavy. He knew, and had been told by many, that material possessions could be replaced. But he also knew the things important to his mother— the silver used by all the McGregor women—and things meaning- ful to his father—the photographs of three American presidents who had visited their home over the decades would be no more. And Beechwood's private collection of art, once described as an American treasure, was now merely dust mixed with the rest of the debris. The enormity of pain numbed him. More than the death of his wife and the destruction of his home, it was the painful realiza- tion it all had been destroyed under his watch. The grandeur of his family home had been erased. Forever.

The investigation into the cause of the fire was straightforward. Law enforcement talked to just about everyone in town before issuing the official statement, which quickly became the talk of every beauty parlor, barber shop, poker game, golf game, and bridge tournament. A variety of people were interrogated and most testified they had never heard Murphy McGregor say an unkind word about his wife or her habits. Most of those same people testified they had witnessed Marianne McGregor in varying degrees of rage aimed at anyone within her sight, and it was no secret she was a drunk. Everyone knew she was, but it went unspoken.

The final report specified the cause of the catastrophic fire was electrical, beginning in the master bedroom on the west wing. No one ever knew for sure how it started, including Lily Mae, but everyone certainly knew how it ended.

AFTER

"I have no right to ask you this, and I fully expect you to turn me down, but I wonder if you would consider staying on with me, here at Beechwood, although Beechwood Manor technically is no more."

Lily Mae nodded as she answered, "I wondered if you might need me to stay on. I'll be right here to help with anything you need."

Wanting, needing really, her companionship more than anything else, he said, "I don't even know where to begin. Maybe help me figure out how to set things straight if you think you're physically strong enough."

"Doc said these bandages will be off in a day or two."

"So you're alright with this idea?"

"I'd already decided. I knew before you asked me. You can't do this alone, no matter how strong you think you are. We'll travel this together and figure it out, piece by piece. Clarence and I both had decided you need us, even if you hadn't already reached that same conclusion."

Although Murphy's ancestral home was now destroyed, he still had several options if he wanted to continue living on McGregor land. The two original guesthouses and the vacant caretaker's cottage were still operable, as well as the barn house that once housed the equestrian staff. Even the chauffeur's cottage was an option although it had been a great while since it had seen occupancy. In the end, he chose as his temporary residence the larger guesthouse designed and built by his parents only three decades earlier. Its warmth and peace gave him the solace he ached for while grieving the death of the big house and everything within it.

It was much larger than he needed but miniscule in comparison to Beechwood Manor. The entire back wall of the two-story cottage was framed in tall windows, opening to the vast expanse of Murphy's favorite of all the lakes on the property. Massive old trees encircled the fieldstone and shake-shingled guest house, tempting many an artist to try to capture the charm of the house among the trees. The interior woodwork—the mantels, crown molding, paneled ceilings and ceiling-to-floor bookcases—were all works of art, envied by all visitors. Never in his wildest dreams could Murphy have expected to one day leave Beachwood Manor and live in the guesthouse, but he had learned that life's journey could sometimes push one down an unexpected path. And such was his life now.

He spent hour after hour, for a considerable number of weeks, penning heartfelt thank you notes to the infinite list of those who did what friends do in times of disaster. It was a tedious task, but it kept him busy and compliant as he wrestled with his emotions.

He felt culpable as he internalized how much easier life was without Marianne. But in time he accepted that being alone wasn't a bad thing at all. His mind was eradicating the pain and skepticism that had slowly seeped into every cell of his being during his days of living with an angry addict. Bit by bit, he was now unexpectedly discovering a more relaxed, tranquil version of himself. One he did not expect.

He avoided town entirely, with two exceptions. He found great solace in his weekly appointments with Father Drew at St. Thomas, just as Doc had suggested. Murphy was drawn to Drew's wise counsel, and he depended on it like salve to a wound.

And he and Baxter joined Katherine and Doc at the clinic for early morning coffee five days a week. Other than his homestead, it was the one place where he could count on just being himself. There he felt no pressure to disentangle his emotions or to explore any plans for the future. He was simply one of three people enjoying the early dawn hours of another day of life. He depended on their simple wisdom to help him maneuver around the obstacles in his path. Doc and Katherine felt a responsibility to provide a serenity that would aid his recovery. Doc provided the humor and wisdom, while Katherine was gentle and nurturing, and Murphy absorbed all they had to offer like a sponge. It was his daily nourishment; fueling his strength and charting his course. And although he didn't know it, one day shortly it would become very clear exactly where that course would take him.

And if they helped him chart his course, Lily Mae was his anchor and Clarence was his first mate overseeing the demolition of Beechwood Manor's charred remains.

Everyone recognized his status as a wealthy and eligible widower, causing women from a variety of age groups to regret they were no longer available. Within hours of the fire, women began sending lavish and uninhibited sympathy notes attached to their casseroles and cakes and bottles of wine. Personally delivered, of course.

He shared all this with Father Drew as a lighthearted ending to their first counseling session after the fire. The previous hour had been painfully raw as Murphy began to work through his emotions while reliving the cause of Marianne's death. Both men were ready for a distraction, and they laughed heartily at some of the blatant proposals Murphy was already receiving thinly disguised as condolences.

"May I suggest that perhaps you and Lily Mae work out some sort of plan, out of necessity I suppose? If you see an approaching car with a male caller, then by all means you should answer the door. But, if it is a solitary female guest, married or unmarried, then perhaps it should be Lily Mae who answers your door. I've seen her in action a few times, and I have no doubt she could deter anyone with ulterior motives. I'm certain of it."

"That's exactly what we'll do, and I promise you, she will undoubtably love this plan. If the next few days of visitors go anything like the last few since the fire, I'll have plenty of stories to report at next week's session."

Turns out it was a good plan. Lily Mae delighted in her role, swearing up and down that the man of the house was not at home. "Well I'll be sure and let him know you made these chicken and dumplings all by yourself," or "Oh, I sure will, I'll tell him just like you told me . . . you were sitting at home making one of these cakes everybody loves when the idea popped in your head that maybe Mr. McGregor would like some all to himself."

Lily Mae could outfox the foxes. What she said and what she thought were two different things. She wanted to tell them they weren't fooling anyone, and certainly not Mr. Murphy Egan McGregor. They came traipsing out to the McGregor homestead all dressed up in their cocktail party clothes with their curled hair and polished nails and lipstick to match, making sure they looked beautiful from head to toe. It was all very orchestrated, and Lily Mae was not fooled by a single one of them.

She always ended with "No, I'm not certain where he went or how long he'll be gone. Probably several hours, at least." And if they acted like they might just stay and wait it out, she always added "and he might not return till tomorrow, but I sure will tell him you came by."

About ten days after the fire, Murphy and Lily Mae were organizing leather-bound books in the guesthouse library when they heard a car coming down the tree-lined drive. They both instantly recognized the sleek gray sedan and its well-known driver who considered herself one of Kingston's elite—obviously only one of her flaws.

"I've got this," said Lily Mae immediately. "You stay right here. I've known for a mighty long time this woman has a drought in her soul, and I'd rather you not be a part of what's about to happen." Closing the French doors behind her, she added under her breath, "Lord, forgive me my trespasses, but especially this one and forgive me for all these years I've been wishing for this moment to come my way."

Lily Mae sashayed to the front door and stepped out on the

porch, blocking the door's entrance, as she told the woman she needed to take her delivery right back home. It was being refused.

With an incredulous voice, the visitor asked, "You won't *accept* it? Is that what you just said?"

"That's exactly what I said."

"What on earth do you mean you won't accept…does he not eat cobbler?"

With a voice lacking all emotion, Lily Mae expounded, "Oh, he likes cobbler all right. Matter of fact, peach *is* his favorite. And he likes a nice thick crust on top, just like this one, but I'm making the decisions for him today." Lily Mae paused to make sure her next words were plainly heard, "I'm telling you, we don't want *your* cobbler in *this* house." Lily Mae's glare could have peeled paint off a porch.

The woman had not seen this coming, and it took her a second to process it all. Indignant, she stomped her high-heeled foot and screeched, "I have never seen such rude behavior in my entire life!"

Lily Mae cut her off. "I'm not real sure how you did it, but you've somehow convinced some people in this town that they should bow down and follow your orders, but in my eyes there's nothing about you worth listening to. You're absolutely nothing to me, and I'm not afraid or ashamed to say that aloud."

The cobbler was still warm in the woman's hands, but she no longer noticed. Seething with anger, she let loose on Lily Mae. "You'll wish you had never said that to me. I guarantee you'll rue this day. Why, you're nothing but an ugly, rude, old…"

By now Lily Mae was loaded for bear. Stepping further out onto the porch, she was close enough to smell the woman's hair spray. Pointing her finger in the woman's face, she said, "You think that's ugly? Let me just tell you what ugly looks like AND smells like. Ugly smells just like tar. You ever smelt ugly old tar? Take yourself a long way back. I heard tell about a girl so full of meanness and the devil she smeared ugly tar all over a little girl's rabbit fur muff because she just couldn't stand to see someone else have something nice. I never have forgotten that story. You remember that, Wanda?" Lily Mae was bellowing by the time she said that repulsive name.

"Oh, for God's sake, I can't stand you. You just wait until I let Murphy know how you've talked to me." With a vicious smirk and sweaty palms, she deliberately threw the entire cobbler at Lily Mae and watched the syrupy peaches and crust drip all the way down Lily Mae's legs to her shoes.

Murphy emerged just in time to observe Wanda's deliberate intentions of bringing harm to Lily Mae. They watched in tandem as she left tire marks on the circular drive.

Beaming, Lily Mae couldn't resist. "Guess you can tell I've been saving that one up for a very long time, but it sure did feel mighty good. These clothes and this porch can be washed off and they'll be good as new. And I'll probably sleep better tonight than I have in years because I've been wondering for a couple of decades now just how the Lord intended me to get square with that woman, and today He opened that door and now it's done."

They both laughed long and hard with the kind of laughter that cleanses. A sense of lightheartedness seemed to fill the air even after the sound of their laughter subsided.

The food parade lasted a good eight weeks. The avalanche of written correspondence lasted even longer. Emulating his father, Murphy had always checked his post office box daily. But soon after the fire, Postmaster Haynie suggested he might need to check it a couple of times each day until, as he put it, "the newness of the fire wears off."

Lily Mae tried to describe it all to Katherine. "There are hundreds of cards and letters. Most are from old friends and relatives, some are business acquaintances, and some are from people I've read about in *Life* magazine. Important folks, most of them. Famous people. People in politics and Hollywood and sports and even some writers. To Murphy, they're just people, but I know they're the kind of folks the rest of us would call famous."

And Lily Mae was right. Often those she categorized as prominent sent long commiserative notes reminiscing about the events they attended at Beechwood Manor over the years, encouraging him to rebuild the house and make her as majestic as she once was.

More than a few cards came from conniving single women cleverly disguising their ulterior motives with words of condolence. Murphy read a few aloud to Lily Mae one afternoon, and the two of them laughed so loud Baxter got up and moved into another room, which only made them laugh louder.

> Murphy,
>
> I stay up late every night just worrying about you. I'd be happy to open a bottle of wine if you ever need to come by and visit and let your heart out. Please call.

Or another

> Murphy,
>
> Sometimes all a friend can do is listen — I'm here for you, day or night, around the clock. Nothing would mean more than for me to wrap my arms around you and let you relieve some of your pain. I just know Marianne would want me to help you get through these tough times.

The only decent sympathy card from a single woman came from Katherine. She sent a very simple card.

```
Murphy,

I'm so sorry for all your pain.
I hope you will take time to find
yourself again. Be still and
listen. I know God will direct
your path.

Fondly,
Katherine
```

Murphy was touched by her unpretentious sincerity, and it affirmed what he already knew. She was the most intriguing woman he had ever known. He kept her card on top of the stack of those he intended to keep, the ones he would rely on for comfort during the dark days ahead.

Lily Mae noticed Katherine's card began to look as though it had been handled and read multiple times which prompted Lily Mae to offer some insight to Murphy, the kind she thought he needed to figure out his new direction. "Couldn't help but notice my Katherine's note to you, Murphy. She knows exactly how to say what she thinks. She's always been smart that way."

Murphy looked up over the top of the morning paper and smiled at Lily Mae. "In some ways I feel like I know her well enough to read her thoughts before she says them, and other times I'm bewildered by what she says and does."

"What exactly about her do you find bewildering?" Lily Mae's back was to him as she was working on the breakfast dishes, but he could hear the smile in her voice just the same.

"For starters, I've always wondered why she never married. I know for certain it hasn't been for lack of choices."

Lily Mae turned and looked him straight on. "She fell in love once. Happened in nursing school while he was in med school. I liked him a lot, but I had a funny nag that ate at me. Something about him I couldn't quite figure out. Turns out I didn't have to say anything to her about it because the romance ended about the time she was finishing nursing school. She moved back to Kingston and told us, me and Doc, to never mention his name in her presence again. The closest she ever got to explaining it was when she said, 'I gave him everything I had in my heart. Turns out it wasn't enough.' So, to answer your question, I guess she just never had the courage to try again. You know this firsthand, I know, but love gone wrong can just about kill you. Takes an awful lot of courage to decide you're willing to risk it all again."

Murphy sat silently for quite some time, contemplating what he had just learned. "What about you, Lily Mae? Why did you never remarry? Didn't you tell me you became a widow at age twenty-four?"

Lily Mae studied the slight breeze blowing through the limbs right outside the kitchen window. Much softer than usual, she answered, "Why did I never remarry? That's easy. Never wanted to venture out to see if there was another man out there as good as my Robert. Not many people, male or female, as good as he was. He treated me the way God wanted a man to treat a woman. When you've been treated that way, you know deep down there's no way you'll find another that good, so you just don't try."

Neither spoke for quite a while. Each was caught up in a different world. Lily Mae was remembering her Robert and all the hopes and dreams they had as newlyweds those many decades ago, and Murphy was caught up in his own thoughts—not of Marianne, but of the young nurse whose heart was broken because she wasn't enough for someone.

It was exactly six months to the day of the fire that Murphy received two invitations to the Winter Escape, the biggest soiree of the year at the Kingston Country Club. He turned both down with kind and respectful notes explaining he'd already planned a fishing trip out of state. Then the profusion of invites to the other six or seven spring and summer traditional social events around Kingston began to arrive. They were not the least bit tempting to Murphy. He found it all quite annoying. Plus, he knew nothing would instigate gossip quicker than being seen around town with a lady on his arm. He found the idea of a social gathering exhausting and wanted no part of it.

But people just couldn't stand to see him alone. In their eyes, it didn't seem healthy. What they didn't know was Murphy was enjoying his quiet life free from all the pain that came with living alongside someone with an addiction. And he stayed busy. He was free to do as he pleased. He could stay up till four in the morning reading a novel, and it would bother no one. He could eat leftover fried chicken for breakfast, sitting on the back porch in nothing but his boots and long johns, and no one would scold him. It was an intoxicating freedom, and he felt privileged to receive it. He vowed he would never take it for granted.

And so about ten months after the fire, over lunch on the back porch, he shared something with Lily Mae and told her she was the first to hear the news. "I've been encouraged by a lot of old family friends from around the country and from almost the entire town of Kingston to rebuild Beechwood Manor. It's been a real struggle to figure out the right thing to do."

"I've watched you walk the boundaries of the old place time and time again, and I knew you were wrestling with it. Knew it was hard for you to study those ruins. Sorrow sought you out and tried to latch on." She let her voice trail a bit and then continued, "When something's belonged to your blood kin that long, it'd be hard to part with, but I guess you already know that."

Looking out over the lake, Murphy nodded and continued, "If I choose not to rebuild, I'm erasing off the face of the earth the grand place that housed my family for generations. It was a majestic place, and she hosted some wondrous events in her day. I thought the decision would come easier to me when they bulldozed the charred skeleton of the house, but I can still see her footprint and in my mind she's standing tall and proud, the only way I've ever known her."

Simultaneously, they looked toward the former site of the majestic manor, silently imagining her standing in all her glory.

Then Murphy continued, "But the world's a different place now, and I guess I'm not the kind of McGregor who needs such a place to entertain. I won't have any descendants who'll fill the house with noise and laughter and conversation, so I think I'm just going to stay right here, in the guesthouse, for the rest of my days." And then he turned and focused on Lily Mae before finishing. He needed to see the wisdom in her eyes when he asked, "Am I doing the right thing, Lily Mae?"

Her nod indicated she thought he'd chosen wisely. "I believe you are. I don't see you building it back just to live in it alone. And the town of Kingston's already on the map, it doesn't need you to create something to prove what your people have done for this town. I believe this beautiful, peaceful house you're in right now is a healthy spot for you. It's plenty big, and Lord knows the way it sits looking right over the lake seems like it was meant for you to live here. The woodwork and rock in this house are a craftsman's masterpiece, and this house is more you than the marble and the crystal and the flocked wallpaper in the big house, even though she was the most magnificent thing I'd ever seen in my entire life. A few of those chandeliers were larger than the room I was born in." She paused and let those words sink in because she knew she had one more thing to say, and she wanted him ready to take it in. "My only advice is for you to stop calling this house the guesthouse because you're not the guest. You're the man of the house now, but I guess you've lived your whole life calling your house by a name so I think it's only right you think hard on it and give this place a name of its own."

Later, returning from a long walk across part of the lower south quadrant he announced he had decided on a name. "Cross Creek seems to fit this place for me."

"Cross Creek." Lily Mae liked the way it sounded when she heard her own voice say it aloud. "I like it. What's it mean?"

Nostalgia swept over him like early morning fog on a pond. "Well, part of it refers to the spring creek that feeds into the lake. I spent countless hours in that big creek when I was young. I tossed around the idea of calling it the Creek House, but I thought more on it. The McGregors would never have owned this land if Donovan McGregor had not crossed the ocean to come to America, and some of the beech trees from this land became track ties that allowed the railroad to cross from one end of the country to the other. I've always thought of this as hallowed ground which makes me think of a cross. So, there it is. Cross Creek."

A hush swept through the trees, acknowledging his wisdom.

ROMANCE

It was the day love laid its branches of hope and tenderness on the ground, and they crossed right over. Of all places, it started in the cemetery.

It had been one of those nights when Murphy suddenly found himself wide-awake at a quarter till three. He woke rested and energized. The trouble was, most people wouldn't start their day for another two or three hours, so he did what he'd always done. He got up anyway. The day was his, and he could do with it as he pleased. It had been twenty-two months since the fire. If he had learned anything, it was to not let a single day be lost to melancholy.

This Saturday promised to be one of those grand late March spring days where anything and everything with life would respond to the glory of the day. Miss Nina, his octogenarian neighbor and dear friend, brought him a propagated gardenia seedling a few weeks back—an old-fashioned Belmont variety. Gardenias were his mother's favorite, and while Beechwood had more than twenty varieties scattered throughout the lawns, he intended this one to grow its roots deep into the soil next to his mother's grave.

At first light, he loaded a variety of gardening tools, a cooler of water, and his worn leather gloves into the back of the faithful old farm truck. Nestling the seedling in his lap, he left plenty of room on the truck's bench seat for Baxter.

It was half-past six by the time they drove through the ancient ivy-covered gated columns of Holly Grove Cemetery. The fact that his ancestors purchased the land for the town's burial ground explained why his people's plots were nestled under the shade of a large grove of trees at the crest of the highest hill. Theirs was the heavily shaded section surrounded by a beautiful antiquated black iron fence with an ornate gate. The enclosure sent a message that the ones buried there were bound together, as connected in death as they had been in life. Other trees and benches were nestled in and around the expansive cemetery, but as an adult Murphy seldom traveled past the McGregor tombstones. He knew what was out there. The place was filled with markers that gave credence to the lives of those that now slept under their stones.

Holly Grove was one of Baxter's favorite spots because, if they arrived early enough, he was allowed the freedom to run and sniff and explore. On this particular day he stuck fairly close to the truck as his master unloaded his assortment of gardening tools, but when Murphy became preoccupied with his digging, Baxter took off down the first hill and over the second.

Murphy pruned some shrubs and then raked the last of winter's debris from all the plots in the McGregor's gated area. He carefully planted the gardenia seedling just outside the ancient iron gate, positioning it so the giant pin oak would provide plenty of shade and shelter during the heat of summer but also allow an ample dose of morning sun. He patted the soil lightly around the gardenia's freshly mounded home and gave it a hearty drink from the cooler, emulating what he'd seen his mother do countless times when he helped her plant at Holly Grove and Beechwood.

Murphy stood back to study what he had accomplished. Turning to a grave, he stood and studied it for quite some time. Removing his cap and kneeling before her headstone, he began, "Mother, I never should have married her. Should have trusted my gut. I guess I'll never understand why I didn't take a stand and call the whole thing off. Well, to be fair, that's not entirely true. I didn't take a stand because of you, Mother. I just didn't want to disappoint you. But you do realize now, don't you, that was not a good idea. It would have been more honorable for me to call off the wedding and break Marianne's heart than to marry her and let her ruin my life and Beechwood Manor. I followed your rotten advice, and it nearly destroyed me. But I'm not here to blame you, Mother.

Just here to remind you I love you and to offer your favorite gardenia as a peace offering and to tell you I'm glad you didn't live long enough to see the ugliness of it all." There was nothing more to say. Those words had been welling up inside him for a long time, and they needed to be said, regardless if she was above or below the ground.

"Darn old curious dog, where'd you wander off to this time?" Murphy gathered his tools and the box of collected leaves and twigs, realizing Baxter had been out of his sight almost since their arrival. The familiar whistle, which usually brought Baxter galloping his way, produced no such response. A second whistle amounted to the same. "You little rascal. This better be something really magnificent you've discovered."

Murphy's head rotated back and forth as he slowly drove the expanse of Holly Grove. It wasn't until he reached the crest of the second hill that he spotted whom Baxter had chosen over him. It was Katherine. Only he saw the sudden grin on his face when he glanced in the rearview mirror. And what a grin it was.

She was in dungarees and a cotton button-down shirt with a sweater tied around her neck. Her blonde hair hung loosely around her shoulders instead of the coiffed chignon he was so accustomed to seeing under her starched nurse's hat. She was kneeling at someone's grave, and Baxter was lying right next to her, supervising her every move. Woman and dog looked up simultaneously when they heard the engine coming over the hill. Katherine waved and Baxter wagged, but neither of them moved from their positions.

As he cut the truck's engine, he thought *Leave it to Baxter. Good dog!*

Her beauty in those casual clothes almost took his breath away. Murphy grabbed his gloves and clippers, hoping Katherine might let him help her in some way. He was surprised by the excitement he was feeling. Or was it a tinge of anticipation? Whatever it was, it was a feeling he thought he was incapable of experiencing at this point in his life, especially over someone twelve years younger.

"Nice dog, lady," Murphy said, laughing. Baxter's snout appeared glued to his front paws, but his tail beat frantically against the dirt; apparently amused he had led his master to this very spot.

They were congregated at a gravesite with Katherine's last name on the monument. The stone bore witness to her mother's birth and death but included only the date of birth for her father. *How do you bury a body when you have no proof the person ever died?* he wondered silently.

"Do you visit here often?" he asked.

"Oh, about once a month. I like to keep things tidy." She looked up at Murphy with a comfortable smile and a twist of her head, shielding her eyes with a gloved hand as she looked up at him.

"I see you have a supervisor." They both looked at Baxter, and he barked at them in response, wagging his tail to indicate he, too, could play their game.

Murphy felt a magnetic pull to her like he had never experienced. The beat of his heart began to accelerate, and he suddenly became very shy. He had never acted this way around Katherine. For that matter, he had never acted this way around any female, and he had known many. He realized some time ago he'd come to adore her, but he always assumed he would be able to disguise it. It was seeing her in a different setting that was tilting his axis.

Dusting herself off, Katherine gave her handiwork a quick glance and decided she'd done all she intended to do. When she turned, she realized he was staring at her, and she blushed.

"What is it?" She swatted at her hair, assuming something had just landed on the crown of her head.

He reached over and brushed her hair just above her right temple and pretended to shoo something away, happy to tell a little fib that would excuse him for staring. He wasn't expecting to react so strongly to the touch of her hair. He instantly wanted to hold a handful of it and not stop until he gathered her in his arms. He felt the blood rush to his cheeks and was amused to discover he was still very much alive, at least around her.

"Just an early spring ladybug…want to throw your bike in the back of the truck and grab a cup of coffee?" He hoped he didn't sound too pubescent. Even reminding himself of their age difference did nothing to extinguish his lighthearted mood.

"Sure, if you think there's room for me and this beautiful dog." She rubbed behind Baxter's ears, who by this time had scooted so close to her side he blocked all daylight between them.

Katherine and Baxter climbed into the cab as Murphy loaded her bike and then climbed in next to them. He drove slowly up and down the hills, out the arched entrance, and made a right turn.

"Aren't we going to the clinic for coffee?"

"Oh," he paused, realizing he assumed they would do something different this time. "Well, we could but I thought we might go down to The Grill on the town square for some coffee and pancakes. What's a good Saturday morning without a stack of flapjacks?" he asked, looking her way while hoping she wouldn't refuse him.

"Sounds delicious." This adventure felt fresh and invigorating, and she was happy. And something more. Giddy with a twinge of what? She refused to process it all but was willing to at least marvel at how comfortable she was at that very moment in the truck with a man she knew so very well.

Turns out the pancakes and coffee and easy conversation were just the precursors of the day. From there they stopped by old man Baker's bait shop and bought three dozen minnows, just as many crickets, a couple of made-to-order sandwiches and cold drinks and then on to his place to grab his tackle and a pair of rods and reels. They walked as a threesome; man, woman, and dog, to the largest lake on Murphy's land and, much to her delight, she spent the next several hours out-fishing him.

"This isn't your first fishing derby, obviously. Who taught you to fish?" he asked, realizing he was envious of the lucky person who'd taught her one of his favorite pastimes.

"I fished as a child with Lily Mae using cane poles, and Doc taught me how to fish with a rod and reel. Lily Mae fished for supper. Doc fished for fun. I like being on the water, it reminds me of those two. Especially early in the morning. I've found that whatever worries you might have in the middle of the night seem to evaporate when you sit on the water's edge with a fishing pole in your hand. It's delightfully peaceful."

Murphy thought it ironic she'd chosen those last two words to describe the water. He would have used the same words to describe her, along with several other words for her can't-stop-staring-at-you loveliness.

When the bait was gone, they wandered to the boathouse and cleaned up. Eventually, they launched a rowboat and after Murphy had rowed quite a distance, they dined on the bologna sandwiches and cold drinks he'd picked up earlier. Murphy couldn't think of anything that felt more natural than to have her right there with him. Baxter sat between them, his tail thumping softly each time either one of them laughed aloud. They rowed over to the spillway and he showed her where the big channel catfish gathered and told a couple of stories of catching some as a boy. They eventually made it back to shore and sat in the rockers on the deck of the boathouse.

"I'm proud of how you've handled yourself these past months since the fire. I know it has been difficult, but you seem to have come out on the other side even stronger than you were before."

"Thank you for all of that. I guess you surely must know, that you, Doc, Lily Mae, and Father Drew are the ones responsible for my...for my rebirth, if you will."

"I can't speak for everyone, but I think I can speak for Doc and myself. We want nothing more than for you to be happy and healthy, and if a cup of coffee and some conversation five days a week has been part of your prescription, then we'll be saddened if you ever decide we are no longer needed."

"You can get that thought out of your head right now, that I'd ever reach the point when I would stop my coffee counseling with two of the finest people I know." Murphy smiled at Katherine and took great pleasure in seeing a blush cover her cheeks.

Katherine tried to redirect the conversation, hoping Murphy wouldn't notice the sudden color. "Yes, I like Father Drew very much, and I like what he's done for St. Thomas. He arrived as a bachelor, but I'm not sure he'll remain that way. He's young and wise and very handsome, but most importantly, we all, meaning all the congregants of St. Thomas, find his charisma irresistible. More than that, I think he understands the brokenness of the world. People come to him drowning in darkness, and he helps them turn on the lights."

Murphy agreed. "I couldn't agree more. I don't think I'm telling anything I shouldn't, but in the course of my counseling sessions with him, I've gained a friend. We spend time almost every week fishing, hunting, or birdwatching here on my land. I've learned our favorite member of the clergy needs and deserves the luxury of removing his collar." After a quick pause and the emergence of a devilish grin, he added, "As well as bingo."

"Bingo?"

"Yes, bingo. It's his secret addiction, but I don't think he'd mind me telling it. I've heard him say it in public. Almost every night of the week he has church commitments of one type or another. If it's not a vestry meeting, it's the Christian education committee, or a premarital counseling session for a young couple, or it's Wednesday night evening prayer, or it's, well, it's endless. So, every now and then when he has a free evening, he sneaks over to the bingo hall over in Burke and plays bingo. There's a group of old, worn out, down-on-their-luck ladies who save him a seat every night, just hoping he'll show up. They have no idea he's a minister, which makes it even more fun for him. He occasionally cooks up a batch of fudge from his grandmother's recipe and takes it to those he affectionately refers to as 'his bingo girls'."

Katherine was hanging on every word. "I love it. I love every single bit of that story. I love that he has a life outside the church, and I love that he has a gaggle of women who adore and coddle him without ever really knowing who he is or what he does. That's genuine."

"And every now and then he wins! He won $1,200 about six months ago. Do you know what he did with it?"

"I'd love to know."

"He took it to a car mechanic in Burke and told the guy to call a particular bingo-playing lady, Margaret Weir, and tell her some nameless person came through town and left money for her much-needed car repairs."

"Do you think the guy did it?"

"Oh, I know he did it. Father Drew wore his collar the day he visited the mechanic and as he firmly shook the guy's hand he said, "Praise God, from whom all blessings flow." Then he gave him cash and told him he expected to see a repaired car within the week."

"Oh, I love this story. How did it end?"

"The next time Father Drew played bingo the ladies swarmed him and told him about Margaret's guardian angel who paid for her car to be repaired." Murphy's eyes danced as he added, "And he never let on."

She smiled and said, "One act of mercy at a time. That seems to be the secret to life."

They both sat back and took it all in. The story of a good man doing a good deed. Katherine knew there were countless stories like that involving Murphy, and he knew the same about her. There was so much they knew about each other, and yet so much more to learn.

They talked of many things that day. She told him some of the humorous events that had happened over the years with Doc at the clinic and a couple of throw-your-head-back-and-laugh stories about Lily Mae. He delighted her with story after story of his boyhood escapades growing up at Beechwood. She laughed easily at his antics and prodded him with questions wanting to know more. Between stories, they sat quietly just enjoying the water and the breeze. He'd always loved his family's land, but today he saw it with fresh eyes and realized the fire had not destroyed what he really loved about Beechwood. It was a majestic place full of trees and shade and colors and smells, and it possessed a pull that made a body just want to sit back, rest, and let it fill your pores. And stay.

His adult life had been spent fighting two wars, one on the other side of an ocean, and the other with Marianne on this soil. He was so busy trying to correct the wrongs of others he forgot to notice what he had all around him. The blinders he had worn seemed to disappear, and he fell in love with the land all over again.

"We'll have to take a walk through the woods sometime. There are so many fascinating things to explore," he said with conviction in hopes she would agree.

"Oh, please, yes, I would like that. What kinds of things are out there? Can you name me six things without stopping?"

Her eagerness was contagious. "Well, a beaver's dam for one; two would be a rock wall built by a battalion of civil war soldiers who made camp here for almost two weeks; three would be the call of the whippoorwills that lull me to sleep each night; four would be an elm tree with a knot shaped like an Indian's head; five would be the old barn with a 1924 Farmall tractor, the very first combustion engine ever driven on this land; and, six would be my very own natural history specimens my mother allowed me to collect and chronicle including snakeskins, a hornets' nest, and an almost entirely intact skeleton of a groundhog."

"You rattled those off so fast I think you could have named fifty! I'm impressed!"

"Is that a challenge? You want fifty? I can deliver fifty without even pausing between each one." And taking a deep breath, he successfully produced a list of fifty of the most fascinating, enticing things Katherine had ever heard.

Something happened between the two of them during his reciting of the fifty wonders. He looked deep into her eyes as he spoke, and she matched his gaze. They never stopped looking at each other and maybe didn't even blink. He felt her look deep within him and saw a heart that was beginning to thaw. At the very same moment, he looked into her eyes and felt her beckon him to join her in a life that was healthy for his soul.

Katherine broke the spell when he finished his litany of wonders. "I think I have a glimpse of who you were as a boy living on this land and who you'll be as an old man, and the only difference between the two will be years and nothing else. This land will take care of you because you love it so." She said it with such genuine warmth that he knew it was perhaps the truest thing anyone had ever told him. And he knew it came from a woman who would cherish the land enveloping her.

He reached for her arm and said, "I'd like to show you something you probably don't even know exists, but it's directly related to you, in a sense. Feel like walking?"

Intrigued, Katherine nodded eagerly, secretly hoping it wasn't already written across her face that she was ready to follow him anywhere. They ambled down the winding lane that had at one time served as the drive connecting the mansion to the guesthouse. Massive trees lined each side and their branches reached across high above the pavement as though they'd linked hands to form the thick canopy of limbs and leaves. While the pavement was plenty wide enough for a vehicle, she realized they were walking so close their arms often brushed against each other and she repeatedly felt his hand brush against hers. The sensation caused her to inhale deeply and she tried her best to savor the moment, knowing this incredibly delightful day might never happen again. At least not for her. Common sense told her Murphy McGregor was never going to find contentment with a woman who'd lived such an ordinary life as hers.

The final turn landed them at the entrance of Cross Creek. Something seemed so familiar to Katherine as they walked up the expanse of the flagstone curved front steps that she caught herself wrestling with a strong sense of déjà vu. Murphy opened the door and stepped aside, allowing her to enter first. Together they stood in the foyer that opened up into what she thought was the most beautiful room she'd seen in her life, transfixed by the dark walnut woodwork throughout the room and the stately bookcases laden with books flanking each side of the fireplace.

She fought hard to suppress a sudden wave of dizziness, instantly sensing her father had at one time been in this very room. His hands had crafted the raw wood into works of art, and here she was, finally, seeing it for the first time. She inhaled a deep breath and tried to steady herself.

Murphy said nothing as he stood behind her with his hands gently resting on her shoulders. He was willing to stand behind her for the rest of his life if necessary, for her to understand that her father, missing now for decades, had created this beautiful room.

In a voice as soft as dew he almost didn't hear her when she said, "I think my father…" but couldn't finish the sentence.

With pride and affirmation, Murphy nodded and replied, "He did."

She ventured farther into the room and reached high to delicately touch the massive layered walnut mantel, as if placing the star on top of a tree. She whispered, "You'll never know what this moment means to me."

When her eyes became misty, his did the same. Murphy knew then he was right in showing it to her and silently berated himself for not doing it years earlier when he first made the connection.

She studied the bookshelves, running her fingers along some of the titles. She inspected the collection of bird eggs and rocks Murphy had placed intermittently among the books. Clearly, he was beginning to rebuild his natural history collection, and she silently nodded, affirming the importance of it all.

He wasn't certain how long they stood in that room, but he knew it was more than a minute and less than a lifetime. And when she turned to face him with a brave closed-lip smile, he said, "We can come back here as often as you wish."

He offered her his hand before she descended the front steps of the house, and as she reached for it, she said in a barely audible voice, "My heart has never stopped missing him. I always thought I'd find him one day, or what happened to…" and when her voice faltered, she said no more.

Apparently miffed he had been banished to the outside, Baxter sat on his haunches on the first step and let out a long howl as they walked past him. One of those howling-at-the-moon scenes the coyotes do so well. They both laughed, and just like that, the heaviness of the mood was lifted.

They paused at one of the ponds on their walk back, and out of habit Murphy picked up a smooth stone and tossed it easily back and forth from one hand to another before letting it rip across the water, pulling off a fourteen-skip throw. Katherine eyed him and suddenly the twinkle in her blue eyes returned. She met his throw and upped it by one. A fifteen-skip throw.

Murphy threw his head back and let out a walloping cheer that echoed across the pond. When was the last time someone had out-skipped him? Probably forty years earlier at that same spot with his best buddy, Walt. It felt good to be young again and on the land that was so much a part of his being. He wanted to somehow re-wind those difficult years when he was entombed in a miserable marriage and have a second try at living them a different way. It began to dawn on him that the years ahead could give him that chance.

Murphy was disappointed when Katherine said it was time to get back home, but it was after all late afternoon.

Reluctantly, the three of them loaded up in the truck and drove back into town. Murphy drove much slower than usual, and he contemplated aloud, "You know, this is the first time in all the years we've known each other that we've truly been alone, and I'm sorry it has taken so long."

As if on cue, Baxter let out a loud sigh and rested his snout on Katherine's lap. She knew if anyone happened to see them, it would be obvious how happy they were together in the old farm truck. She couldn't imagine being any happier.

He unloaded her bike and put it away in the shed and together they walked up the flight of stairs to her apartment entrance above the clinic. When he thanked her for being his fishing buddy, things suddenly became awkward. He didn't really want to leave her, but she offered no invitation to come inside. Baxter sat on the welcome mat at her door, his eyes begging to be taken inside. Murphy had to look away from Katherine for fear his own eyes begged the same.

"Load up, Baxter. We've got to run."

Baxter didn't budge.

"Load up, boy, let's go for a ride." Murphy jingled his keys as an enticement for the old dog. No luck.

"Why, you old traitor," laughed Murphy.

Katherine held her hand over her mouth, attempting to hide her giggle, which only made Baxter thump his tail harder. She gently took him by the collar and led him back down the stairs to the cab of the truck, at which point he became his obedient self again.

She stood at her doorstep and waved goodbye as Murphy backed down the driveway and was surprised to see him hit the brakes. Hopping out and standing at his truck door he said, "I've thought this all day but didn't say…I like your hair down. You're prettier than any Breck girl I've ever seen." He saw the smile and wonder spread across her face as she unconsciously touched her hair, and he waved as he drove off.

Later in the evening Murphy reached for the bar of soap at the boathouse sink and saw her wristwatch lying on the counter. He held it in his hands as if it were porcelain. Just a round clock face with an hour, a minute, and a second hand on a simple brown leather band. You couldn't find a plainer woman's wristwatch if you tried. Something told Murphy that if given the choice of a hundred bejeweled watches, Katherine would still select this simple design. The thought pleased him.

As tempting as it was, he did not drive back into town to return her watch. He wanted to give her some space, and he thought he'd wait until Monday morning when he would join her and Doc for coffee at the clinic. By the end of the weekend, Murphy knew all he wanted to do at this point in his life was to spend more time with her. As in the rest of it. Coffee and orange juice and flapjacks every morning, as long as she was sitting across the table...*their* table.

Murphy checked his hair in the mirror twice and whistled as he drove to the clinic early Monday morning. Wishing he'd brought a handful of flowers, he wondered if he could have pulled it off without Doc teasing him. And what about Doc? Wonder what he'd say about this new turn in their journey. Doc's reaction would be pivotal.

He spotted her through the window when he pulled up to the clinic's back entrance. She was in her starched nurse's uniform with her hair pulled up in the chignon that worked so well with her nurse's cap. He watched her for just a moment. Her back was to the window, but he knew her hands were busy preparing coffee in the percolator for the three of them to enjoy. His legs could barely carry him quickly enough to be in her presence again.

She turned and faced him when he walked in, and they looked eye to eye, searching to see if the other gave any indication of regret for the long hours they'd spent together just two days before.

"Good morning." There was a brightness in her face and her voice.

Handing her the watch, he found his eyes in hers. "One of the best mornings of my life. Thank you."

She reached up to straighten the lapel of his jacket and allowed her hand to rest there a moment as she responded, "Thank you. For everything."

It was in that instant they both knew the direction their lives were headed and neither was afraid.

Katherine handed Murphy his coffee cup, and they settled into their usual chairs as she explained Doc's absence. He'd taken a call in his office about fifteen minutes earlier and, surprisingly, he was still on the line. Doc liked phone conversations to be succinct, believing a telephone call should take less time than the three minutes it takes to soft-boil an egg.

It was a welcome break from tradition for Katherine and Murphy to have a few minutes alone. He was dying to know how she spent the rest of her weekend but didn't want to pry. Turns out he didn't have to. She volunteered that she ate dinner at Lily Mae's Saturday night, and the two of them talked so long into the evening that she ended up sleeping over and together they went to Bethel A.M.E. Church just as they had so many of the Sundays of her childhood.

Doc walked in with his hand outstretched, waiting for his coffee cup, just as Murphy was beginning to recount his uneventful Saturday night, and promptly the conversation broadened to three.

"You were on the phone much longer than usual. Everything in order?" Katherine asked as she dropped a sugar cube in his cup, expecting him to at least identify the caller.

Doc boomed in a voice several decibels louder than they were used to hearing from him so early in the morning, "All is good in this world of ours, and I'm certain God's watching us! Now, let's start this day off right and drop another cube in my cup. This is going to turn out to be a two-sugar-cube day for all of us!"

Doc's obvious pleasure with the day set the tone, and Murphy delightedly told Doc all about the fishing conspiracy he'd discovered. "If I'd only known you'd been teaching your nurse to fish I wouldn't have been so eager to show off my own fishing skills. She out-fished me from the start."

Doc lifted his coffee cup in midair to prevent spillage on his lap and roared, "That's my girl! I hate to tell you, but I think she could out-fish the professionals. She gets around a body of water and performs some kind of hocus pocus, and those fish seem to fight each other just to get on her hook. That K Syndrome's potent even on fish and fowl.

Murphy was more than eager to add evidence to the K Syndrome. "Turns out it works on canines too. Baxter formed an alliance with her and would've changed residences if I'd allowed it. I'm thinking of changing his name to Benedict."

With a grin, Doc offered some wisdom. "Son, I'm not sure if I've ever mentioned this to you, but I advise you not to try to impress her with your rock skipping skills because that's another one of her gifts." The resulting avalanche of laughter from the other two let him know his advice was poorly timed.

"Oh, just stop, you two. Blah, blah, blah! You're full of tomfoolery today, both of you!" Thinking she could change the subject, she added "Doc, I brought us meatloaf sandwiches for lunch with some of Lily Mae's leftovers from Saturday night."

That did the trick. The triad then began arguing over what constituted the best meatloaf sandwich. Mustard? Mayonnaise? A touch of catsup? A slice of onion? They debated it so long they were each on their second cup of coffee before Doc threw out an invitation.

"Murph, how'd you like to have dinner tonight?"

Murphy first looked at Doc and then glancing at Katherine he said, "I'd be honored to have dinner with you two tonight."

Katherine's widened eyes darted to Doc, who quickly rectified the assumption. "Just you and me, Murph."

Trying hard to maintain the enthusiasm in his voice, he told Doc, "Sounds like a grand plan. What time?"

Katherine stood with her back to the men, washing the percolator and cups, listening as Doc instructed Murphy to be at his house at 7:00. If Doc needed to postpone or give a rain check, he would let Murphy know.

The coffee group ended just as it always had. Doc announced, "It's time we turn this coffee house into a clinic. May the Lord bless us with wisdom and patience and an occasional patient wanting to pay a bill."

Murphy turned to head out the door, just as he had innumerable times before. But this time he turned and gave Katherine a wink, which set off a chain of events. It made her blush and act bashful—a new look for her—and Doc witnessed it all.

He couldn't resist. "Say, Murph, I'm looking forward to tonight, and I'm giving you an assignment for today. Go by the library and see if you can research that K Syndrome. Seems like it's pretty potent on *everyone*." Doc laughed so hard at his own joke he had to brace his portly self against the door frame while he watched Murphy chuckle all the way to his truck and drive away.

"Very amusing," she said through a grin. "Want me to call Lily Mae and see what she can fix for you and Murphy tonight?"

"No. I think I have it all taken care of."

"Well, need me to come over and set your table or make some iced tea?"

"Nope. I'm in good shape."

No matter how hard she tried, she couldn't think of a way to find out what Doc was up to, but she knew old Doc Bishop well, and she could tell by the look in his brown loving eyes that he was up to something. Neither of them mentioned the dinner for the rest of their busy day, and before they realized where the day had gone, they were sending their last patient out the door at 5:30. Wanting to neither pester nor invade his privacy, Katherine hurriedly tidied the examining rooms, said her goodbye, and out the door she went.

Murphy was dressed and ready to go at 6:00 and then watched, or at least pretended to watch, Walter Cronkite's evening news, finding it hard to concentrate. The clock eventually struck the three-quarter chime and off he went, carrying a bottle of brandy, because his upbringing required it, and because he knew Doc enjoyed a toddy from time-to-time.

PARTY OF THREE

Doc greeted Murphy at the door wearing one of his late wife's aprons over his pleated slacks and comfortable flannel shirt. Murphy immediately detected the aroma of greens, corn bread, and what? Pot roast? Salisbury steak? Some kind of beef with a gravy. His taste buds performed a roll call.

"Alright, Doc, I'm salivating just smelling what's coming from the kitchen." And it was then he spotted three place settings around Doc's dining room table.

"That's right, there will be three of us," Doc said as he followed Murphy's eyes. "When I invited you I thought it would be just the two of us, but I had an offer from someone who insisted on joining us, and I didn't have the words in my vocabulary that would allow me to tell her no."

Doc knew instantly from the pleased look spreading across Murphy's face that the poor guy was going to be in for a surprise. A big one. As if on cue, she headed out of the kitchen coming straight for him. Murphy made an effort to maintain his happy expression, despite knowing that this was a woman he was going to have to reckon with.

"Lily Mae! So, that's how Doc made sure his house smelled like heaven when I walked in. Now I know how you spent your day off."

Lily Mae walked up to him and wagged a wooden spoon in his face. "You think I'm going to let you two men folk have a dinner without me busting in? No, sir. I'm thinking we've got *lots* to talk about!" There was a grin on Lily Mae's face, but her eyes were fixed hard on him. She was a paradox of mixed signals, and Murphy was intrigued. And anxious. He knew he was dining with the two most important people in Katherine's life. The outcome of this evening could possibly determine how he would live out the rest of his days.

The night progressed, and the three of them enjoyed the sinfully delicious meal she'd prepared. Murphy had a second helping of everything. Doc took seconds on the greens and added a big slab of butter on his second helping of cornbread. Lily Mae ate like a bird, nibbling at everything on her plate but finishing none of it.

They had feisty conversations about the governor and the fate of Doc's college football team. A little of this and a little of that. Doc was wise. He waited until they'd gathered in the den with plates of Lily Mae's strawberry shortcake to begin his discourse directed entirely at Murphy.

"Murphy, Katherine spent Saturday night with Lily Mae, and they stayed up half the night talking, which then prompted Lily Mae to call me early this morning. We had a good long talk, about fifteen minutes' worth, early this morning, but I think you probably already suspected that. We have reason to think your friendship with Katherine might be taking a new turn."

Murphy's head nodded, and Lily Mae muttered something under her breath, which he could not understand. He glanced her way, quickly surmised he didn't know how to read the look on her face, and immediately shifted his attention back to Doc.

"I'm certain you know what Katherine means to me. I couldn't love her more if she were my very own. She brings softness to the hardened ones, and she brings hope to the terminal ones and I don't just mean my patients. I mean everyone she comes in contact with. The girl has seen more than her share of hurt, and she hasn't let it destroy her. And if you didn't know, she's had more than her share of men who wanted to love her. Some I approved of, but she didn't pursue any of them. It's been painful to see how hard some of the young men in this town have tried to get her to notice them. She's kind to everyone, and many a young man has taken that as a sign of her interest. Hell, I wish I had kept a tally of the number of men whom I had to pull aside and advise to move on. Some people are meant to love a few, and every now and then you meet a person who was put on this earth to love them all. In all my years, I've never known another person with her goodness. I'd commit murder with no regrets if I ever thought anyone wanted to deliberately harm her. Do you have any idea how truthful those words are, son? I literally would be able to kill someone if they injured her in any way. She's a strong woman. She was more mature at age seven when her father disappeared than many old people are on their deathbeds."

Not knowing how this was going to end, Murphy looked at both and interjected, preventing Doc from continuing. "I guess I've known for a long time what kind of woman she is, but I never thought I was worthy of someone like her. With permission from both of you, I'd like to see where this goes. I know I'm older and I know down the road that could be unfair to her but…" He stopped and peered into both faces trying to determine if he should continue.

Lily Mae encouraged him. "Go on. Say what you have to say, and then it's my turn to talk. I'm keeping my tongue still till you finish with all that you want to tell us."

Murphy couldn't tell from her tone if she was about to burst into tears or rail at him, but he could tell she was holding something back. The room seemed still and tense, and he had an uneasy feeling it might end poorly. He tried to gulp down a few swallows of tea before he could squeak out more thoughts.

"I guess when we started meeting for coffee at the clinic my world was tumbling down on top of me. I remember leaving one morning after one of our visits and wondering what about her made me feel so peaceful in her presence. I grew to depend on the light I saw in her. I needed Doc's wise counsel, and I sought the gentleness she offered so freely. After the fire, I was one of the walking wounded I'd always heard about. I wanted to begin living again, but I didn't really know how. Throughout my life, people have cast me in different positive roles. As Donovan Colin McGregor's descendent, I was the keeper of the land my family cultivated for generations, I was a pilot in the war, and the list goes on. But then all that changed, and the positive things I had accomplished were negated by the stigma of my wife. I was the husband of a woman so full of hate and disgust for me that she was willing to kill herself and take with her everything I valued. People told me healing would just take time, and I gave it time. You both know all I did to try to find my place again. You were there beside me every step of the way. I didn't feel I belonged anywhere. I guess you could say I was rudderless. I got down on my knees time and again asking for direction, to help me find my way. How was I supposed to know God intended for me to love the woman who…"? Murphy couldn't say more. His eyes were puddling. His voice would not cooperate.

No one said a word. Silence slipped in the room, and calm prevailed. Then Lily Mae decided it was her turn to talk.

"Murphy McGregor, I have prayed and prayed to the good Lord for him to send someone to love my Queenie. I won't live on this earth as long as she will, and the good Lord knows Doc will be going to heaven sooner than the rest of us if he keeps sneaking seconds and thirds of all those sweets." She glanced at Doc and sent him one of her know-it-all looks she was so famous for.

Then she turned back to Murphy and said, "I want it to be you. That seed got planted in my head way before the fire, but I told the good Lord he was going to have to figure that one out on His own. Sure enough, what happened? Tragedy came upon you like you were carrying a cloud of locusts above your head. You were hurt and lost and all alone while half the country was sending you condolences. I watched you every single day and didn't know how I could take all that hurt away from you. One day, after you moved to Cross Creek, I studied you out by the lake. Sitting there with Baxter at your feet looking ahead as if you saw nothing before you when actually the good Lord had laid out one of His most beautiful sunsets ever made. The water was still. The crickets seemed to be begging to be used for bait, and the fish were jumping. But you just sat there and didn't see a bit of it. I knew that was the most sorrow I'd ever seen anyone encounter, and it dawned on me my Queenie would be just like that if she's all alone when Doc and I are gone. Now, what do you think that did to me? It made me get sassy. I told God Almighty that I was ready for Him to get this man healed and get his sight back because he needed to see what was right in front of him. One of God's very own angels fixing him coffee five days a week and trying to put some sunshine in his life, and he was too numb to see it. And you being fifty-one years old and my Queenie thirty-nine, you best hurry up and marry her because we all know you're on the other side of young. But let me tell you something. If I ever thought you weren't good to Queenie, old Doc here wouldn't have to go to prison for killing you because I would have already done it. Nobody's going to hurt my Queenie." Realizing she'd said all she intended to say, she slowly sat back down and began humming under her breath, smoothing the pleats of her apron as if they suddenly needed pressing.

Doc took over once again. "She has a peaceful life now, and she says she has all she's ever wanted or hoped for. I know she means that, but I want her to know the kind of love I had with my Mary Nell. It's the kind of love that everyone hopes for, but few people really have. I won't let her go to you unless you can prove to me you'll be able to give her that. But son, if you aren't able to or you don't want to be invested in that kind of love, I want you to walk away and never come back for coffee or visits or even medical care. She only just realized it herself, but she was falling in love with you when you first started coming by to get a sliver of the peacefulness we have early in the morning. That means she's loved you a long time and never acted on it. Don't break her heart because if you do, you'll break all our hearts."

Murphy could only nod his head. He struggled to control his emotions. "I grew up in a family of great people. You know all about that. Sitting presidents have broken bread at our table. Generals from both world wars have hunted on our land. Buildings, parks, and roads throughout our state were named after people I knew only as my Poppy and Mams. Neither of you have ever heard me boast like this, and I don't say it to impress you. You are aware of the advantages that have been afforded me throughout my lifetime. But I tell you now, none of those people were of the same caliber as Katherine. And when we were together at Cross Creek, I swear I could hear the trees whispering that a truly great one was in our midst. And I have fallen in love with her."

That was all he needed to say to convince her two greatest admirers to give him their permission to love Katherine. A woman who would have loved him if he owned nothing but his name. A woman who could spend the rest of her days showing him the gentleness of life.

On his way home Murphy drove past the clinic to see if any light shone from her apartment, and he realized he had the willpower of a fat man. He wanted to tell her of his evening, and look into her eyes, and make sure he hadn't imagined it all.

She was opening her door on the landing as he hit the top stair. There she stood with her hair down around her shoulders. Her smile told him she was already his. In the doorway, for the entire world to see, he cradled her face in his hands. Leaning in towards her, he kissed her gently. When she responded with a soft sigh, he kissed her hard. And when she stepped into his embrace and wrapped her arms around him, he knew. And so did she.

"I have fallen in love with you, Katherine."

It took her breath away. His simple words of love opened spaces in her heart that had never before had life.

Katherine looked deep into his eyes, took his hand, and guided him inside. "Oh, Murphy McGregor, I so wanted you to love me." And she knew in that instant, her world had changed.

Beauty Shop

"Just wanted to be sure we're still on for a trim today at 10:00." Marge had been cutting her hair for at least ten years and had never called before to remind her of an appointment, but on this particular day, she did.

"Yes, I'm looking forward to it, and as a matter of fact, Marge, if you have time to do a little more, I'd love some curls today."

"Oh? Something special happening tonight?"

"Well," Katherine hesitated, knowing any details she shared with Marge would soon be repeated. "Just in the mood for something a little different, I guess. That's all."

"Then why don't we plan on you getting here at 9:45 so we can get started a little earlier,"

"Wonderful, see you in just a bit."

Someone was going to cast a pall over what should have been a beautiful day, but Katherine did not to detect it. She was too busy anticipating the night ahead when she and Murphy would announce their wedding date to Doc and Lily Mae.

Katherine knew Marge would do her best to find out what was so special about this night. And she also knew that every beauty shop customer for the rest of the day would learn the details of whatever news Katherine revealed, so she reminded herself to guard against any impulse to share.

Marge shot her an uneasy look as she walked in the door, a look Katherine couldn't quite read.

"I'm not quite ready for you, Sug. Just sit in that red chair and wait for me to finish with Sarah. Another ten minutes is all I need." Pointing with the end of her rat-tail comb, she continued, "The red chair on the backside of the row of dryers."

Settling in, she was vaguely aware of the three women in the chair backs adjacent to hers. But she immediately recognized Wanda Sullivan-Langston's caustic voice. The voice that long ago had taunted Katherine for being the girl whose father had deserted her. How unfortunate that on this perfect day she was going to have to listen to a voice that rippled her skin.

She could not say the exact moment she realized that Wanda's litany was directed specifically at her. Judging from the decibel level of her voice, she intended the entire beauty shop to hear every word of the bombastic speech she was delivering.

"I know this. His mother, grandmother, great grandmother and all the other women from that family would literally die if they weren't dead already, knowing that he intends to bring *her* into his family. Just die, I'm telling you. Can you imagine that conversation? 'So, tell us about your family, dear.' And then she could drop the bomb she tried so hard to hide, 'Well, actually, my mom was crazy, and my father ran off and left us.' Oh, can't you just picture it?"

She was on a roll, enjoying her gapped-mouth audience. "For Christ's sake, the girl has only lived in two places almost her entire life…above a diner and over a doctor's office. It's disgraceful to think of the prestigious people who've been entertained by that family, and now it will all be in the hands of a complete idiot who doesn't even know how to set a table. Little-Miss-Came-From-Nothing. She probably couldn't even name the pieces of a silver service unless someone glued names to the bottom of each piece. They never married trash before, and I swear to God they'd put a stop to it now if they had a way to rise from the dead. It's sinful what he's doing to the dynasty his ancestors worked so hard to establish. She'll be a laughingstock in Kingston the first time she tries to pull off some event. I'll refuse the invitation, and I expect all of you to do the same. We'll show Murphy McGregor what we think of his taste in women. That'll remind her of her place in this community. Has no one bothered to tell him she grew up on the other side of the tracks? I'm sure *she's* certainly never told him."

The sound of Wanda's maniacal laugh made Katherine sick. She kept herself composed until she backed out of the parking lot and then lost all sense of dignity as the tears and nausea began.

While Wanda's monologue was vicious and mean, Katherine knew deep down that there was probably some truth to it, although she had never allowed herself to admit it. What did she have in common with the McGregor women who came before her? Nothing really. Who was she kidding? The thought of disappointing Murphy was unbearable. He would one day wake up and realize he had married a woman who had lived her entire life in a different kind of world.

She managed to drive herself home and get inside before heaving her guts out. Feeling faint, she sat on the cold tile bathroom floor, gulping for air. The last time her body ached like this was when her father went missing. It was the kind of pain a heart is not supposed to endure, but one God had sent her way twice.

She wanted to run to Lily Mae or Doc and plead for their wisdom, but deep down she knew it would be pointless. Neither would be impartial, and they'd only try to quell her fears rather than speak the truth as Wanda's wicked tongue had done.

Wanda. The thought of her voice and the ugliness of it made Katherine vomit. How could any one person be so manipulative and corrosive? And why? Why had the girl, and now the woman, spent so much of her energy trying to make Katherine miserable? This time though, there was some truth to her savage words. Katherine really wasn't from stock a McGregor was expected to marry.

She knew there was only one thing to do.

He was surprised and elated to see her car coming down the curved driveway. The thought of her living at Cross Creek pleased him. He eagerly walked to greet his betrothed. His everything. His greatest blessing in life. But when her eyes locked on his, he knew instantly something had gone terribly wrong.

He guessed at the truth. For her to be so violently pained, it had to be the unexpected death of Doc or Lily Mae. Still unaware of what news would unfold, he held her and cried with her.

She tried to speak but could utter only animal-like sounds of pain, so he gripped her even tighter to his chest, protecting and soothing as best he could.

Eventually, she was able to speak a sentence. It was concise, powerful, and utterly ridiculous.

"I'm afraid I'm not enough for you." Her voice was hoarse, her body shaking, and her pained eyes refused to meet his.

"Did you just say you're afraid you aren't *enough* for me? Is that what you said?"

She pulled away from him and dropped to the ground on her knees, weeping. He was immediately beside her and pried her hands from her face. Bewildered he said, "What has happened? What on earth made you say that?"

She didn't want to tell him. She didn't want to be so naive that she had to accidently overhear it to realize she wasn't enough. The truth was, she had never once worried about it before. She just assumed they would tackle life together, hand in hand, and there would be nothing the two of them couldn't figure out. But after hearing Wanda's words, she realized for the first time there was more than just Katherine and Murphy at stake. It was the generations of McGregors who had begun with nothing, had worked and toiled and given back when they were blessed, who eventually amassed a sizable fortune through their determination and fortitude. The community, the state, and many across the nation held the McGregor name in high esteem and regarded them as people of compassion and dignity. They were top-shelf, and Wanda wanted her to believe she was on the bottom.

Murphy read the hesitancy in her face, and an anger rose within him.

"Tell me, NOW, Katherine. I'm not asking you. I'm demanding it." Murphy was seething, intent on getting to the root of this insanity. "I want to know what made you think that. Has someone said something to you? I want to hear it from you because if you don't tell me, so help me God, I will not stop searching until someone tells me." His voice thundered, shaking as intensely as his hands.

She slowly began to unravel the story. It was in the retelling that she realized the call from Marge must have been part of a greater plan to ensure Wanda the opportunity, and audience, for her tirade. She told him in detail of the jabs about the McGregor women not approving, and how inadequate she would be in trying to host anything he might plan, and how she had lived on the wrong side of the tracks.

He paced back and forth, listening without comment as she replayed the monologue, stopping every now and then to regard her with utter disbelief. He knew it wasn't the long list of untruths causing this explosive anger to rip through his body. It was the realization that the spiteful words were intended to annihilate the person he cherished more than life itself. He was certain he would have his vengeance.

When she finished, she was devastated to see the pain in his eyes. She reached out to comfort him, as he dropped to his knees and wrapped his arms around her waist, desperate for her embrace to temper his rage.

"In this world, you are all that I love. The rest of the things that clutter my life are belongings, obligations, and memories. The world of expected frou-frous ended when I married for the wrong reason, then my parents died, and my home burnt to the ground. I have never once missed that life, but if you want to live in that world, I know all the matriarchs of Beechwood would envy your grace, charm, and skill. And why do you think that is important to me? You've heard me tell all my stories of growing up in that lifestyle, but you have never once heard me long for those days when the house and lawns were full of hundreds of people? I cherish the peacefulness and intimacy of the two of us being alone. We don't spend our time planning events to include half the town. We make plans that will take us around the world. Our time together is not forever on this earth, and I'll be damned if I'm going to let Wanda Sullivan-Langston and her small-mindedness destroy what I have searched for my entire life. And besides, if you must know, I wrestle with my own fear night after night. My greatest fear is that Doc and Lily Mae will decide I'm not enough for you."

Turns out, those were the words she needed to hear. Their love could outlast the wicked tongues of any spiteful biddies that coveted what they felt for each other. They spent the rest of the day outside under the trees, making plans for the rest of their lives. But Murphy's desire to drive into town and find Wanda was dynamite with a lit fuse. Nothing peaceful would come of it. He secretly devised a scheme he would initiate come Monday morning.

He planned to call in the troops, declare war, and turn the tables on Wanda. Murphy's first stop was to Marge to try to understand why she allowed, and supposedly participated in the planned ambush. Turns out Marge herself had been blackmailed in a sense. If Marge did not agree to provide Wanda and her cronies with the date and time of Katherine's appointment, she threatened that she and all her friends would take their business elsewhere. Afraid of losing a large portion of her family's sole source of income, she provided the information to Wanda.

Murphy softened his tone with Marge when she told him of the fireworks that occurred after Katherine left. Marge told Wanda she was ashamed to be connected with Wanda's cruel display in any form or fashion, and that she would never again be welcome in her shop. Marge reminded Murphy she would rather live in the poor house and still have her pride than live out the rest of her days knowing she had to be around the maliciousness of Wanda Sullivan-Langston.

Then Murphy set step two of his plan in motion—initiating the purchase of an entire city block in downtown Kingston, including the building that once housed Grapham's Diner, the building where Katherine had lived as a child, with plans for it to become Kingston's finest park.

He paid a visit to his longtime friend, J.C. Westmoreland, Kingston's prominent real estate developer. "I want swings, slides, merry-go-rounds, seesaws, everything any son or daughter of Kingston would want in a park and then I want a train for people to ride that encircles the park. Some folks in this town need to be reminded there's no such thing as the wrong side of the tracks. Tracks were meant to cross over and take you places rather than serve as a dividing line of injustice and poverty. I'm going to be out of the country honeymooning for most of the next two months, but I'd like to break ground as soon as I return. Whatever you do, make sure the massive pin oak isn't damaged when you tear down the diner. I want a bench under that majestic tree. I plan on sitting on it often with my wife beside me as we marvel at the journey we've been given."

The Right Reverend Drew Keller officiated their ceremony. Lily Mae and Doc were the only others present who witnessed the moment she officially became his. Their wedding night brought a new level to their love. She had never been intimate with a man, and Murphy realized he had never really made love before. She gave him every inch of her body to discover and claim. And then the afterward became just as intimate and divine as the act itself. They melted in each other's arms, exhausted. Her foot rested in the arch of his foot, as they breathed the same air. They slumbered through the night, their bodies always touching, as if magnetized.

Seventeen months later federal agents raided Wanda Sullivan-Langston's home. After being indicted by a Federal Grand Jury, her husband was charged with eleven felony counts of money laundering and fraud. The IRS frowned upon business owners filing fraudulent claims for small business disaster loans.

Doc and Baxter

They lost both Doc and Baxter the week after their second anniversary. First Baxter, then Doc. Their hearts broke as they watched Baxter close his weary eyes and take his last breath. They'd lost a piece of who they were. The house was still and quiet now, and his absence made the air hard to breathe.

They had no way of knowing a tsunami was just days away. An unpredicted storm of heartbreak was headed their direction.

Doc finally booked his retirement gift from Katherine and Murphy, a long-awaited fourteen-day deep sea fishing trip to one of the British islands near Cuba. It was something Katherine had heard him talk about frequently after he'd read Hemingway's *The Old Man and the Sea*. Something he "one day" intended to do, and they knew if they didn't give it to him he'd never get around to going.

He called them long distance half way through the trip. "I wish we were all here together to enjoy this beautiful island. Words don't begin to do it justice, and I'm certain you'd love it."

"Are they treating you right over there, Doc?" Murphy watched as Katherine shook her head in his direction and silently mouthed, "Don't tell him about Baxter. Save it."

"I'll put it this way son, I don't know what you told them or how you arranged it, but I think I'm getting better VIP treatment than if ole Hemingway himself were here."

"No one deserves it more than you, my friend. I'm putting Katherine on the phone now. She's hanging on to my every word and smiling from ear to ear, so anxious to hear your voice."

She couldn't get the phone to her ear quickly enough. "You've only been gone seven days, and I miss you terribly. I can't wait to get you home so we can all sit around the table and listen to your stories. How many have you caught, and how's the food?"

"The second day at sea I caught a sixty-eight-pound wahoo, and my guide took it to an old cook and told him how to prepare it. It was enough to feed most of the entire north shore of the island, and I've never seen so many happy people trying to thank me. Not many here speak English, but they sure seem to understand it. This is the fishing trip of a lifetime, and I thank you."

"Seems like you've been gone a month! We'll be at the airport to meet your plane on Saturday, and then Lily Mae will join us here for dinner. We want to hear every detail. I love you, Doc. Not counting nursing school, this is the longest we've been away from each other since the summer I was seven, and I can't wait to get you home."

Doc could hear the longing in her voice, and he knew exactly how she felt.

"I couldn't love you more, my dear. It's funny you mentioned that summer so long ago. My solitude this week has given me some time to reflect on the different paths I've chosen in life. Been thinking a lot on some of those forks in the road and pivotal decisions, especially about the events from *that* summer." Doc paused, and just as Katherine was beginning to speak, he continued, "and I'd like to share something with you when I return. It's something I overheard all those years ago, a few months after your father disappeared. I'm positive of its validity, and I think it's time you learn what I've known all this time. I can't justify why I've never talked about it, and I'm not proud that I've never had the courage, but now the memory has reared its ugly head and I'm troubled." Katherine heard his voice choke, but he recovered and continued, "But, we can't go backward, can we? So, no more of this kind of talk on a long-distance penny. I'm eager to see all of you in just a few days. Goodbye, my sweet Katherine."

They did go to the airport on Saturday, and they watched his plane land, but they wouldn't realize for another twenty-five minutes why an ambulance met the plane on the runway. Doc suffered a fatal pulmonary embolism and died just minutes before landing.

The next few days were a blur. Murphy never took his eyes off Katherine, knowing her world was upside-down. Sleep evaded him that week as he watched her wrestle fitfully in her sleep. Lily Mae had always been the balm for Katherine so Murphy asked her if she would come to Cross Creek for a few days. He was worried he wasn't doing enough to help her.

"I keep wondering who on earth I would have turned out to be if he had not been in my life? He could have simply chosen to look the other way after my father disappeared."

Lily Mae held Katherine tightly in her arms and reminded her, "Never question the good Lord's doings, Queenie. Doc's love for you wasn't by accident. The Lord knew you needed Doc as much as he needed you. And now, all these years later, the Lord knew to give you a strong man before He took your other one away."

"Now I guess I'll never know what it was he wanted to tell me about the summer my father disappeared."

Lily Mae winced and stiffened her back, turning suddenly to look at Katherine. "What makes you think he was going to tell you something about all that?"

"He mentioned it on the phone. Our last conversation. It had to do with overhearing something a long, long time ago and now wrestling with himself about never doing anything about it."

Lily Mae blew out a puff of air she'd been holding in. Speaking softly, she thought aloud, "The Lord must not have thought you needed to know what Doc was going to tell you or else he would have arranged for it to happen while Doc was still with us."

And then, she held her tighter as Katherine shed more tears. Lily Mae cried with her, knowing she now might have to be the one to tell her what Doc meant for her to know. She knew full well what he intended to divulge. She just wasn't sure she had the strength to see the aftermath.

Katherine and Murphy weren't the only ones Doc had called long distance. He also called Father Drew. It was a brief phone call but long enough for Doc to allude that he needed to get something off his chest when he returned. He warned it was the kind of news that would knock all of them, especially Katherine, off their foundations. He worried she would not understand why he had feared telling her before, and for that he had no answer.

When the autopsy report indicated an advanced stage of colon cancer, they realized the embolism was actually a blessing. They were thankful for a quick, painless death for the man who attended the bedside of countless terminal patients, watching as their lives faded, waiting for death to finally knock on the door.

PART THREE

1977 — 2014

SAVANNAH

"Hello," was the only word he spoke, stopping to see if continuing would just be a waste of time.

"Well, hello. How are you on this beautiful day?" Katherine's response encouraged him. What kind of day was it? He noticed very little, as his haunting memories overshadowed the present.

"My name's Hollis Walker, and I heard you're looking for a caretaker. I hope you don't mind I drove out without calling first but I was driving through town and stopped in front of a church that was hosting a BBQ fundraiser for their benevolent fund and one of the church ladies sat down next to me and we talked for quite a while and when we said our goodbyes she gave me your name and drew me a map to get to your place and well, here I am. Have you hired already?"

She heard the urgency in his voice, and she knew she liked him from the start. There was something about his eyes that held a mixture of honesty and eagerness. She saw pain mixed in there also. He was soft spoken and small framed but handsome with a dose of shyness sprinkled in. Good manners, strikingly appealing, and gentle. A trifecta. Katherine could immediately tell he was genuine. She knew Lily Mae must have seen it too or else she wouldn't have made up the part of a fictitious job.

He sat on the porch swing and waited while she fixed them both a cold drink, asking the typical get-to-know-you questions. His answers were remarkably clear for a man who appeared completely distracted, keeping his eyes steadfast on his older model black Volvo station wagon parked under one of the enormous pecan trees near the house. All the windows in his car were rolled down which led Katherine to assume he had some sort of animal accompanying him, perhaps a loyal old dog to provide company. Whatever it was, he listened and watched alertly for any signs of movement.

The second he detected a faint sound, he bounded off the porch, taking two of the broad steps at a time. Leaning into the back seat, he began talking to the dog in a soft, soothing voice. Katherine rose to see if she could bring the animal some water or assist him in bringing the dog to the porch where she was sure he would be much more comfortable. Their porch had been lonely for a dog since Baxter died.

When he turned to face her direction, she saw what he held in his arms. Katherine was certain she had never seen a more beautiful creature with thick ringlets the color of sunshine, eyes of darkened slate, and lips like those painted on a china doll's face. One lone dimple suddenly appeared when her father whispered something to evoke a smile.

Katherine kept her ears open as the three of them visited, anxiously awaiting the sound of Murphy's truck winding down the driveway. When he did finally arrive, her husband was more than surprised to find a well-groomed young man on one of the porch rockers and a four-year-old child snuggled up next to Katherine on the porch swing, enjoying a glass of Katherine's lemonade. He studied his beautiful wife's face as he climbed down from the truck's cab, and her smile told him that this pair of unexpected strangers made her jubilant. And that alone let him know all was right with the world.

He felt a confident handshake when the two men exchanged introductions—always a positive sign, in Murphy's rulebook.

"Lily Mae met Hollis in town at Bethel's plate lunch fundraiser, and she suggested he drive out to Beechwood and apply for the job opening."

That was all she needed to say. It was then Murphy knew he would create some job that needed to be filled someplace on the grounds of his homestead. "And who is this little bit sitting on my swing?" Murphy asked with a big dopey grin, trying to emulate the voice of a gentle giant from one of the fairy tales little girls tend to love.

Giggling, she buried her face in the crook of Katherine's arm, peeking out sheepishly while Hollis introduced his daughter, Savannah. Murphy and Savannah locked eyes and that was that.

The two men went on to have what Murphy later referred to as a job interview, but in actuality, it was a vegetable dinner prepared by Katherine. Squash casserole, corn on the cob, sliced tomatoes, black-eyed peas, pickled okra, spoon bread, and blackberry cobbler for dessert. It felt natural to share the garden's bounty and to have two more chairs at their table.

Murphy reached over and squeezed Katherine's hand. "Hollis, it sounds like you would be well suited for our general caretaker's job. It would involve exactly what the title says. I need someone with fresh eyes to supervise the care of the north quadrant."

"Sir, I can't tell you what that means to me. I'm honored. Now, you need to know, I've never done anything like this before, so I might need some time to learn the ropes."

Savannah looked up from her bowl of peach cobbler, and with a smidge of it on her chin, she proudly announced, "Daddy can draw, and he makes me books. Don't you Daddy? I get to go to school next year, but I already know how to read because my daddy taught me, didn't you, Daddy?" Hollis leaned over and wiped the cobbler from her chin and planted a kiss on top of her head.

"I pity that teacher next year because, well, you know what they say about the proverbial sponge." He faltered for a second and then asked, "Would my job allow me to take her to and from school when she begins next year?"

Those few words told Murphy and Katherine that no other parent would be joining the girl and her father.

Katherine heartily answered "Of course!" at the exact second Murphy responded with his own hearty, "Absolutely!"

"That's funny!" said Savannah as she threw her head back with a laugh, causing both Katherine and Murphy to wonder what it might be like to watch her grow up at Cross Creek.

After dinner, they all walked a portion of the north quadrant and then climbed onto the old restored '24 model Farmall tractor to venture out and inspect some of the timber and a couple of the irrigation ponds.

During the restoration of the tractor, Murphy had replaced the traditional seat with a padded bench seat providing ample room for Katherine and Baxter at that time to sit comfortably with him. This ride, however, consisted of three adults and a tow-headed bundle of giggles. Savannah snuggled in her father's lap next to Katherine; until she climbed completely unsolicited into Murphy's lap to help him maneuver the eighteen-inch steering wheel. A sixth sense seemed to tell the four-year-old that that particular lap had been waiting fifty-five years for her to claim as her own.

Along the way, they watched a hawk launch from a branch high above and glide right over them. Savannah was fascinated. "What is that giant bird? Is it an eagle? That's America's national symbol."

They all chuckled, and Murphy explained, "That was a Cooper's hawk. They're fond of beech trees and that is the kind of tree you see all around us so you'll see a lot of hawks around here, too. Did you like it?"

Savannah was enthralled. "I love it. Do you know more things about Cooper's hawks?"

Murphy was fueling her curiosity. He stopped and picked up a feather and measured, showing her it was longer than the distance from her wrist to her fingertips. Pointing to a nest about thirty feet off the ground, he said, "I know their eggs are bright blue, and they usually lay three to five. Those eggs are called a clutch. What do you know?"

Savannah absorbed it all, her mind racing to store the new information in files somewhere within her head. Without missing a beat, she replied. "I know the American bald eagle lives up to

20 years. That's a very, very, very long time. Can I please keep this feather?"

Katherine's heart was full. She loved listening to her husband talk with this inquisitive well-mannered four-year-old bundle of energy with a barrage of questions. Something in her gut told her that the "I know/what do you know?" routine would become a daily part of their lives if Hollis accepted the job.

They rode over to the caretaker's cottage to see if Hollis thought it would be a suitable place for them to live comfortably. An aged country cottage with high ceilings, it had a wood burning fireplace, an abundance of large windows, and beautiful hardwood floors. Katherine and Murphy began removing the sheets covering the upholstered furniture, revealing a room that was warm and inviting. Hollis saw a place he and his daughter could call home. A fresh start. A rebirth.

Everything Hollis and Savannah owned was packed neatly in the back of his car. They had no destination until Hollis, by happenstance, drove through the town of Kingston and saw a young teenage boy standing outside a small church building waving a poster advertising a BBQ plate fundraiser. And a lady greeted him like she'd been expecting him to walk through the door. She then sent him in the direction of Cross Creek, and with all the remnants of courage he had left, he knocked on the McGregor's back door.

It came as no surprise to Katherine when Murphy asked Hollis if he would like the job. No reference checks, no forms to sign, no negotiating, no bargaining, no union representatives, no bonus signing packages.

It was simply, "Son, would you like to work for us?"

"I'm honored, sir. Could you and I step outside for a minute or two?" Murphy detected a clouded look on Hollis' face, indicating trouble of some sort.

Katherine gave both men a nod to let them know she and Savannah would be happy catching a few lightning bugs in the backyard, deliberately positioning herself so she could still see both men as they conversed.

There was a little bit of the old boot kicking at the dust and a little gazing up at the night sky but, for the most part, one was talking and the other was listening, intently. It ended with a long, agonizing stare-down, and then Murphy extended his hand as a gentleman's agreement, and Hollis accepted. The two men walked side by side as they headed to the backyard in search of the lightning bug collectors. Both looked at Katherine, and she realized it was the first time she had seen Hollis genuinely smile. It became very clear where Savannah had inherited her lone dimple.

When they were finally alone and she was certain they were out of earshot, Katherine blurted, "Well, tell me, what was that all about?"

"Seems there's been a bit of trouble he wanted us to know about ahead of time."

"What kind of trouble could that sweet man have encountered?"

"He left behind a successful architectural career in Kentucky. His wife's death, or maybe the circumstances of her death, nearly destroyed him. I don't know a whole lot more than that. Maybe it was because of the ghosts in my own closet before you rescued me, but my gut tells me the accident was the beginning of one set of problems and the end of another. He's intelligent, you can tell by his conversation. He was brought up right, you can tell by his manners. I can only imagine he must have been going through hell on earth if he left it all behind. It's my hope the peace that surrounds us here will also envelop them."

She slipped her hand in his. "Fresh starts are good."

Lily Mae, Clarence, and Father Drew came for dinner the next evening. Katherine stood back and watched as Savannah ran to Lily Mae with open arms as if they'd been friends forever. Lily Mae nestled her into her bosom as they embraced, and Katherine stood and watched, knowing full well what that hug felt like to a little girl. It was clear; Lily Mae had a new little girl to love and guide along the way.

That evening at dinner, perched atop two Sears and Roebuck catalogs, Savannah grinned broadly and announced, "I know granddaddy long-leg spiders eat mosquitos and that's a good thing. What do *you* know?" and she didn't stop until each person had shared one solid fact.

"I know there's no such thing as a *grandmother* long-leg spider, but I'm not sure why that is," said Lily Mae, and they all laughed.

Next came Clarence's turn to play the game. Chuckling, he said, "I know no matter how harmless they are or how old I get, I still shudder if someone throws one my way." That brought a round of laughter at the thought of a man the size of a mountain jumping at the sight of a harmless spider.

Father Drew raised his glass and winked. "I guess there were two granddaddy long-leg spiders on Noah's ark, but I have a feeling one surely must have been the female version, if there is such a thing!"

"I know only the female mosquito sucks blood," said Hollis. Judging from the look on everyone's faces, he had enlightened all of them with something new.

"I know a mosquito uses *her* saliva to coat our skin when she bites us, the nasty little blood-sucker!" said Murphy.

And when it was Katherine's turn, she offered, "I know this is going to be a daily dinner table routine, so my advice to each of us is to always be prepared."

Soon after dinner Lily Mae announced she needed to get back home. "Still have some studying of the Word to do before church in the morning."

Savannah protested, "But I don't want you to go. I want you to stay here with us. You can sleep in my bed, I promise I won't take up too much room. Please?"

"Child, you're making that sound hard to decline, but I've got my own house and my own bed." Aiming her head toward Katherine, she asked Savannah, "Did you know Katherine used to sleep in my bed at my house when she was just a little bit older than you are now?"

"She did?" Savannah was mystified.

"I sure did, and I loved it, too. Lily Mae used to wrap her arms around me and hold me tight and sing me to sleep. I can still hear her voice when I close my eyes at night."

Savannah nestled next to Lily Mae and whispered something into her ear. Lily Mae pressed her forehead against hers and softly responded, "Because her mamma was gone during those days when she used to sleep in my bed."

Savannah quietly said to no one in particular, "Just like mine," and a thick frozen stillness suffocated the room until Lily Mae broke the hurt that surrounded all of them.

"You wait till you get a little bigger and then you can come spend the night at Lily Mae's house, and we'll do all the things I used to do with Katherine when she was my sweet little gal."

"You promise?"

Holding her right-hand high in the air, Lily Mae said, "I do promise that to you, sweet girl. And I keep my promises." Lily Mae then looked at Katherine and they both knew she was reliving a memory of another little girl from long ago.

Katherine put her arms around both of them and announced, "You girls aren't going to do any such thing without me, so you better make room since I'm Lily Mae's first girl!"

Savannah squealed with delight, hopping from one foot to the other. "When, when, when? Can I Daddy? Please?"

"I'm sure you can, one day, but not tonight." He looked at Lily Mae and said, "You're very kind. I can tell you have quite a history with Katherine. The happenstance of meeting you overcomes me. I don't know what else to say."

A look of wonder spread across Lily Mae's face. "That was no happenstance, son. You write this down. That was a day, an hour, a minute, and a second that was meant to be. That plan was made by God Almighty before you even pulled off the highway. Nestle that in your heart and keep it there. You'll see. Won't he?" She looked at Katherine and Murphy for affirmation.

With complete authority, Murphy told Hollis, "As certain as the sun rises and sets and the earth revolves around the sun, that woman speaks the truth. That's the only way she knows how to live."

The next day Murphy came home with an invoice for a new set of World Book Encyclopedias, and he and Hollis began work on a built-in bookcase for the nook in the Butler's pantry right off the kitchen. A handy location for a set of books that would be referenced often during their nightly "I know/what do you know?" discussions around the dinner table.

It wasn't long before Murphy and Savannah began filling up the bottom shelves of the bookcase with loot from their daily walks—a discarded bird's nest, the fossil of an ancient snail, an entirely intact butterfly—treasures of the land that enticed them both.

Katherine and Murphy noticed there were a few things banished from the caretaker's cottage, by Hollis' choice. The absence was glaring. No television, no photos of Savannah's prior life, and no alcoholic beverages. Katherine would one day be glad she didn't know any of the details of Savannah's mother's death so she could honestly plead ignorance when pressed for details.

Life on the farm was healthy for all of them. Hollis prospered from hard work and the endless supply of things to accomplish, and Savannah flourished with the unending devotion of Murphy, Katherine, and Lily Mae. Her insatiable curiosity meant she spent her waking moments discovering all that was around her.

As she grew, Hollis established physical boundaries for Savannah. Facing east, she was not allowed to venture past the barn, and facing west, she was not permitted to go past the garden. The flagpole near the pond's edge was her northern boundary, and her southern border was the old concrete bench under one of the live oaks.

Savannah shared the news of the boundaries with Lily Mae, anxious to know what Lily Mae thought.

"I like those boundaries, Savannah. They give you a freedom to explore but at the same time they give you a sense of limits. Folks who follow life's boundaries are often the ones who enjoy it the most."

"But what about people who don't stay in their boundaries. What happens to them?"

"Oh, they're either risk-takers or rule-breakers or sometimes both. Some turn out successful. Some don't. It all seems to boil down to how much they value the rules of life."

"Don't worry about me, Lily Mae. I'm going to stay in those boundaries. I'm good about following the rules."

Lily Mae looked at the others gathered in the room. She had wisdom she was bursting to share. "Our girl's got a gypsy soul. Boundaries or no boundaries, the gypsy is deep within her. You watch and see."

They exchanged glances, each wondering if that prophecy would end up as a blessing or a curse, knowing only time would tell.

Several things changed around the farm after Savannah's arrival. It just seemed right to add a swing under one of the giant oaks and, of course, a child's size table with four chairs and pink dishes for tea parties on the porch.

That was just the start of new things. Lily Mae constantly sewed, always replicating Savannah's new outfits with identical ones for her dolls. Next came bikes in several stages, an ant farm, a microscope, and a set of walkie-talkies that mainly just squeaked and squawked, but Savannah loved them, so the noise didn't seem to bother anyone.

Her inquisitive mind never rested. If Hollis didn't know the answer, she had three other adults standing in the wings, hoping to help her solve all the mysteries around her.

A tree house was erected in one of the pecan trees which included a rope ladder, a trap door, and a bucket with a pulley that stretched from the tree house to the kitchen window. Many an evening Katherine or Lily Mae put homemade cookies or frosted brownies in the bucket and whisked them to the two occupants in the tree house, never knowing for sure who loved them more, Savannah or Murphy.

Only once did Hollis talk with Murphy and Katherine about

their roles in Savannah's life and the absence of her mother. They had been living in the caretaker's cottage for over three years. He started with hesitation in his voice, knowing it would be difficult to genuinely express all he felt.

"I arrived here a broken man hoping to find work. I never dreamt I would find the healing you've provided. Savannah's life changed drastically when her mother made a desperate split-second decision, and then her life changed again when her father made his own split-second, poignant decision to turn down this long driveway and knock on your door." Hollis studied their faces intently, hoping they would hear the sincerity in his words, "You took us in, you gave me work, and you slowly breathed life back into us. I was drowning, and I didn't know how to come back up for air. I sometimes sit and watch Savannah sleeping, and I now realize she could have lost both her parents before she ever celebrated her fifth birthday. This house, this job, this land, and your nourishment saved my life, and I will forever remember what it felt like for me to find peace again. You gave us a place to plant our feet, and you gave us roots so we could find our strength. I don't speak of Savannah's mother, but that doesn't mean I don't miss her every day." He paused, trying to swallow the lump that seemed to be growing at an alarming speed. "I know you're not Savannah's grandparents, and I'll never ask you to assume that role. You've provided her with so many miraculous things, but I wonder if you are aware of the most incredible of all your gifts."

Murphy and Katherine exchanged looks, neither knowing what to expect.

Hollis explained, "You model for her what true love looks like between a husband and a wife. She watches you and absorbs everything you do for each other. The respect you have for each other is like a mist from a spring shower, the kind of rain you stand in so your skin can soak it up. Savannah knows first-hand what love looks and feels like between a husband and wife, thanks to you."

There was much Murphy wanted Hollis to understand. "We never want to step out of bounds, and we expect you to tell us if we ever do. What you have to realize is you've added life to our years by allowing us to be a part of yours and Savannah's."

They reminisced about the day they first met and what a pivotal day that was in all their lives. Katherine couldn't resist asking something she and Murphy had always wondered.

"Hollis, we've never seen a picture of Savannah's mother. I'm sure you have a good reason for that. If you don't mind me asking, does Savannah look anything like her mother?"

Hollis pursed his lips, pausing, thinking how to best answer. They could tell by the longing in his eyes he intended to answer. "You've never seen a photograph of her because it was excruciating to look at her picture when we first arrived. But now, we take her picture out of my dresser on the second day of October, the day of her birth, and study her face, and then we return it to the drawer. Even after three years it rips my heart open to hold a photo of her face in my hands, knowing I'll never touch her again. But in a sense, you have seen a copy of her face. Savannah looks more like her mother every single day. Her hair, her eyes, her little nose, her intelligence, her curiosity. It's as though her mother lives on." And then painfully, he added, "We celebrate the date of her birth. I have never told Savannah the date of her death. I hope she'll never inquire."

Murphy sucked in a hint of breath, ready to ask his reasoning, but changed his mind. Later, in private, he and Katherine thought of an endless list of possible reasons why Hollis would keep that information from his daughter, but neither of them could conjure any reasonable answer.

As Savannah grew and matured, her interests matured also, and her boundaries all but vanished. The walkie-talkies were replaced with a 35mm camera and eventually her own dark room for developing innumerable rolls of black and white or Kodachrome film. Sometime during her sixteenth year, the boathouse acquired a new canoe, one she could maneuver single-handedly as competently as any grown man.

While the rest of the country seemed to depend on television to help raise the younger generation, Hollis and Savannah spent their evenings immersed in books and music. Big books, little books, comic books, poetry collections, encyclopedias, anything in print. Over time came the diaries and journals that Savannah meticulously wrote in each and every night.

Dear Diary,
Today is really a lucky day. It's my 6th birthday and can you guess how many turtle eggs I found today? Hint, Daddy guessed 12 and his guess was too high and Lily Mae guessed 10 and it was too low. Think you know? Another word for a guess is an estimate. It's called a synonym.

Dear Diary,
Today is the first day of second grade; Daddy says my teacher will be surprised I already know how to use a dictionary. What will I do if we don't have one in our classroom? *

Signed,
Savannah the Second Grader
* I hope we have a nice thick dictionary in our classroom, not the skinny kind for grade school kids.

And over time the diaries were replaced with journals. Her curiosity was documented in a thousand different ways.

Sunday, the last day of winter
I've been told on many occasions that I'm very observant and I can tell they mean that as a compliment. When people refer to my dad, they call him Hollis. I'm the only one who calls him Daddy and it sounds childish. I sometimes shout HOLLIS in

a very loud voice if I need to get his attention. Believe me, that works. I think I'm going to ask him if I can call him Hollis just like everyone else.
Postscript: I asked, and he said I could make my own decision about that. From now on that's what I am going to call him.

The twenty-third day of the Moon of Popping Trees
Murphy told me the Lakota Indians had different names for different seasons. Some names were about the people and some were about animals. I think my favorite is February because they called it the Moon of Popping Trees. It isn't hard for me to imagine how the ice and snow on the tree branches made them pop and break. That's the same sound we hear each winter when the snow and ice weigh down all the beechwood limbs. A beechwood tree can live 300 years. Think what these trees all around me have seen and heard. Murphy said I need to listen because they have a lot to tell.

Thursday, the fifteenth day of August
I've spent most of my entire day reading everything I can find written by or about Marguerite Higgins, the first female Pulitzer Prize winner for International Reporting. She worked for the Associated Press across the world. Hollis provided me a lengthy explanation on what that means for a journalist. I'm trying to imagine what it must have been like for her the very first time she saw her byline proceeded by AP? What a glorious moment it must have been. I think we march to the beat of the same drum.

Sunday, June 17
I have a hunger to be able to go back in time and record all the thousands of stories Lily Mae has shared with me in my lifetime. I've always been spellbound listening to her

stories—and the ones that rock me to my core are the ones she tells from a time long ago, the ones she begins with "after freedom came to my people." Her stories are not in any of the history books I've ever been handed in a classroom. Times were hard before the end of the civil war, and they were awful for a long time afterward. Some of her folks barely survived. They were hungry and cold, and the only thing they had was hope. I asked her how long it took for her family to forgive the sin of slavery. Her answer was simple. "We aren't responsible for the sins of others, only our own. The good Lord loves us all too much to make us accountable for those things in which we had no say." I hope I'll always remember that. Her words are strong and good and wise. I want them to be long-lasting.

It wasn't just the replacement of journals over diaries that made it clear to the rest of them she was growing up. Over the years, their daily "I know/what do you know?" routine morphed into lively philosophical, political, and analytical discussions, and it was very clear to all of them how brilliant she had become.

During her sophomore year of high school, she decided to pursue a vocation that would allow her to travel the world. One Thursday evening after dinner, Savannah shared some important news. "I don't think I was meant to settle down. I will one day, I'm sure, but there's so much I want to see. I hope I'm not disappointing any of you when I say I'm eager to leave here. Not leave *you*, of course. But I want to see the places we've talked about, I want to follow the maps we've studied in our encyclopedias, I want to fill up a passport with stamps from around the world. My wanderlust came from you and all the things we've talked about around this very table all these years. You planted the seed, and now I want to water it and watch it grow. Can you blame me for wanting to see this great big world of ours?"

Hollis studied the rim of his coffee cup, trying to choose his words carefully before responding to his daughter. "The world as we now know it is completely different than the world in which I grew up. Who would have ever imagined someone might attempt to assassinate the President of the United States and then be found not guilty by reason of insanity? We never worried our American diplomats and citizens would be held hostage in a land clear across the world for 444 days, and who would have ever dreamed a group of Legionnaires would attend a convention and 34 of them would die from a form of pneumonia that would later be named after them. I want you to see this beautiful world of ours, but I want you to be careful, Savannah. There's an equal abundance of wonder and ugliness. I know I'll never be able to hold you back. I've known it since you were just a little girl."

Lily Mae took Hollis' hand and studied his eyes before speaking. "That gypsy soul has taken hold. All we can do is lift her high in prayer. Those boundaries are about to be no more, I'm afraid to say. I want you to ponder that and ponder it hard." Hollis nodded, knowing the truth of her words.

Katherine looked at Murphy, in anticipation of his wise response. He didn't disappoint her. "The old proverb says a rolling stone gathers no moss." As his voice cracked a bit, he finished, "You know life with moss. We want you to go and explore, and I know in time you will return. This moss, this land, is a part of who you are."

Perhaps it began with her inquisitive mind, curious about all the mysteries of planet earth or maybe it was the plethora of books at her fingertips, but the combination of the two would one day result in an award-winning journalist who would travel places worldwide and make a staggering discovery that would change her life forever.

LEAVING

They knew she was leaving them all behind when she enrolled at Northwestern to study journalism. Just as it should be, they reminded each other.

Her writing only intensified at the leading school of journalism, and her curiosity fueled her drive to explore. Phone calls were frequent, but most cherished were the letters she sent weekly, without fail. They gathered and listened as Hollis read each epistle aloud. The format was familiar. They could hear her voice.

Dear Ones,
This I know:
   –I can survive on four hours of sleep and still function fairly well. Why sleep when I could be exploring? I bet Hollis is shuddering right now as he reads this.
   –Student government is invigorating. Clark Courtway and I are working on a debate together – Cuban trade embargos. He's actually been to Cuba. Fascinating! I'm sure Murphy has been. Anyone else?
   –Remember what I told you earlier about my English professor, Dr. Lance? He's top notch. He returned everyone's writing assignment today except mine, asking me to stay after class so we could discuss it. Turns out he thought it was the strongest style and voice he's seen in a long while from any of his freshmen writing courses. Wants me to consider having it published! I know you're smiling. So am I.
   –Would you mind if I brought someone home with me for fall break? I'd like for Clark to see my home and my people. You'll like him. Everyone does.

So......what do you know?
    –Hollis?
    –Katherine?
    –Murphy?
    –Lily Mae?
I'm waiting to hear! See you Friday, next!
All my love,
Savannah
p.s. Lily Mae's cookies were a hit! Clark is incredulous that anyone can cook like that. My response? "Welcome to my world!"

Not a single letter arrived without a mention of Clark. They met the first week of school and had a couple of classes together their first semester. Several years older than Savannah, he had served in the Air Force for four years, and now attended college on the G.I. Bill. Murphy, Katherine, Lily Mae, Clarence, and Hollis instantly liked him. He was solid and genuine, and they wondered how long it would take Savannah to realize Clark walked around in a complete state of adoration of her.

Dear Ones,
This I know:
    –Clark instantly fell in love with each of you. You are all he wants to talk about. Looks like I'll be bringing him back again. All your kind comments about him were so apropos.
    –We lost three girls on my floor after fall break. Two decided the rigor of Northwestern was more than they could handle, and one discovered her funding fell through, but I think secretly she was glad. Thank you for allowing me the privilege of being here.
    –I've already started planning my schedule for next semester, and I have my fingers crossed I get Dr. Jordan for my lit class. Murphy, she said she knew you. Who doesn't, is what

I wanted to ask but decided against it. After all, she is the dept. chair. You raised me well!

*This I **don't** know:*

    –Hollis, what do you mean you noticed the way Clark stands back while I command a room with my stories? I don't get that. He's not a back-of-the-room kind of guy. Katherine and Lily Mae, do you agree? Is this one of those male-vs-female observations?

So....what do <u>you</u> know?

    –Hollis?

    –Katherine?

    –Murphy?

    –Lily Mae?

All my love,

S.

Each time she departed Beechwood they all marveled at the way she was changing, becoming even more beautiful, more magnetic, more dynamic than before. She had morphed into a breath-taking, charismatic, confident young woman.

Dear Ones,

This I know:

    –How can my first year of college be ending so soon? It's just not possible. Wasn't it only yesterday we arrived on campus for move-in day? I didn't think the nine months of my senior year of high school would ever end, yet these nine months of my freshman year at Northwestern have flown by with the speed of Haley's Comet.

    –Lily Mae, I told Clark what you said about him being the one who understood my "brilliance" (yes, I used quotation marks when I said that word aloud). He laughed and told me to tell you he figured out a long time ago he knew

he'd never be able to tame me if I decided to go in a direction that didn't include him. I don't know what to think about that, actually.

—I found out today I was chosen to interview Dr. Samuel Renburg when he comes to campus to share his story about his experiences at Auschwitz. I'm thrilled but shocked. I had to audition, and I think everyone assumed an upperclassman would get the assignment. Believe me, I've done my homework on this one. Remember all the dinner table conversations we had over the years about the Holocaust? Little did we know what was in store for me.

So . . . what do you know?

—Hollis?

—Katherine?

—Murphy?

—Lily Mae?

All my love,

S.

Home on Christmas break her sophomore year, Savannah and Katherine talked late into the night after everyone else had gone to bed.

"I'm so glad Clark was able to join us for Christmas. It's very kind of his family to share him with us. I'd like to meet them one day. You like them very much don't you?"

"I do. They're good people. I think Clark loves his step-mother as much as he loves his father. They've been together most of his life."

"I only know bits and pieces about that. How did that come about? I remember you told me his mother died, but that's all I know. What happened?"

"Well, Clark shouldered responsibility at an early age. He was seven when his mother died from complications after a car accident and, as the oldest of three children, a great deal depended on him. Late at night when everyone else was asleep, he grieved. His father remarried Julie just a year after his mother's death, and he said it was as though she brought a glue to help them put the pieces of their lives back together. Clark has always loved Julie, but as a young boy he still grieved each night and longed to have his mother hold him. He slept with her picture under his pillow every night for years. He said the pain lessened in time, but the hole remained."

Katherine listened intently. "That's what grief does to us. I remember missing my father so severely I wouldn't go to sleep for fear I would wake up and forget everything about him. Doc and Lily Mae had to help me realize he was permanently fixed in my heart, but it took years to fully grasp his mortality, if it's at all possible. How unusual that you two have something so painful in common, losing your mothers so young."

"When Clark first told me about his father and step-mother and younger brothers, I envied the warmth in his eyes and the tenderness in his voice. And when he told me how difficult it was to lose his mother, I wept with him. He shared with me things he had never told anyone. He said it seemed as though he was waiting to release it until he found someone who knew the enormity of the pain."

"Oh, Savannah. Only ones who have had someone stolen from them would come close to understanding those words."

"In his eyes she was perfect. His father never tried to bury her memory or diminish his pain. He feels blessed to have been loved by two mothers."

Katherine suddenly worried she might know where this was headed, and she was right.

Savannah searched her face before continuing, "The enigma for me has always been the wonder of how my life would have changed if Dad had remarried or if I had had siblings. I envy Clark for having actual memories of his mother. I don't have any of that. It's as though all of my mother's belongings died with her when she left this world. I have one photograph of my mother, and I used to see it only once a year, October 2nd to be exact, her birthday, when Dad would pull it out, and we'd look at it together. It was always too painful for him, so I rarely asked him to tell me about her. When you initiate a conversation that makes your father cry, you tend to stay away from those things. I once took a picture of that photograph and developed it in my dark room, but Dad never knew. You know what I used to do with it? I slept with it under my pillow at night."

PROPOSAL

Dear Ones,
This I know:
 –With your blessings, Clark and I and four others are planning to spend two months this summer backpacking in Europe, sleeping in hostels, dining with the locals, and soaking up all the history and architecture. I am chomping at the bit to capture all the sights with my new Nikon—thanks again, Murphy!
 –I'm almost finished with two applications...one for grad school at Boston U and the other for an internship at The Boston Globe. I'm inclined to put them both in the mailbox at the same time and just sit back and see which one materializes first. Such a gamble!
 Advice? Don't hold back.
 –Would you believe the new priest at St. Peter's went to seminary with Father Drew? We are having dinner with him next week. He insinuated, with a delighted grin, he has a lot of dirt to divulge on Kingston's illustrious clergyman. Tell Father Drew I will keep nothing from him!
So . . . what do you know?
 –Hollis?
 –Katherine?
 –Murphy?
 –Lily Mae?
All my love,
S.

Dear Ones,
This I know:

—Are you really sure I can handle both at the same time... grad school and internship??? Katherine predicted they would both open up for me, and we all know she's never wrong! I think I'm going to give it a try, but I really want to know what each of you think.

—What was turning into a debacle trying to plan the travel itineraries for six seems to be working itself out. Everyone is dropping like flies so it appears it will only be Clark and me taking the backpacking sojourn. Fine with us!

—Murphy, thanks for the list of contacts for our trip. How is it possible you know people all over the world? YOU are the precise reason we are beginning our trip in Ireland.
So ... what do you know?
—Hollis?
—Katherine?
—Murphy?
—Lily Mae?
All my love,
S.
P.S. You do realize my postcards will consist mostly of abbreviations while we are traveling?? We will have so much to tell and such limited space. How well you decipher will be a test of how well you know me!
Another P.S. Tell Father Drew his secret is out! Who knew he was known as the seminary prankster at Sewanee?

Postcard from Salzburg
D.O.-
T.I.K-

—Having the time of our lives. Realize how young America is in comparison. Have seen buildings erected B.C. Impressive

*and mind-boggling at the same time. Thank you for instill-
ing art appreciation. Such a blessing.*

*–Have not eaten anything we don't love. L.M.'s advice to
sample everything was spot on.*

*–Had dinner last night with Ambassador Tucker at the
embassy in Austria. Charming man. Considers Murphy a
dear friend.*

–See you in ten days. So much to tell!

So, W.D.Y.K? H? K? M? LM?

L, S & C

So, somewhere in-between classes and weekends and dates with
other people, football games, debate tournaments, cramming for
finals, and their summer in Europe, it all became clear to Savannah.
The realization she didn't intend to live a life without Clark seemed
to calm her to the core. And she told him just that when they came
home to Beechwood in October of their senior year.

Fishing together in the canoe she asked him, "Do you want to
journey life beside me? Because I can't imagine me trying to live it
without you."

"I cannot believe you, Savannah! You wait until I reel in a fish
the size of a deep freeze, and then you throw that at me? If that's a
proposal I'm going to ignore it because I'm going to do the propos-
ing, and if you think I'm going to ask you to marry me then you
better wipe that little mess of catfish bait off your forehead and for
once, sit still and stop talking!"

And by the time they paddled back to shore they were engaged.
Nothing had ever felt more right in her life than that very moment.
They celebrated that evening with all the other important people
in Savannah's life. The giddiness in the house was contagious.

"We're thinking maybe sometime in the fall, maybe even here
on the farm, and I'm hoping Lily Mae, if she's willing…"

"Your wedding dress? Oh, child, I'll gladly take my thimble out of retirement if it means I get to make your wedding gown. These old hands have been aching for something to make them feel useful again. Strike up the band and ring the bells!"

The light danced in everyone's eyes. The chance to watch a grown up Savannah wed Clark on their land, wearing a dress made by Lily Mae's expert hands, in the season when the land was the most impressive, was a series of beautiful gifts wrapped up in one glorious package.

They all looked to Hollis, the father of the bride. With pride in his voice he said, "We better get busy. We have a wedding in about eleven months."

"Not *next* fall, Dad, we mean the fall after Clark finishes law school and I finish grad school. Four years away."

Murphy was dumbfounded, and his argument was a strong one. "So, why do you two want to wait to begin the best years of your life? Why not marry as soon as you can? But what do I know, I'm just an old man who still can't believe the nurse fell in love with a dopey guy like me. I would have married her twenty years earlier if I could have."

"We don't think there's adequate time to plan a wedding, move to Boston and both of us begin something new this fall. I'll be adjusting to law school, and Savannah will begin her internship with *The Boston Globe* as well as grad school and neither of us wants to lessen the importance of any of it by compromising our time."

Savannah stood next to him, resting her head on his shoulder. "I can tell you're disappointed that it's not going to happen in a few months, and I hope you understand why. Let's just say we're sure there won't be a wedding this year, but it will happen sometime in the next four years."

Hollis raised his glass and offered a toast, "Here's to the bride and groom and their wedding at Beechwood, whenever it might occur. God speed!" After a hearty round of cheers, the room divided into two camps with the women talking wedding dresses and the men talking Harvard Law.

When they drove Lily Mae back into town that evening Katherine noticed she was deep in thought. "What's on your mind? There's something you don't like. What is it?"

"I'm not sure. I felt it when I hugged Savannah just now. It's powerful, and I don't want to say the words aloud."

With a heaviness in his voice, Murphy said, "Tell us, Lily Mae. We know the power of your intuition, and I clearly hear the worry in your voice." He found her statement foreboding. He had witnessed Lily Mae's intuition time and time again and knew it possessed power. He pulled off his glasses and rubbed his eyes, anxious to hear what was coming next.

"I don't think this will happen. Not anytime soon at least. It's in my gut. Something's telling me we won't be around to see it happen. Actually, the Lord's telling me."

The three of them never spoke again of Lily Mae's prediction. They waited to see what the future held for their Savannah. It would be three years before the pieces fell together. A bomb would rock their world. Even Lily Mae's prophesy had not prepared them for the depth of its destruction.

JOURNEY

Their first clue came when Clark called Hollis to ask if he had heard anything from Savannah in the past twenty-four hours. Something was terribly wrong.

"What do you mean? No, I haven't…what's this all about? Is she missing? What's happened?"

Clark's tremulous voice was pained as he tried to explain. "She isn't missing, but I don't know where she is. She sent me several emails last night and this morning to let me know she's okay but that she's not coming back to the apartment."

"Where is she?"

"I was hoping you might tell me."

"Not coming back to the apartment…has something happened I don't know about? Are you splitting up?" Hollis pummeled him with questions, knowing full well that law school could cause relationships to buckle under the pressure.

"No, it's nothing like that; at least I don't think so. Everything's great, as far as I know. We spent yesterday morning at the harbor having brunch and laughing and talking for hours. There was nothing wrong. There never is. We never argue about anything, and if we get on each other's nerves, we talk about it. That's one of the things we do best. We communicate. My God, Hollis, you know better than anyone how well she can communicate."

"What happened after the harbor?"

"I left to meet my study group at the library, and she was headed back to *The Globe* to see if they had her new assignment ready. She had a couple of things she wanted to research on her own and was hoping she wouldn't receive her new assignment until Monday so she could have some time to work on those other things."

"What were they?"

"I have no idea. She didn't say. She wasn't evasive, she just didn't mention it."

"So, she just emailed and said she wasn't coming back? Do you know who she's with?"

"I'll forward you the emails, and you see if you can make any sense of them. She didn't tell me if she is with anyone, and I've called everyone I know. You were my last call; I didn't want to scare you, but I haven't seen her in twenty-seven hours."

"Let me see if Murphy or Katherine knows anything about this. Forward me those emails. I'll call you right back."

It was only a matter of minutes before Murphy was calling. "Clark, Hollis told us everything. The three of us are on our way. My pilot is fueling the plane now. We'll be there in three hours. We'll find her, son. I promise."

By the time the plane touched down, they were raw with desperation. They shuddered when they saw the profound fear that had permeated Clark's entire being. He had a copy of what appeared to be a new email in his hand.

They were met at the airport with a car and driver, and they climbed inside to listen as Clark tried to read it aloud. Struggling, he pressed it into Katherine's hands. Gathering all the strength within her, she read it aloud.

Darling, I know you will never understand this, but I must go. I've decided we can't have a life together. I need to move and settle someplace where I can make a new start for myself. I will love you always, and I hope one day you will forgive me. I think if you ever discovered who I really am, your love would turn to hate, and I'm not strong enough to handle that. Do not waste your time trying to find me. I will let you know when I settle, but know this…you and I will never be in each other's presence again as long as we live. I'm so sorry.
Savannah

As tormenting as it was, they had to hear it read several more times for it to sink in, but even then, it was impossible to understand.

"Let's get to the hotel and check our emails to see if she has responded to any of us. And son, we'll not keep anything from you, no matter how brutal, if she shares anything with us she hasn't told you."

But that was part of the problem. She didn't divulge any additional morsel of information. She refused to talk to any of them.

Murphy had already communicated with Nathan Landis, Boston's most acclaimed private investigator, and he was waiting at the hotel with fragmented news to share when they arrived. She unexpectedly resigned from her internship on Saturday afternoon, just hours after spending the morning with Clark at the harbor. Landis drilled Clark about that day, about their lives, about their relationship.

Clark told him everything...how they both put long, arduous hours into their studies, Harvard Law was what they both expected, plus some. Clark's immersion into law school provided Savannah with the opportunity to invest unlimited time into grad school and her internship at *The Globe*. She began making a name for herself, allowing her editor to see her as the quality journalist she had already become. Accordingly, she was given full access to some of the best archival data in the world. Her research took her frequently to D.C. and London and other exciting places she had always wanted to explore. It invigorated her. Savannah loved her career, and neither of them could imagine being any happier than they were in Boston. No matter how busy, they made time for each other. Their contentment came when they were wrapped in each other's arms breathing the same air. Each marveled at how quickly the first year passed, then the second, and suddenly they found themselves in the middle of their third year in Boston.

Landis took copies of the emails and asked a series of rapid-fire questions before departing. That evening he returned to the hotel suite and laid out the facts he had uncovered.

"She flew out of the country this afternoon at 2:20 on Emirates Airline flight MP2684 to Johannesburg, South Africa." He paused, letting that sink in before continuing, "She's completed two credit card transactions since arriving but neither purchase was for lodging. The last event I can trace from the card is a withdrawal of money from her bank."

Katherine was shocked. "South Africa? Why so far away?"

Clark's voice was thick as he thought aloud, "She just finished researching a piece for *The Globe* on Nelson Mandela, and she's talked a great deal about it, but nothing that would make me think she was going to South Africa."

They needed time to absorb what Landis had divulged. Nothing made sense to them. He arranged for them to meet with her boss and the editor at *The Globe* at 8:00 p.m. that evening but nothing was resolved.

"She worked from her own computer on Saturday afternoon and used her *Globe* password to access our archival database. We can see she logged out only twenty minutes after her initial login. There's no indication she has attempted to access our database since then."

They spent the next few days talking to her friends who were just as traumatized as the rest of them. No one understood or could have predicted anything of this nature. Just the opposite. Savannah's departure made them wonder how well they knew the people they loved.

She never returned to Clark. Johannesburg became her home. It was where she lived and sought therapy as she battled the demon that forced her to leave behind everyone and everything she loved. Her career flourished and eventually AP appeared on her byline, just as she had dreamed.

About every six months Murphy arranged for a visit to Africa. Sometimes he sent Hollis. Other times he and Katherine visited. They all returned with the same report. She was established and thriving in her life across the world, but the light had disappeared from her eyes. That part of her was dead, no longer playing along with the "I know/What do you know?" game for fear it would involve news of Clark.

There was a time they thought Clark might not survive the combination of the pain of losing her and the intense demands of Harvard Law. But he did, and he eventually moved to Kingston. With Murphy and Katherine's support, he established a non-profit serving those living below the poverty line by ensuring equal access to justice. Occasionally, they would overhear someone say they thought it a bit unusual that Clark earned a law degree from Harvard and applied it to a non-profit, but Murphy and Katherine couldn't think of a grander way to use it.

He stayed busy and became involved in many things in and around Kingston, yet none of those involved romance. He dated many but committed to none. No one knew about the piles of notebooks in which he chronicled all of Savannah's AP articles. The first bookmark on his computer was her webpage. She was clear across the world, but for a few seconds every now and then, when he mustered the strength to look, her photo seemed to peer right back at him.

SAM

Murphy was watching as she pulled in the drive. J.C. Westmoreland had called to alert him about the incident outside the Kingston Post Office which had happened just minutes before.

"I knew I shouldn't have let you go to town by yourself."

Now she was curious. "I don't know who called you, but news sure travels fast around this little town. Who was it?"

"You'll have to bribe me if you want to get that information and need I remind you, my love, I always give in to your bribes?"

She cocked her head and flashed a smile, and he gave in.

"J.C. gave me the lowdown on what happened. Are you alright?"

"I'm perfectly fine, but I would like to know what he told you. I'm anxious to see if he had the same impression I did."

"Well, let's see. He said you were almost to the bottom step when some guy came barreling around the corner on a rickety bicycle and practically ran you over. I think he referred to him as 'afflicted in some way, or something similar.'"

"For heaven's sakes, J.C. made it sound worse than it actually was. Imagine that."

"Did your mail fly through the air?"

"Yes, but we picked it up."

"Did you nearly fall to the ground?"

"Yes, but that's what handrails are for, aren't they?"

"Did you have a small band of gawkers gathered around you?"

"Yes, several of them picked up our mail. Thank goodness Father Drew happened to be there and saw the whole thing. I kept telling everyone I was fine, but they didn't listen to me."

"The guy on the bike…any idea who he was or what he was doing?"

"I'd never seen him before. It seems the old red bike is his means of transportation, and he uses it to carry discarded aluminum cans he finds stashed away in hidden places."

The phone rang as they entered the back door. It was Father Drew with a bit of information he learned from the church secretary at St. Thomas. "She only knows him as Sam. She described him as maybe being mentally disabled, and he typically rides his bicycle around town, usually about sunrise or sunset, collecting aluminum cans to make a few dollars. She spotted him one evening rummaging through our dumpster and watched him from the window, ready to give him the what for if he scattered litter in the parking lot. But I have to tell you, she was pleasantly surprised. Not only did our scavenger make sure the dumpster was in good shape when he finished, he also picked up the stray pieces of litter around the entire parking lot that had been there before he arrived and deposited them into our dumpster. She says he's harmless."

"And did you get the same feeling? That he's harmless?"

"I did. It sounds to me like he's just a guy who does what he has to do to make some extra money. He's lived in Kingston for about ten years, I think."

"Katherine said basically the same thing. She thinks he seems to be invisible to people. Maybe we pretend not to see him. I'm ashamed to say that maybe not noticing him prevents folks from getting involved with someone who might be a bit different from the rest of us."

That evening over dinner Katherine and Murphy talked a great deal about the incident. He could tell the man on the bicycle had evoked a sense of wonder in his wife, and he predicted they were on the cusp of a new adventure.

She barely had the second bite of pie in her mouth when she slowly lowered her fork and studied it hard. "If you rely on finding aluminum cans to buy your groceries, how often do you have the pleasure of eating a slice of *pie*?"

And she knew then and there that the accidental meeting was really no accident at all.

They spotted Sam from a distance several times over the next few months. He was always trying to maneuver his bike with different types of contraptions attached to the front—sometimes a cardboard box, other times a torn black trash bag, and occasionally a couple of grocery sacks slipped around the handlebars. His dedication to his quest for aluminum cans was clear.

One Saturday they stopped for a late lunch at the Burger Barn. The smell of patties sizzling on the griddle made it almost impossible to resist ordering the supersized Double Decker, Real Deal, or the gargantuan Hub Cap.

Katherine spotted him balancing a lone burger atop a red plastic tray. No fries, no shake, no drink. He walked with slow, deliberate steps as if carrying a five-tiered birthday cake all ablaze in candles. Mesmerized, Katherine and Murphy watched as Sam carefully unwrapped his burger and removed something from his pocket, which he used to divide his burger in half.

Katherine whispered to Murphy as they watched his every movement, "Is that a pocketknife he just pulled out of his pocket?"

"Probably. Most men carry one, but I'm only guessing."

They witnessed him wrap half of the burger and put it into his pocket, along with the set of nail clippers he'd used to divide it. They could guess the other half would serve as his evening meal. She now understood what she needed to do. And Murphy knew too.

Besides, she desperately needed something to focus on other than Savannah's absence. It had been three years since Savannah's departure, and she still felt an emptiness that nothing else could fill.

Later the next day Katherine drove to the aluminum recycling station, eager to learn the going rate for aluminum cans. The gentleman, although he didn't seem to be very gentle, eyed her up and down, did the same to her vehicle, and then slicked back his greasy dark hair before answering.

"Thirty cents a pound is the rate today. Tomorrow it might be a little more or a little less. How many you got, lady?"

"How much money do you think I would get if I brought you a lawn size trash bag filled with aluminum cans?"

"Smashed or whole?"

"I don't know. Is one kind more valuable than the other?"

It tickled him when intelligent looking people asked dumb questions. He took her for one of those snooty women who kept her beer cans in a special trash can at home, not wanting her neighbors or the garbage man to know she was a drinker. He'd seen plenty of her kind before. Some people were so high and mighty it made him sick.

He gave her a snide once over and explained, "You can fit a lot more smashed cans into a bag. My shift ends in about five minutes so let's see what you got." Swiveling his finger in midair, motioning her to pop the trunk, he continued, "I can tell pretty close just by eyeing them how much money you'll have coming to you. Open up."

Katherine explained she didn't have any cans, not a single one, but intended to start saving them immediately, and she was going to tell all her friends to save them also.

"Some folks have more money than they do sense," he muttered to himself as she drove off. "That broad acted like I'd just let her in on the secret of picking the winning ponies at the track." But in the long run, it didn't make much difference to him, all he wanted to do was go home and crack open his own cold one.

With her new knowledge in the art of recycling aluminum cans, she devised a plan. Friends of Sam developed into a secret kinship of seventeen folks who started saving their aluminum cans for a man who was oblivious to it all. Katherine and Murphy carefully selected nine of their friends and Lily Mae chose six of hers. Everyone was eager to be part of the covert mission. All the participants put their sacks of cans on their doorsteps every Friday morning and Katherine and Murphy drove to each house, collected the cans, rain or shine and placed them neatly, row after row, in the barn. Now all they had to do was wait for the opportunity to find Sam and tell him about the gift with his name on it.

They saw him again the evening of the annual Kingston Christmas parade. Murphy always provided a flatbed trailer for St. Thomas' float, and he liked to personally ensure it had been hooked up securely before the truck began the parade route. The crowd had already begun mingling, and the air was thick with holiday excitement. Katherine and Murphy were standing in front of S & A's Hardware off the square when they noticed a man lurking in a darkened storefront entrance.

"Look who's standing in the doorway at Jenifer's Antique Shop. I think that's our man." Katherine was beside herself.

"Let's casually walk his way and see if we can strike up a conversation. Maybe he'll let us buy him a burger at you-know-where." Katherine was already two steps ahead of him.

Sam spotted the strangers looking keenly towards him, headed his direction, so he scuttled away. He didn't do well with strangers. Often his encounters had bad endings, so he avoided them at all costs.

But then, two months later, when she least expected it, Katherine officially met her Sam. Murphy was away for a two-day meeting at Weber Springs, and she was in town running a few errands. She saw the rusted bike in the parking lot of Davis' Drug Store and knew there was only one person in town with a bike like that.

She walked up and down each aisle until she spotted him near the eye care products. Slowly approaching, she asked silently that she be given the right words to say so that the Friends of Sam project could enter Phase Two.

"Hello there."

Just a stare in response from Sam, maybe he was expecting a rude insult to follow.

"My name's Katherine, and, am I right, you're Sam?"

"Hey." His voice was wary, apprehensive. His shaggy bangs fell well past his eyebrows, hiding the brilliant color of his green eyes. His cotton shirt was tucked neatly into his jeans, a western belt holding them up. He wore tennis shoes with Velcro fasteners and at his right ankle was a rubber band around the hem, his insurance to prevent his pant leg from getting caught in the chain of his bike.

"I think I've seen you riding your bike with a box of cans." She omitted the fact that he had almost laid her out cold in front of the post office last summer.

Only the slight trickle of an upward curve on his lips accompanied his stare.

"I have some cans a few friends gave me, and I wondered if you'd like to have them? Or better yet, why don't you let us bring them to you? My husband and I. If you'd like. I don't mean to be a bother to you though."

"What kind a cans you got? The pork 'n bean kind or the soda pop kind?"

"Oh, aluminum cans, like soda pop, the kind you can recycle. Would you like to have them?"

He wanted to know more but remained wary. "How many you got?"

Grinning, she said, "A few sacks" and then added, "Completely full."

"They crushed or whole?"

"A little of both. Some cans are already crushed, and some are still whole."

"306 Potter Road. What time you gonna bring 'em?" he asked, looking at his analog wristwatch. The curve on his lips appeared again.

They sorted out the details, and he gave her directions. Pointing to the intersection outside the drug store, he said, "You go down that road and turn by Seely's Seafood, the eatin' place with the big fish on the sign. Stay on that and then turn right by the water tower. You know where that is?"

Katherine nodded, being very familiar with the water tower.

Sam continued, "Turn when you see the mailbox with the pony on it. That's Potter Road. My house is on that street. I'll be watchin'—306 Potter Road. Don't forget."

Katherine immediately headed home to orchestrate the beginning of Phase 3 of the Friends of Sam project. With Murphy gone and Hollis and Clarence working on a project on the west quadrant, no one was around to help her, and it took longer than she expected to load the bags into the farm truck.

A new worry crept into her mind. She had already forgotten segments of his directions. Remembering the restaurant and something about a pony on a mailbox she found herself in a neighborhood she knew nothing about and was completely lost, wondering how on earth she would ever find Sam's house. And then she spotted a mailbox on a street corner with a Budweiser Clydesdale on it.

"Well, hello *pony*. Aren't you a Godsend!"

After turning onto Potter, she saw Sam standing at the end of his driveway at the far end of his dead-end street. She thought, *how long has he been waiting? Or for that matter, how long have I been waiting for this moment?* She realized then how very much she had wanted this day to arrive.

His house was run down, in need of several repairs but not really much different than the other houses in his neighborhood. She envisioned what a difference a good spray wash and a few gallons of paint might make.

"You get lost?" he asked as she pulled into his driveway. Standing in the summer's heat made his dark hair sweaty and his green eyes shine above his reddened cheeks.

"Just a little, but I was glad to see you standing there. You saved me."

He wrinkled his bushy eyebrows and said, "I won't let ya get lost again." Katherine heard the sincerity in his voice. It was thick and intentional, like pouring molasses from a jar.

Sam's face transformed when he realized the mountain of cans in the back of the truck were for him. All of them.

They unloaded the truck bed silently and reverently, stacking them in the carless carport. Mutely, Sam handled each sack with deliberate care.

"There are plenty more where those came from."

Sam shot her a bewildered look and then shyly smiled, "You sure drink a lot of soda pop and beer."

"I'm a member of a club, and the purpose of our club is for all seventeen members to collect aluminum cans."

"What kind 'a club?"

"Funny you asked. We actually call ourselves Friends of Sam."

"Well, my name is Sam, but I ain't in no club."

"If you think you would like to be in this club, I could arrange it. Since you would be the only club member actually named Sam, we would probably need to make sure we bring all our cans to you each week; and you can do anything you want with them. What do you think about that? Would that be okay?"

"Could I keep the money that I get for 'em?"

"Oh, of course! We would love that!"

"What day you gonna bring me some more cans?"

The weekly rendezvous to 306 Potter Road began. As the weeks and months passed, Katherine, Murphy and Sam's Friday encounters turned into can collection from the Friends of Sam's members, lunch at the Burger Barn, a drive over to the aluminum recycling center for can redemption, and usually a long, leisurely ride through the countryside, reminding Sam of the rural home he lived in as a boy.

It was clear Sam lived a simple life. There was a distant relative who checked on him about once a month to make sure his bills were paid, but he was detached from Sam's day-to-day existence. Sam had some cognitive issues, obviously. Some things he just didn't understand, and he read only a small number of words. But he was wise in other ways. His ability to judge a person's character was as sharp as a butcher's cleaver.

It didn't take Murphy long to realize Sam had an uncanny sense about maintaining his bicycle. He didn't seem to know the actual names of some of the parts, but he understood their function and how to repair them if needed. He referred to the cogset as the "round thingy" and the fender as the "backend," but he could explain the function of the gear shifting system with exact accuracy, in his own simple words.

"Have you ever thought about working in a bike shop? You know so much about bicycles, and I bet you…" Murphy stopped when he saw Sam's face fill with fear.

"I don't want no job at a bike place. I don't like being around strangers. I always do something that makes 'em mad, or they pick on me and I don't like that." Sam's voice was rising like mercury in a thermometer on a hot day in August and his entire body seemed agitated.

"Whoa, whoa, whoa! No one is going to make you do anything you don't want to do. I just thought you would have a lot to offer, but I realize now there is more to it than that." And they never mentioned it again.

The weekly contributions from the Friends of Sam didn't stop his quest for cans he found tossed here and there around town. It was ingrained in him. He had a passion for rummaging.

Sam became a loyal friend to Katherine and Murphy, worrying about them when the weather turned angry, always the first to call and check on them when a storm had passed. He cautioned Katherine when the cold fronts were headed their direction, always afraid she might get cold and then sick. He gravitated to Murphy, longing to have male companionship, and Murphy never tired of his Friday comrade.

Without fail, Sam insisted on washing out the truck bed at the end of each can redemption day. "If ya' pull in that car wash there,

I'll spend my money to make that water hose work and I'll wash out the truck, so you don't get no flies. People don't want a truck full of flies."

"Sam, you are loyal to the core, and I admire that about a man. Murphy and I are proud to call you our friend."

"My mama taught me you're supposed to take care of your things." He halted and looked at both of them, maybe waiting to see if he needed to tell them more. "I guess you're one of my things now."

Driving back home, Murphy smiled at Katherine and said, "Isn't it funny how it all worked out. We thought we were taking care of Sam, and it turns out he's the one taking care of us."

MURPHY

Thankful she had thought to grab a cardigan, she wrapped it around her shoulders as they walked a section of the fourth quadrant. Murphy always liked to walk a portion of his ancestral land before setting foot on another country's soil, and they were leaving the next day for another African adventure, more specifically, another trip to see Savannah.

The breeze was crisp, and nature's paintbrush had been busy, as the earth prepared for winter. A thick carpet of leaves crunched underfoot, and the bushy-tailed squirrels gathered and hoarded acorns in haste. The ducks could be seen flying in their aerodynamic V-flight formation. In the distance, someone was busy burning a pile of leaves.

Murphy always spoke with nostalgia during the walks prior to any long departure. He said it rooted him, and Katherine was certain she knew what that meant, loving the land as much as he. As they walked the acreage, he often told stories of his family all the way back to the first McGregors—the early ones who homesteaded the land. There wasn't a story she had not heard, but each one was worth repeating forever. On this day, however, he was quiet. She didn't have to offer a penny for his thoughts. She could read his mind.

Hand in hand they stopped to examine the rub marks left by a rutting buck on the bark of a tree. He pointed to the deer tracks in the mud near the creek, and silently they followed until the tracks disappeared.

Stopping for a moment to watch another formation of ducks fly overhead, Murphy thought aloud. "No matter how old I get, I'm still fascinated by the migration of birds and their instinct that tells them it's time to go and how far they must travel before returning home to us."

"It's one of those marvels many people overlook, too busy with their own lives to ponder the mystery," her soft voice coaxed him to say more.

"How do they know when they've made it back home?"

"They know. Just as you and I know."

"I wish Savannah had a bit of migration in her. Not the part that takes her far away. She already has that. The instinct that helps her navigate her way home is what she's lacking."

"I could tell you were feeling melancholy this morning, and now I know why. I miss her terribly, too. Do you think she hasn't returned because Clark chose to settle in Kingston? Surely after all these years she wouldn't let that stop her." Murphy wrapped his arms around his beloved, resting his chin on the top of her head while she continued, "You would think after six years, one of them would have married. Clark used to always ask about her, but he doesn't anymore." After a pause she said what they both knew to be true, "The hurt is still there, I can see it in his eyes."

"If Savannah did migrate home, do you think Clark would want to see her? After leaving so abruptly? I think the pain that still simmers within him stems from not understanding the why of it all. Maybe she, herself, didn't understand what she was doing. Something was driving her to get out of his life immediately and move far, far away. Africa is about as far away as one could get, I guess. But I'm still surprised she's never come back for a visit. I wouldn't be able to leave this place and not return. This land pulls me like a magnet, and I really thought she loved it, too."

"I still say something happened. Something that devastated her. I thought by now we would understand it better, but none of it makes a bit of sense." Katherine turned toward Murphy as she continued. "I do think I am better able than most to wrap my brain around the mystery since I've contemplated my father's disappearance my entire life. I hope Clark has been able to work through the anger. It's stifling and debilitating to feel such anger at someone you can no longer reach out and touch."

They embraced for several more minutes, soaking in all things autumn. "All I need in life is to stand with my feet planted on this ground and have you in my arms. I can't imagine needing or wanting anything more than what I have right here." Katherine tightened her grip around her husband's waist.

She knew a topic that would lighten the mood. "Let's think of brighter things. So, our favorite Episcopal priest is going to marry the Bishop's daughter! And to imagine we get to witness the union soon after we return. I guess the last time I felt this good about a marriage was when you proposed to me."

"Drew and Mary-Claire. Theirs will be a happy home. I knew he was smitten the very first time he told us about her. Do you remember? He said he finally understood the real meaning of all the love songs on the radio?"

"I do remember. It will be quite the wedding. The whole town will turn out and probably every member of the clergy in the diocese. Get ready to see our beloved bachelor Father Drew wear a wedding band." She touched Murphy's band as she said it, and it brought back all the emotions of placing that ring on his finger so many years ago.

"And get ready to meet his bingo ladies. They've all been invited and, according to Drew, they promptly went out and bought new hats. Big ones with feathers and wide brims. Every color of the rainbow. They'll be ushered up to the very front to sit in the family pew." Murphy laughed. "I'm looking forward to sitting with those colorful ladies. I have a hunch we're going to love them." In his best preacher voice he recited, "Dearly beloved, we have joined together in the presence of God and Drew's bingo ladies to witness and bless the joining together of Drew and Mary-Claire."

On the walk back, Murphy said, "I need about fifteen minutes to run the tractor over those vines in the garden and then I'll be ready for lunch. I'd like to get that done before we leave for Africa in the morning."

"That gives me time to fix lunch. Meatloaf sandwiches okay?"

The grin and the kiss on her forehead were his way of reminding her he still found her captivating. "Your meatloaf sandwiches make me miss old Doc."

"Me, too. Which reminds me, I need to call Lily Mae and Sam and tell them what time we're picking them up for dinner tonight."

While Murphy headed back to the barn, she listened as he tried to coax the bobwhites to answer his whistle. The land and all its glory ran deep in his blood.

After making the sandwiches, Katherine decided she'd surprise Murphy by pulling out the old, musty canvas folding chairs that had once belonged to Doc. She carried them to the lake's shore, stopping just long enough to watch a third V formation of ducks fly overhead, squawking at her as they passed.

"Safe journey, my friends. Until we meet again, next year."

Then she stood at the kitchen window, watching for Murphy's return, waiting to carry the tray of sandwiches and drinks to the lake. Glancing at her watch, she thought of fifty things that might have postponed his return. She began to worry when an hour had elapsed, and fifteen minutes after the anxiety set in she decided it was time to find him and bring him home. But first she called Hollis and Clarence to see, if by chance, they had run into him in the vicinity of the garden.

She set out on foot and then thought better of it. *Might wish I had a vehicle*, was the thought that seemed to perch in her mind. Grabbing the truck keys off the hook in the garage, she drove the same route she last saw him travel.

When the bend in the road revealed the parked tractor up ahead, she felt a tremendous sense of relief from the dread brooding deep within her, but the relief was short-lived. The tractor motor was still running, and the tractor was missing its driver.

She called his name, looking for tracks or clues to indicate which direction he might have headed once he climbed down off the tractor. Stepping up to remove the key from the ignition, she saw what was lying on the other side.

Murphy lay motionless on the ground where he had fallen, and his face firmly planted in the dirt. She struggled to pull his limp body over to confirm the premonition that she had lost him. And she had. He was already gone. The blood that ran through the veins of the person she loved most on this earth was as motionless as a frozen fountain in the dead of winter. Sitting cross-legged and holding his head in her lap, she cried, allowing her tears to fall onto his face as she told him again how much she loved being his bride.

Hollis and Clarence were there with her when the coroner arrived to take his body away from his beloved homeland for the very last time. Katherine managed to say through her tears, "Safe travels, my love, until we meet again. You migrated home without me."

The funeral was four days later. The initial details all hinged on Savannah's intent to arrive from Africa, so they were astonished when she chose not to make the trip home to tell Murphy farewell. That alone was heartbreaking for Hollis and Katherine. Savannah believed she could not face burying Murphy and seeing Clark face-to-face. Neither of them could argue that.

The funeral at St. Thomas was all one would expect for a man of prominence and a great deal more. He was buried in a simple box made of timber taken from his beloved land, crafted by Hollis, Clarence, and Father Drew. The smorgasbord of people in the congregation mingled as one. The tailor-made suit with a monogrammed cuff sat next to another monogram of sorts, a uniform displaying the Waffle House insignia. The faces in the crowd were a sea of shades of white and black and brown and red. The ages were a continuum of infant to elderly. The vehicles in the parking lot ranged from work trucks to limousines. Katherine knew the gathered crowd of mourners served as a beautiful representation of the man who loved them all. In the strongest voice she could muster, Katherine addressed the massive, varied crowd.

"We are united this day because of our love for the man we all referred to as Murphy, upon his insistence. Mr. McGregor was entirely too formal a name for him, although he was immensely proud of his Irish heritage, as you well know. I think the reason so many have congregated today is because each of you had a genuine relationship with him. Murphy had a way of conveying how special we were to him, every single one. If you were the cashier who rang up his groceries, he called you by name and asked about your family because he had listened to your response just a week or two before and now he wanted an update. If you came to our farm to work on a leaky pipe, he made arrangements for you to return with your children before the week's end so they could catch some large-mouth bass. And you somehow knew he would be crushed if you didn't take him up on the offer. Look around you. You were just as important to Murphy as the person sitting on your left and your right. It's possible you might have already sized up the person sitting next to you and perhaps surmised you have nothing in common with them. If so, that's how you differ from Murphy. He found something in common with every single person he met. Some of you might have been seated with him as a lobbyist at a dinner table in Washington, D.C., and he earnestly wanted to know your feelings on the matter at hand, not what your company or your political party expected you to say, but what you thought deep in your core. Some of you sat down to dinner with him in a crowded diner in a small town anywhere in America. His sincerity of wanting to share his table with you was irresistible, and before you parted at the end of the meal, you had exchanged names, numbers and addresses. You always received a Christmas card from him. Then he would check on you anytime he drove back through your small town.

And there is another characteristic he shared with the world. He read several newspapers each morning, and he could converse with anyone on any area of business, sports, and politics because he understood the way those worlds orbited. He was reared and educated to be the CEO of the family business. He never once considered doing anything else; except the years he served our country during the war. His father and grandfather instilled in him that he was the seventh generation of the McGregor clan to honor the land that had been passed down to him. But they both hoped he would do more than honor; to love it as deeply as he could love a living being. And he did just that. So, while each of you knew him in one capacity or another, deep down he was simply just the young boy who grew to be a man who loved his homestead with all his heart. No matter what other accomplishments he achieved, he was most proud to be the guy who could navigate the backwaters and take you straight to the best fishing hole or rebuild the carburetor on the tractor or dig the irrigation system with a shovel or a backhoe, depending on the need. He cleaned up well, and I never ceased to be delighted by his good looks, but truth be known, he was most handsome to me when he had a smidge of axle grease above his eyebrow or a splinter that needed to be extracted after an afternoon of chopping wood. Especially knowing that that axle grease was from someone's broken down car on the side of the road or the cord of wood was needed to warm someone's house for the children's sake.

Obviously, Murphy's gifts were encouragement, faithfulness, hospitality, and friendship. There is a small plaque sitting on Murphy's bedside table. It is a replica of the one that sat beside his father's and grandfather's bedside tables. It says: *Love every being God sends your way. Walk beside them, or carry them if needed, but love them as though they were your own.* He loved all of us with his entire being. To me, that is the measure of a man. My man, Murphy Egan McGregor."

Katherine rested her head on Lily Mae's shoulder as the driver lead the long procession to Holly Grove for Murphy's burial. Very little was spoken during the drive. Lily Mae hummed softly, never ceasing to rhythmically pat the sorrowful hands resting in her old brown ones.

She nudged Katherine to look out her window as the funeral procession entered the magnificent ornate gates of Holly Grove cemetery. The trees were in full glory, each looking like it wore its own version of Jacob's coat of many colors. Just to the right of the gate's entrance stood a man, his hat pressed over his heart with one hand while holding his bike upright with the other. His tear-stained face looked straight ahead, like a sentry on duty. Sam had come to tell Murphy goodbye in his own simple way—one friend telling another friend goodbye. The image and the sentiment settled in Katherine's heart and remained there prominently the rest of her life. She conjured it anytime she heard mention of the word "loyalty."

HOLLIS' SECRET

It was a late November evening, and she stopped by the caretaker's cottage with a pan of apple crisp, still warm from the oven, to share with Hollis. Knocking lightly on the door, she could see him through the large front window holding a glass in one hand and a large photograph in the other.

"We both know how much Murphy loved apple crisp." That's all she could say. It was all she needed to say. Hollis watched as her blue eyes clouded with tears. He hoped she would not ask him how long it takes to recover from losing the love of your life. His answer would be too grim for her ears. "I've not seen this. Did she send it recently?" The black and white photograph showed a barefoot Savannah in pedal pushers and a striped cotton blouse, grinning right at Katherine with that infectious smile that could melt any heart.

"Katherine, that's not Savannah." Hollis paused, trying to decide if he really wanted to open Pandora's Box. With a thick voice he continued, "That's her mother only a couple of months before she died. My poignant reminder that today's the anniversary of her death."

Katherine stared at the face of the woman, a replica of Savannah's. There was so much she and Murphy and Lily Mae had always wanted to know but had refrained from asking, fearing it would be too painful and too private.

"Oh, Hollis, all these years we've been so close, and I never knew November 29th was a difficult day for you. I wish Murphy and I had known so we could have given you support on this day each year."

"I know. I wish I'd told you from the start, but I made a big mess of the whole thing by not being honest with you, and worse, with Savannah. When she was about eight, she wanted me to tell her the date of her mother's death. You remember how inquisitive she was. Still is. I made up a date because I was still trying to protect her from the truth. So, I pulled February 28 out of thin air, and from that point forward Savannah thought that was the date of her mother's death."

"That doesn't seem like such a terrible mistake. I bet if you explained it to her exactly the way you've just told me she would understand. But when you say "protect her from the truth," what are you referring to? Something more?"

Hanging his weary head, Hollis said, "Katherine, the web is so tangled. I've done a miserable job of being honest. It was so much easier to tell a lie than the truth. Even after all these years I wish I could hold fast to the lie rather than the ugliness of the truth."

He poured himself another glass of wine and offered one to Katherine. She could tell he was wrestling with some sort of agony that had tortured him for many years. He picked up the photograph and stared, in hopes those frozen lips would speak to him and tell him to come clean, to free what he had kept trapped for so many years.

"Abigail. She was the most beautiful, talented, creative woman I had ever met. A true artist's soul, and I loved her from the very day I met her. We were married for nine years before she became pregnant with Savannah. Nine years is a long time. They were wonderful years." Hollis stopped and took a slow sip of wine. It seemed to revitalize him. He lowered himself onto the ottoman next to Katherine's chair and inhaled a long, labored breath as the memories washed over him. "My God, we loved being Savannah's parents. And Abigail was an incredible mother."

"I'm sure she was," Katherine said in a tone that honored the woman who gave life to the child they all adored. "Hollis, you did what you had to do at the time. You were in survival mode. Savannah would surely understand that now. Anyone would."

He laughed ruefully and looked at Katherine for forgiveness. "But would *anyone* pull a date out of thin air and make up a fictitious cause of death, or would they have the integrity to tell the facts? I sure didn't."

"I obviously don't know the full story, but can't we agree at the very least you did what you thought was best at the time. Please stop tormenting yourself."

"Your kind words do nothing to placate my guilt. I told her the cause of death was a car accident, and that was only a morsel of the truth. There *was* an accident on a cold winter night, and her mother did die, but her mother was drunk, and the driver of the other vehicle was killed." The silence in the room was thick as he struggled to tell more. "She went with a friend to a gallery opening and later called me to come pick her up after she'd had a few glasses of wine. Too many. I was mad at her because I didn't want her to go in the first place, so I told her I didn't intend to wake Savannah and put her in the cold car."

Painful sounds escaped his throat, and they sucked the life from the room. Sobbing, he continued, "I told her to call a cab. I said those awful, selfish words to my wife. To Savannah's mother. To the love of my life. But she didn't call a cab. She got behind the wheel. My God, do you have any idea how many times I have wished I could have taken her place?"

The painful facts were exhausting. To tell and to hear.

Eventually, Katherine asked, "How much of this does Savannah know?"

"She thinks her mother lost control on an icy turn and hit a bridge embankment. No other car involved. I tried so hard to protect her from the truth of what actually happened."

"She's never asked again? I'm surprised her ravenous curiosity didn't get the best of her."

"I think I know why. I cried pitifully as I told her, and I think it was more painful for her to see me cry than it was to hear me explain the cause of her mother's death. It's surreal to think Savannah is now older than Abigail lived to be."

Katherine tried to offer hope. "The emotional triggers that arise during grief are a blessing and a curse. Eventually, we keep the ones that aid and abet the good memories, and we slowly let the traumatic ones lose their impact. In the end, it will be the cherished parts of the relationship that will remain. At least, that's what it feels like to me."

Sharing the story with Katherine was the beginning of a lightened conscience for Hollis. They talked of it frequently in the months ahead and each conversation brought him more peace. He wondered why he kept the truth buried within him so long and was now eager to expunge what had eaten away at his heart. It was time to tell Savannah. But news like this needed to be told in person, for the listener's and teller's sake. They decided he would share the tangled story with her the next time he visited Africa.

DELIVERY

The note said:

Katherine,
I have decided. Call me.
Blessings,
Drew

Three months prior, Katherine had given Father Drew an assignment and asked him to contact her when his decision was final. Obviously, he was ready to share.

Katherine was giddy with excitement as she poured their coffee. "I must admit, I barely slept last night. It felt like Christmas Eve when I was a child. I must have heard the big clock chime every single hour."

Father Drew tried to sip the too hot coffee before responding. "You know you gave me a very difficult assignment...think of something we could purchase for St. Thomas that would make the lost feel welcomed, yet I was to tell no one where it came from. That was the hardest part of all."

"There is no reason for anyone to know it's from me, but there is every reason in the world to make the lost feel welcome." Her tone indicated to Drew that the decision was final.

He smiled at Katherine as he made his announcement, "What would you think about a life-size crèche to be displayed during Advent on the grounds outside the church, the side facing Main Street. And we could offer warm cider or cocoa and Christmas hymns to anyone who wanted to come visit?

He saw the excitement light up her face.

"If our nativity scene could help just one…and yes, of course, it should be life-size." She faltered for a moment trying to absorb it all. "I cannot think of anything I would rather purchase for the church right now. Anonymously, of course."

He was barely out of the drive before she was opening a new page in her journal and labeling it "The Christ Child." After two busy weeks of long distance and international phone calls followed by written correspondence, Katherine secured her order for a life-size custom crèche from Groppetti's, a fifth generation Italian company located in Tuscany, specializing in magnificently hand-carved nativities. The order was a large one. The holy family and manger, three wise men – two standing and one kneeling, a seated donkey, a camel, a kneeling ox, a standing sheep, and a shepherd boy holding a lamb. An order of that size would take five months to create and approximately two months for delivery across the Mediterranean Sea and the North Atlantic.

Four days shy of thirty weeks from the date of the conversation with Father Drew, a phone call came.

"Katherine McGregor?"

After she verified, he went on to explain he represented TFO Freight and needed to schedule a delivery headed her way with a total of ten vast shipping crates. "It's really quite simple. I just need to verify the delivery address and make sure the location has either a loading dock or an accessible forklift on standby."

The caller found himself stalling, not wanting to terminate the call, as he enjoyed hearing the excitement in her bubbling, elderly voice while she explained the destination was the Episcopal church in Kingston. Although it was none of his business, and he knew better, he couldn't help but ask what on earth was housed in the crates that could possibly excite her so.

"Young man, you have in your possession something that will remind the good folks of Kingston that love is all around us.

Sometimes, you know, it just takes a little nudge. When you climbed out of bed this morning did you have any idea you were chosen for such a remarkable job?"

There was a long pause, and Katherine wondered if the phone had disconnected in the midst of her rambling. "Are you still there? Hello?" As she moved the phone away from her ear, she heard the caller clear his throat.

"Yes, ma'am. I'm still here. I'm just trying to take it all in. I don't really know what to say other than I've just decided to assign myself the honor of being the driver who'll deliver your cargo. Your *precious* cargo. I originally planned to give this job to another driver, but now I think I'll see if I can't rearrange the routing schedule and let this gig be mine all the way through."

He was shocked to hear the words coming from his own mouth. Most of his workdays were spent in the office scheduling routes, yet he tried to schedule himself at least one good long delivery each month. The other drivers respected the fact that he enjoyed handling a rig, no matter how high up the chain he'd climbed, and he liked the freedom of the road. But he generally didn't decide on the spur of the moment. It was usually well planned, seeing as how he didn't care for surprises. He immediately began second-guessing himself and wished for a rewind button.

"I think that is a tremendous idea you have, young man. I didn't even catch your name."

"William. William Clay."

"Well, Mr. William Clay, when will I see you face-to-face? This promises to be an event I will not forget."

That startled him even more. It had been a very, very long time since he was involved in anything that would make a woman remember him for the rest of her life.

Glancing at his calendar he said, "Looks like I'll be pulling into the fine town of Kingston in four days, which means you'll see me late Tuesday afternoon."

"William Clay, please drive very carefully. I want you to arrive safely. After all, you are an important man in my life these days. Be careful, son."

Another pause and a clearing of his throat, and all he could muster before hanging up was, "See you Tuesday."

William studied the phone. That phone conversation lasted exactly three minutes and fifty-two seconds yet in that timeframe this unknown woman had somehow convinced him he was an important man with an important assignment. He sat still for quite some time. Her words washed over him. *You are an important man in my life these days.* She made him feel as though something good was down the road ahead.

He said aloud to no one, "Looks like I'm swapping routes and headed on a twelve hundred mile round trip to a place I've never heard of, to see a lady I don't know, to deliver cargo I can't imagine spending real money on. Exactly when did I turn into such a fool?"

That night he Googled the town of Kingston. Typical small town. The website was maintained by the Kingston Chamber of Commerce. It was designated the county seat about eighty years after America won her independence. The website touted it to be a great place to live, work, and play. Situated in an area of the state thick in timber and plenty of other natural resources. Photographs of last year's Christmas parade and the county fair were plastered all over the site. It appeared that the downtown merchants all flew American flags on significant flag-flying days, and the photos showed a magnificent display of red, white, and blue along Main Street. There were accolades for the local school system and a photograph of the current Future Farmers of America chapter, ranked seventh in the nation. Good looking clean-cut teenagers huddled together with handsome toothy grins. Another section of the website mentioned the historic home place of the McGregor dynasty located just outside the city limits and showed a picture of the historical marker commemorating the site. The Arts, Culture, and Entertainment section described beautiful rivers and man-made lakes brimming with opportunities for fishing, boating, canoeing, and kayaking. Lots of photos of Kingstonites holding up their catch of the day. William had to admit he was impressed. It almost sounded like a place a person could call home. If someone were looking.

That was the thing about William that many people couldn't know or understand. He wasn't looking for a home. He gave up on that quest at age eighteen when he was considered too old to be a ward of the state and was subsequently dismissed from the foster care system. He was five when his father died, and four years later his mother's death left him alone. He had two older half-brothers on his father's side and one older half-sister on his mother's side who were all grown by the time he officially became an orphan. For a variety of reasons, none of his half-siblings could or would adopt him, so he became a ward of the state.

One day he was someone's son, and the next day he belonged to no one. Adrift. When you share DNA with folks and none of them agree to take you in, it does a number on your identity, and you never really get over it. You spend a lot of your life wondering what you did so wrong that no one wanted *you*. You forget to ponder what was wrong with *them*.

No one adopts nine-year-olds. Young infants or toddlers, yes. Fourth graders, no. He eventually lost count of the number of foster homes. The majority were safe and clean. Others were perhaps clean, but the walls kept dirty secrets, the kind that still brought him terrors in the night. Clean seemed to be the one common denominator between the decent places and the ones that scarred him. He wished the social workers assigned to his case had lived within the system. If they had, they might have looked past the pine-scented, freshly mopped floors and seen evidence of unspoken things that happened when the doors were closed and the television volume was turned up as high as it could go.

Changing foster homes also meant he frequently changed schools. He lost track of how many times he entered a brand-new classroom to see the teacher give him the once over. By the time he was in his seventh new school, he realized he needed to choose his destiny. He could be known as a bully, angry at the entire world, or he could be a wallflower no one seemed to notice. Life was already hard enough, so he chose the latter and spent the rest of his adolescence following the rules, focused on being a nobody. Neither took much effort. They seemed to go hand in hand.

The typical events that consume children's thoughts and energy—birthday parties, Christmas wish lists, try-outs, sleepovers, and summer camps were completely off limits to William. Instead, he became a reader of anything and everything he could get his hands on. He read cereal boxes and owner's manuals and any book, magazine, or newspaper he could find, regardless of the topic. Reading allowed him to explore places and events he couldn't even pronounce or possibly find on a map. It was his one escape, and it was a healthy one. The alternatives were not.

After being discharged from the system at age eighteen, he worked two jobs to save enough money to attend trucking school. He figured a big rig would allow him to travel and see the kinds of places he'd always read about.

He was accustomed to his solitary life. There were no surprises. He drove his routes, delivered the freight on time without incident or accident, and came back to his home alone. His was the most meticulously maintained house on the street. The grass was mowed each week. The tomato plants were fertilized the first week of each month in the summer. He flew an American flag by his front door 365 days a year, not just on patriotic holidays. He even surprised himself each year as he eagerly anticipated the chore of hanging Christmas lights along his roofline. An outsider would assume the family who lived there had an Ozzie and Harriet kind of life. Trouble was, there never had been a Harriet.

William had every tangible possession he wanted at this stage in his life. As an adolescent, feeling very much alone, he always assumed he'd be happy if he just had stuff to call his very own. He used to envision one day having a house full of things with his name written on the bottom of everything with a permanent marker. Permanent was the part he wished for the most. Even now, at age thirty-eight, with all the possessions he could ever want, the loneliness surrounded him. It crept into his life the day his mother died, and he held onto it and drug it around like a bucket of cement.

But now, incredibly, he found he was more than willing, actually eager, to trade routes with another trucker to ensure he was going to make this delivery to Mrs. Katherine McGregor in Kingston. *Wait,* he wondered to himself, *McGregor is her last name. What did I read on the website about that name? I wonder if she's related to the family who had the big mansion mentioned on the website.* Too tired to look, he drifted off to sleep, knowing he had a long route beginning early in the morning.

Driving the route to Kingston allowed him ample time to wonder what it was about the woman that made him respond so uncharacteristically, as though he couldn't resist her magnetic pull.

As promised, William made his obligatory call to alert his customer of his estimated time of arrival. He expected to arrive at his destination within the next forty minutes.

"I'm so pleased to hear your voice, William. I'm here waiting, and I'm eager to put a face to this strong voice you have. Be careful, son, and I'll see you soon. Goodbye."

He managed to get in a quick goodbye before the line went dead. Funny she'd said that about his voice when he had been thinking the same about hers. He had a nose for determining the goodness of a person within a minute or two of meeting them, and often it was the voice that gave it away. He could detect phoniness in a voice faster than a metal detector hovering over a land mine. She was probably in the grandmother stage of her life, and he envisioned someone a tad plump with a cardigan resting around her shoulders and glasses on a chain. Hair would be gray and shoes would be practical and possibly she would smell of old lady lilac-scented hand lotion.

He gave himself a good glance in the rig's rearview mirror. Clean-shaven and a wrinkle-free shirt. Not bad. Thankful his short crew cut had recently been trimmed, he popped in a piece of gum to freshen his breath, hoping to cut the aroma of barbecued chips he had been enjoying during the last leg of the journey.

Pleasantly surprised at what he saw of Kingston, he entered from the north end of town and strategically maneuvered his rig through the town's square. The GPS indicated St. Thomas Episcopal Church was just one block east, and he noticed a couple of small directional signs along the route indicating he was on the right path.

Even from a block away he knew he'd found his destination. Not from the posted sign in front of the church but from the welcoming crowd of four standing at the curb. A woman waving frantically with a cleric-collared minister standing to her right. To her left stood a timeworn woman of color standing erect and dignified supported with a walking stick. Next to her was a man with both hands shoved in his pockets, possibly the first woman's grown son. William nodded his head and gave a simple wave as he began to manipulate the tight turn. In all his years of driving cargo, he had never had a welcoming committee. It brought a smile to his face and on impulse he gave the horn a quick blast, surprising even himself, which produced an eruption of laughter and cheers from the eager foursome.

Opening the door to his cab, he looked down and realized his greeters had hastily moved as one ensemble right outside his cab and were looking up at him with great anticipation.

Suddenly everyone began speaking at once. The only silent one was Katherine. She stared directly into William's eyes with a broad, welcoming smile. She was not at all like he had predicted. Her slender body with her blue eyes and hint of grey in her hair were the opposite of what he expected for her age, and he wondered if those good looks had worked to her advantage over the years. He quietly reached up and removed his cap, offered his hand and said, "You must be Mrs. McGregor."

"Katherine, please," she said as she brushed away his outstretched hand and reached up to give him a welcoming hug. Unaccustomed, William responded with the warmth of a robot.

There was a swarm of activity over the next couple of hours, making a beehive look lethargic. The men of the church unloaded and opened the crates as the ever-growing gathering of church members uttered a collective gasp each time a new portion of the nativity was revealed.

William was intrigued by it all, but it was the trio of Katherine, Lily Mae, and Sam that fascinated him the most. Lily Mae bossed everyone present, no matter the age or gender, using her cane as an extension of her pointer finger and everyone seemed to expect it out of the old woman who looked like she'd already seen a century of life. Katherine knew everyone and he sensed a comfortable feeling about her within those walls. He watched her from the opposite side of the room and estimated she hugged at least a hundred people that evening. It seemed to be something she did well and frequently. He envied that. Sam didn't speak much, but he was quick to do whatever anyone asked him of him. On two occasions William observed Sam leave his task and check on Katherine, making sure she was warm enough and not too tired. He guessed Sam was her dutiful son, and he wondered if Sam knew how lucky he was to have such a title bestowed on him.

It was just dinner he agreed to. He had no idea it would become the spark that would grow to illuminate his whole world. It took root at dinner when he shocked himself by promising Katherine he would return in two weeks for the unveiling of the nativity. According to Lily Mae, all the fine people of Kingston planned to attend, and they wanted him to see the magnitude of his delivery. That was all fine and good, but what on earth had he gotten himself into and more importantly, why? He couldn't put his finger on it, but there was something about Katherine that drew him as if she had a web and he was caught within.

So, keeping his word, he did return. He planned to arrive the afternoon of the unveiling, spend one night, and over the course of the next eight vacation days hit as many casinos as possible on his route back home. He called Katherine from his hotel room and was once again struck by the tenderness of her voice.

"Would you mind if I drove to your hotel, and then we could use my car to pick up Lily Mae and Sam? I'd like very much to be at the church in plenty of time before the crowd begins to grow."

He went back through it all in his mind a million times later that night. There was nothing that prophesied the kind of night he would experience and for that he was glad. If he had known in advance, he might have declined the offer.

The evening itself was simple. The emotions that accompanied it were startling. Katherine and Lily Mae sat in the back seat and filled the entire car with chatter. Sam called shotgun as if someone else were joining them and smiled sheepishly as William chauffeured them to St. Thomas.

Quite a crowd had already congregated, but it was small in comparison to the vast gathering that would assemble by the time the unveiling occurred.

"So this is what small town America looks like," he said to his companions.

Lily Mae chuckled. "A little bit of this and a little bit of that and a whole lot of everybody knowing everybody else."

"And a lovely place to call home," Katherine added.

The Kingston police barricaded two blocks of Main Street to ensure there would be plenty of room for folks to gather, but William soon wondered if they needed to consider blocking off a third. The crowd grew rapidly by the minute, and the excitement in the air was electrifying. He couldn't fight the contagious anticipation. When Father Drew stepped to the microphone the crowd began to settle. He tapped the live mic a couple of times and the noise came to an immediate hush.

William listened as Father Drew commanded the large crowd with his amplified voice and was startled when he heard his own name announced over the loudspeaker. Something about "a friend of Katherine McGregor and please join me in giving him a hearty welcome." The crowd erupted in applause.

Katherine leaned in closer and explained, "Kingston is applauding you."

William shot her a bewildered look, puzzled as to why he was worthy of mention before this substantial crowd of strangers.

"You are the one who made the delivery possible, and the whole town appreciates you."

William felt several pats on the back from those standing nearest him. He realized he was smiling back at Katherine as if it was commonplace for him to be the center of attention. Nothing could be further from the truth.

Soon after, the spotlights were dimmed, and an expectant hush saturated the night air. A single female voice began singing "What Child Is This" a cappella as the life-size figures of Mary, Joseph, and baby Jesus were placed in the manger. When the angel and the shepherds were unveiled, a duo of teenaged boys, accompanied by a flute, sang "Angels We Have Heard on High." William felt a warmth spread through his body and wondered if others could feel it too. Then, as the three wise men were revealed, a man and woman accompanied by a string quartet, sang "We Three Kings of Orient Are."

Nothing prepared William for what would happen next. Small tapered candles were distributed throughout the crowd and almost instantly a warm glow of candlelight surrounded the nativity. Drums rolled and trumpets blared while the voices of the crowd joined to sing "Oh Come, All Ye Faithful."

William knew then Christmas was much more than what the big box stores advertised. It was strangers singing shoulder to shoulder as they gazed at the nativity. It was Katherine with her arm linked in his, smiling at him, whispering something into his ear. "Just look what you delivered to our town. Merry Christmas, William."

Words were not adequate at that moment. He didn't know how to describe how he felt, so he did what his gut told him to do. It was the easiest thing, yet also the hardest thing, he could possibly imagine. He slipped his hands out of the pockets of his corduroy coat and casually took Katherine's arm on one side of him and Lily Mae's on the other. They snuggled in closer. He didn't even attempt to wipe the tears. He just let them drip off his face, one after another.

Dinner that night was a bit of a blur. Katherine insisted they all dine with her at Caroline's Landing, Kingston's finest restaurant. William observed several remarkable things over dinner. Sam ordered a hamburger, of course, and no one seemed to mind it wasn't on the menu. The meal was one of the finest he had ever tasted, but the most delicious part of the evening was the telling of the story of how Katherine and Lily Mae and Sam had all become connected in life. And it took the three of them to tell the story to the fullest.

So here he was, sitting at an elegant restaurant, amidst three people who were not one bit related, but they were as fine a family as he had ever seen or read about. "That's just about the most compelling story I've heard in my entire life." And raising his glass he said, "Here's to Doc and Murphy, two fine gentlemen I wish I had known."

He remained in Kingston for the next seven days. Katherine insisted he stay with her, convincing him the old rule about guests and fish beginning to stink after three days never applied to Cross Creek. He soon discovered the house, the land, and the woodland animals. The moonlight and stars were the most glorious things he had seen in his thirty-eight years of living. He felt conected to the land in a good way, making him ponder if his people had been loggers in days gone by. Katherine watched him walk the grounds each sunrise. She hoped the trees were rooting him, giving him sanctuary.

She kept him busy. Each day they ran errands in town, giving Katherine an excuse to introduce him. He shook hands with more people in those seven days than he had in his entire life.

Two of those errand days included Sam and Lily Mae. As if they had done it their whole lives, Sam always called shotgun, and Lily Mae and Katherine huddled together in the back seat telling stories which kept them all laughing—laughing so hard that people in other cars alongside them couldn't help but look at them and smile.

Lily Mae went to the library twice a week to return her books-on-tape and select four more. She introduced William to the young librarian, Annabelle Curry, who seemed to blush when her eyes caught his. It did not go unnoticed, and Lily Mae whispered it to Katherine as William chauffeured. When he caught a glimpse of Katherine's smile and a raise of her eyebrow, he shook his head and laughed, trying hard to conceal his interest.

And just like that, his seven days of vacation ended. It was the quickest week of his life. He awoke, realizing it would be his last day in Kingston and he felt a worrisome nag in his gut. It gnawed at him, telling him leaving was somehow wrong. But he fought the feeling, and showered and shaved and tidied the room. He supposed the source of it came from knowing he was driving away from a place that felt so right.

His real life he was quite different from the life he had lived these last seven days in Katherine's company. For decades, he had convinced his heart that he preferred to live as a solitary man. Over the years, he'd developed a strong defense mechanism that allowed him to shut off the rest of the world when he felt claustrophobic from the laughter and close bonds he witnessed in others. If this mechanism was so strong, why was it failing him now? It was going to take everything within him to zip his suitcase and carry it to his truck.

Nausea reared its ugly head. To calm his stomach, he stretched out on the freshly made bed. His heart was beating rapidly, and his breath was shallow. His brain was beginning to process the terrifying possibility that he might be having a heart attack, and for just the tiniest second, he saw the irony of it all. He might be dying in the very place where he had begun to understand how tired he was of being estranged from an ordinary life. That peculiar thought shot through his body like a jolt from a defibrillator. He heard a loud moan and was petrified to realize that the sound had come from his own mouth.

In an attempt to stop the room from spinning, he turned on his side. After fifty or sixty seconds the pain began to subside, the nausea slowly dissipated and his breathing started to normalize. And then it hit him. It all suddenly became evident. He realized he was lying in the fetal position. All those years ago, his body had reacted the same way when he was told he'd have to leave his mother's house to go live with people he didn't know. Twice now in his life every fiber of his being had convulsed at the idea of walking away from love. He heard another sound coming from within, and this time it was sobbing.

There was no turning back or second-guessing when he bashfully told Katherine he had decided to stay in Kingston. Remarkably, she did not ask all the logistical questions for which he had no answers…where he planned to live or how he planned to make a living or even if he had really thought it through.

She merely clutched both of his hands in hers and said with genuine tenderness, "You know what the Bible tells us in Hebrews? *Do not neglect to show hospitality to strangers, for by doing that some have entertained angels without knowing it.* Welcome, William, and may you never feel the need to leave again. But if you do, may you find your way back home to us." She reached out for him, and their embrace lasted long enough to remind him how to hug back, leaving a little puddle of his tears on her right shoulder.

It wasn't until much later that Katherine learned William's story, but she had sensed from the beginning a brokenness about him— that he had known the meaning of sadness for most of his days.

SETTLE IN

It didn't take William long to settle in. He was a regular around Katherine's table for their Sunday night dinners.

"It feels like we just added the last piece to the jigsaw puzzle, and now the picture is finally complete." Katherine looked at Lily Mae, knowing full well she understood exactly what she meant.

"Except this time, it's not a jigsaw of a lighthouse or ships in a harbor. It's a picture of our lives, you, me, Sam, Hollis, Clarence and now William."

"If only Murphy and Doc and Savannah . . ."

"I know, Queenie, I know. But I haven't stopped pestering the good Lord about that. I'm certain he's got a plan for Savannah, just not sure what it is. But this I know to be true…it's a mighty plan. You and I both know that."

Over dessert, Hollis broached the subject of William joining himself and Clarence in the day-to-day management of the farm. They both thought he would be a good fit since they weren't as nimble as they used to be, and they readily admitted they could use a young buck. William was tempted. He liked the idea.

It was Katherine's turn. "That's an excellent proposition, and I like it from all angles, but I have another idea. One that Lily Mae and I came up with together."

Clarence couldn't contain a chuckle. "This one's going to be good. You combine the gumption of those two old women, and you've got yourself something to be reckoned with. You have to remember, William, I've known Lily Mae my entire life, and Katherine has known her since she was seven. Yes sir, this one is really going to be good. Brace yourself, buddy, and now let's hear it."

Katherine took the stage, smiling. "Well, I have no doubt William would be an asset on the farm, but I'm afraid as soon as you men realize how intelligent he is and how quick he is to catch on to things, you won't want to share him with Lily Mae and me so we want to lay claim on him first."

"Queenie, why don't you let me tell it, since it was really my idea to begin with?"

"Well, of course, Lily Mae. You tell it then and be convincing because we don't want William to turn us down."

In his entire life, he was certain no one had ever fought over him. It was a powerful awakening.

Lily Mae began. "Hear me out. I'm trying to do my part and conserve America's energy. Seems that's what our politicians and conservationists keep preaching about these days."

Clarence chuckled again. "I told you this was going to be good. Lily Mae's about to tell us how William here is going to be America's answer to the energy crisis. Go ahead, Sister."

"Now you hush up and let me finish." Lily Mae's audience was eager to hear her bright idea, recognizing the mirth in her voice. "We're hoping William might decide to work for *us,*" indicating with her head she meant just herself and Katherine. "We've reached the point we could use some help. We've been thinking I might give up my house and move to Cross Creek. That's the saving energy part. He could help me get all settled and then he could manage us, take us here and there, driving us when we needed to go places. Katherine's not too old to drive, but he's spoiled us. We've been having a lot more fun sitting together in the back seat talking and carrying on than when she's doing the driving all around town. Besides, we're hoping we can work around his schedule cause we're thinking he might start taking some college classes and get himself a degree in something. He's got lots more gifts than just being a good driver. Not sure if he realizes it or not, but it's plain as day to the rest of us."

All eyes shifted to William. He quietly studied Lily Mae's face and then Katherine's. "What exactly does *manage you* entail?"

"There you go, son! That question alone lets me know you are a man of intelligence." Clarence nodded as he laughed at his own announcement. "These two gals aren't the kind to be managed, so you should know that up front. I think you better just take us up on the farm offer and forget these two. They'll get you in a heap of trouble without you ever realizing it. I've been there and done that and I'm scared of these two."

It took a while for the laughter to subside around the table.

"That's just about enough out of you, Clarence." Everyone detected the playfulness in Katherine's voice. "Maybe just a trip to the library a couple of days a week, grocery shopping, the drug store now and then, Sam's house every Friday for can redemption and any other day he wants to spend with us, and one other adventure we haven't yet mentioned to you."

Hollis couldn't resist. "And here it comes. You see how these two operate? Ole Doc Bishop used to call it the K Syndrome when he talked about how Katherine could hypnotize people, but I realized years ago she learned that magic trick from Lily Mae. These two have some spells up their sleeves. Don't say we didn't warn you, William."

"Hear me out now," Katherine continued. "Every Monday afternoon I visit several friends who live over at Shady Valley on May Avenue. It's an assisted living facility, not the nicest or best smelling one in town, but one filled with people who have run out of youth and luck years ago. There are a couple of people in particular I want you to meet. Both of them are veterans, and I know how you love American history. I think you'll have quite a bit to talk about."

Sam finally entered the conversation, and everyone stopped to listened intently. "William's new around here. Seems like he should have time to think 'bout what you're saying to him. He might need some time, seems like."

William did need time but not a lot of it. He knew before his head rested on the pillow that night which option to choose. With one condition.

The next morning he shared his thoughts with Katherine. "I'd like to take you up on your offer, but I think I'd like to get a place of my own. Maybe someplace half way between Cross Creek and Sam's place. That way I can get to him quickly if he ever needs me, and the same applies for you. That idea came to me, and it feels right. What do you think?"

Katherine's hug carried with it every word of love known to man. And so, their journey began.

He particularly connected with one of the veterans during their Monday visits at Shady Valley. Royce Thessing had almost no family who ventured his way. He was crusty and curt and had pushed away what little family still felt obligated to visit sporadically once or twice a year. But William was different. If he noticed Royce's offensive odor or language, he never let on. The two men simply talked about the war—where Royce served, the outcome of the battles, his buddies in combat who were like brothers, and much more.

Mr. Thessing didn't realize it, but William gathered all the information he learned each Monday and began to investigate the names and dates. The internet had a wealth of WWII documentation, and as it turned out, Annabelle Curry, the young reference librarian, was more than eager to assist in his research.

It was Annabelle who gave William access to the recently declassified government sites. Together they spent hours, days, and weeks searching, sorting data and compiling information. They became a research team of two, working arduously for Mr. Royce Thessing, without the old guy knowing a bit of it. An air of comfortableness enveloped them when they spoke, and William seemed to linger longer and longer each week at the reference desk.

But it never went farther than that. Just two people researching an old soldier's career and accomplishments from a war that occurred decades before they were born.

"Maybe that's all it's intended to be." Katherine didn't believe it even as the words came out of her mouth.

"Now, I raised you better than that, Queenie. Have you not seen how she brings out the twinkle in his eyes? You watch. Something potent's going to come out of all this research these two have going on. I can feel it."

BABY JESUS

In the first week of Advent of the third year after the debut of St. Thomas' life-size nativity scene, the unthinkable occurred. Someone stole baby Jesus. Right smack in the middle of Kingston. Father Drew called to break the news to Katherine.

It was difficult news to deliver, and it was difficult news to grasp. "That just can't be right. Who on earth in our town would take baby Jesus and why? Now you and I both know teenagers sometimes play silly pranks. Do you think someone just moved him to one of the other churches?"

"I've already sent an email to the churches in the ministerial alliance, but so far nothing's turned up." Katherine heard a rawness in Father Drew's voice she seldom heard. "When I talked to Father John at St. Joseph's he reminded me it's the Catholic tradition to wait until Christmas morning to place the Christ child in the manger, and he wondered if St. Thomas had decided to do the same."

"I wish it were that simple. I'm going to assume someone will call, laughing hysterically, to report that they found it laying in their front yard next to their mechanical reindeer or pink flamingos. I have a hunch this will end well." It was the best Katherine could do. She hoped she sounded more convincing than she felt.

Katherine and William went in tandem to tell Sam, who took the news the hardest. Sam's world was black and white, without a smidgen of gray. Things were right or they were wrong and, in his mind, stealing baby Jesus was very, very wrong. He didn't take their word for it. He had to see it to believe it, so they all loaded up and William drove them to St. Thomas to see the vacancy in the manger for themselves.

"That's wrong what somebody did to Jesus." Sam turned his head, avoiding a second look at the nativity. "Let's go find 'em."

And by that he meant, literally, let's go look for someone walking around Kingston carrying a life-size hand carved wooden infant Christ child. William never even glanced at Katherine for approval. He just put the car in gear and for the next two hours they followed Sam's navigation as they slowly drove up and down any street he directed. William knew it was pointless. Katherine knew it was pointless. But they both knew it would help Sam understand that baby Jesus wasn't just lying on some street corner waiting to be found.

The *Kingston Daily* ran a front-page story the following morning, complete with a color photo of the empty manger. The article included quotes from several prominent Kingstonites expressing their disappointment that vandals would attempt something so blatantly sacrilegious in their peaceful town. The Kingston Chamber of Commerce offered a reward for the return of the missing baby.

The disappearance was the talk of the town. Everyone had an opinion on whether the church should dismantle the Nativity until the missing member of the Holy Family could be replaced. The *Kingston Daily* seized the opportunity to boost sales by providing a daily update. Father Drew reminded the reporter it was ultimately up to St. Thomas' vestry to decide how to handle the disappearance, and they were scheduled to vote on the issue the following week at their regularly scheduled meeting. Until then, the Nativity remained as it was, void and all.

It was five days after the abduction that baby Jesus was discovered under a pile of fetid trash and Styrofoam peanuts in First Bank of Kingston's dumpster. If it weren't for Sam's passion for rummaging in trash receptacles for aluminum cans, baby Jesus would have been flattened by the garbage truck and spent the rest of eternity disintegrating in the Kingston dump.

It was still dark and quite cold, but Sam had a routine, and regardless of the weather he rarely deviated from his schedule of predawn dumpster searching. He almost didn't see the carved body lying under the rubbish. He'd actually already walked away from the dumpster and was maneuvering his bike when he had the strong feeling that something was wrong, which pulled him back to the dumpster. It was a feeling so strong he couldn't avoid it, like it was meant to be. It was Sam who found what Kingston had lost.

He removed his coat and wrapped it gingerly around the wooden replica of the Christ child and then cradled him across his chest as he pedaled back home, just as dawn was breaking.

"You better come see me and you better come now. Jesus ain't lost no more. I got him here at my house. Got him wrapped up in my coat. I thought you'd want to know he's not hurt."

"Oh, Sam." Tearfully, Katherine told him she was on her way.

Katherine and Lily Mae arrived only minutes before William, followed shortly by Father Drew. There he was, the wooden Christ child, lying on Sam's worn Naugahyde couch wrapped in a man's coat, his carved arms and legs outstretched as though he were reaching for Sam.

En masse, they rode with Father Drew to return Jesus to the manger and the word spread throughout town like jam on warm toast. The same *Kingston Daily* reporter now begged to do a follow-up interview with Sam. The headline the next day read, "Baby Jesus Saved" and quoted Sam saying, "I couldn't sleep right knowing somebody took Jesus."

No one witnessed the recovery, but it would be told and retold many times in the following days by Kingstonites who celebrated the righting of the wrong. Overnight Sam's description went from being "the can guy who's not all there" to "one of Kingston's finest."

What Sam decided to do next was not discovered until about midnight several evenings later when Officer Keith Sims was working his night shift. Spotting someone lurking in a darkened doorway about a block from the town square, he parked his patrol car and approached the man positioned in the dim light directly across the street from, and in full view of, St. Thomas' life-sized outdoor nativity.

"Hey, man. What are you doing standing out here in the cold?"

"Just watching." Sam shifted from one foot to the other, never turning his head to match eyes with the policeman. Officer Sims noticed the man's tennis shoes, a poor selection of footwear on this night of below freezing temperatures.

"What are you watching for?" He asked, turning his head to see the view his stranger was so deliberately studying.

"Trying to make sure nobody steals the baby again. They did it already and I'm gonna' watch over Jesus and make sure it don't happen again." Sam never once took his eyes off the crime scene.

"Are you the one who found him? In the dumpster?" It all became clear to Officer Sims, and he was struck by the magnitude of this man's commitment. "Tell you what, I'll keep a good eye out to make sure they're all safe and you can go on home and get out of the cold. I'll make sure nothing else happens. It's already below freezing and they're predicting sleet before the night ends."

"Nope. What if you have to go help somebody else? Who'll watch then?"

"Well, you're right, something could come up and I'd have to leave temporarily but then I'd return and stand watch again."

"Nope, I ain't leavin'. Somebody in this town tried to do wrong to baby Jesus already and I ain't going to let 'em do it again. I know what's right and I know what's wrong and I know God's watching. I thought I might help a little."

And so that's how it went for the next week. Sam slept during the day and stood watch by night. Word got out. Police officers told their spouses who went to work and told their colleagues. They told their neighbors, and it wasn't long before the whole town knew. Everyone got in the spirit. Someone anonymously dropped off a collapsible canvas chair for Sam to sit in while he was on his self-assigned watch. First Bank of Kingston took up a collection and presented Sam with three pairs of insulated socks, a down coat, and new neoprene boots. Katherine packed him a tall thermos of hot chocolate and snacks, and William kept him company several hours each evening.

Some nights were wet and every night was cold, but nothing prevented Sam from standing guard, like a loyal sentry, watching over his sheep. Without fail. He set the kind of example that touched even the hard-hearted. Father Drew included it in an Advent sermon, reminding St. Thomas' congregants that the way the town responded to Sam and his efforts was a touching example of loving our neighbors as ourselves.

Downtown Kingston was always picturesque but especially so at Christmas. Wreaths hung from every storefront, white twinkling lights wrapped each streetlight, the entire roofline and all eight columns of the county courthouse were illuminated in white lights. Everyone anticipated the annual Christmas parade, a fifty-three-year-long tradition. Little about the dazzling event had changed over the years. It was comprised of a couple of school marching bands playing their small reprotoire of Christmas music, at least twenty church floats in a variety of shapes and sizes, several beauty queens, and the ever-popular finale of Santa riding atop the city's most impressive fire truck, throwing candy to all the kids while ho-ho-hoing all the way.

Just days before the parade, Mayor Phillips asked Katherine to arrange for Sam to be present at the Kingston City Council meeting with a promise that it would be a memorable event.

And so they gathered. Turns out it was quite a few friends who came to see what Mayor Phillips had in mind. Katherine and Lily Mae sat on one side of Sam while William and Father Drew and his wife, Mary-Claire, joined him on the other. The remainder of the front row was filled with smiling uniformed police officers and the reporter from the *Kingston Daily*.

The city council meeting was called to order, and the secretary called roll. All eight members were present, including Wanda Sullivan-Langston.

The townsfolk weren't too surprised when she won her first election for city council. Many found her opinionated ways offensive, but they feared her retribution if they crossed her. Her family had long been connected with local politics beginning with her incompetent uncle who had cruelly tormented the area as county sheriff for several decades. The wrath of Wanda Sullivan-Langston was something to avoid at all costs.

Katherine knew that wrath well. She still felt sorrow when she thought of the destruction of the white rabbit fur muff orchestrated by Wanda, the intentional hurtful things that she had said about the disappearance of Katherine's father, and of course her attempt to thwart Katherine's marriage to Murphy.

Rapping his gavel, Mayor Phillips began, "I'd like to welcome you to our December Kingston City Council meeting. I'm especially excited about this evening's events. I have a declaration prepared I'd like to propose to our city council for their approval. We have a well-deserved honor to bestow on someone who has proven exemplary citizenship during this special time of year."

The crowd murmured with excitement. Katherine and Lily Mae looked at Sam, anxious to see if he realized what was about to happen.

Mayor Phillips continued. "We all know the unpleasant news of the disappearance of baby Jesus from St. Thomas' beautiful outdoor nativity. And unless you live under a rock, you've heard the story of Sam Higgins finding Jesus in the dumpster at First Bank of Kingston. But that's really just the beginning of the story."

Mayor Phillips went on to explain Sam's self-appointed role of sentry, standing watch over the nativity, like the North Star.

"This Kingston citizen has reminded our city what valor looks like these days, and his commitment is one of the most selfless things that has happened in Kingston for a very long time."

The audience erupted in boisterous applause. Katherine leaned toward her friend and whispered, "Everyone's clapping for you, Sam, because they admire your loyalty."

Unaccustomed to the attention, he hung his head low, the tip of his chin nearly touching his chest, rocking slowly back and forth, his fingers splayed as they gripped his thighs. His reddened face showed no emotion.

Resting her arm across Sam's shoulders, Katherine looked up to exchange appreciative glances with the city council members. All but one eagerly participating in the applause. Wanda sat stoically with her hands in her lap, looking straight ahead with an icy stare at an unremarkable door jam, as if she were posing for an 18th-century portrait.

William leaned in close to Katherine and whispered, "What's up with that one? The one who refuses to clap or look this way?"

Lily Mae responded succinctly with two words which instantly told him who this glaring woman was. "Peach cobbler."

A thought crossed Katherine's mind, but she shooed it away. Certainly, Wanda knew better than to cause a scene on such a lovely occasion.

Mayor Phillips proceeded to read the declaration aloud, "Hear ye, hear ye good citizens of Kingston. Whereas, the City of Kingston each calendar year shall recognize a member of the community as the Citizen of the Year, and now, therefore, be it resolved, that the City Council hereby appoints this year's…"

Wanda Sullivan-Langston's caustic voice brought the mayor's speech to a sudden halt. "Need I remind you, Mayor Phillips, that you are obligated to follow the established Robert's Rules of Order while conducting the city council meetings? I'm disappointed I have to remind you, but this is a blatant disregard for process. You've failed to ask for a motion, a discussion, and a vote." She turned this time to the audience, expecting their appreciation for her willingness to put a stop to the foolishness of rewarding a man who spent his time digging around in other people's trash.

It was insulting to hear a member of the city council talk to Mayor Phillips in such a way during a public meeting and he had had enough of her. Judging from the crowd's reaction, the town of Kingston had, as well. But he couldn't dispute her insistence on following Robert's Rules of Order, so, in an attempt to mollify her, he called for a motion which he received immediately. He then asked if there was any discussion.

Wanda slowly stood and turned to face the crowd. After a dramatic pause and an attempt to make eye contact with anyone of importance seated in the audience, she addressed them with command in her voice, honing her retort, "This trivializes all other Citizen of the Year proclamations ever presented. A mentally deficient man who lurks around our town does not deserve this honor. If you want to present a proclamation to someone who has brought honor and dignity to Kingston, I suggest you look for someone who is smart enough to understand what they're actually receiving."

She sat back down and deliberately stared at Katherine with utter hatred. Then she diverted her contemptuous stare on Lily Mae. Retaliation at its best.

Lily Mae never took her eyes off Wanda as she leaned over to Katherine and asked, "Are you going to handle this, or am I?"

Katherine gracefully rose from her chair, walked past Mayor Phillips at the podium, passed the bannister, ascended the two steps elevating the semi-circle of city council members, and stopped when she was face-to-face with Wanda.

In a hushed voice only loud enough for Wanda and the other aldermen to hear, Katherine spoke calmly, eloquently, and deliberately. "Wanda, you need to stop that vicious tongue of yours right this minute. I will not allow you to get away with what you're trying to do. How you've gotten away with it all these years I'll never know, but I'm putting a stop to this right now."

Wanda's face was a study of contradictions. Her smirk indicated she was undeterred by Katherine's words, yet her eyes reflected a look of fear. She knew Katherine had plenty of ammunition, but she played her poker hand well.

"Sit down and shut up, Katherine. No one on the city council has given you permission to speak. We don't care to listen to another word from you. For that matter, we couldn't care less about what you think about *anything*," drawing out the syllables for emphasis. She then looked to her fellow council members expecting their approval, knowing they didn't dare disagree with her. She was surprised to find all seven faces regarding her with disdain. Clearly, her power had been eclipsed.

Katherine continued, her voice galvanized with determination, but still hushed enough to prevent the audience from hearing. She had words she'd wanted to say for a very long time. Placing both of her palms flat on the table in front of Wanda, she leaned in and began. "I'm telling you now, and I mean every word of it, if you prevent this from happening, I will stand before this crowd and recite, in great detail, a very long list of things you have done to lie, cheat, and steal your pompous way around this town. Many of them are the cruel and deceitful things you have done to me personally. I know other things regarding some indescretions that Doc shared with me about you over the years. Since he is no longer with us, I won't have a problem telling the gathered assembly here what you thought would never be exposed due to Doc's Hippocratic oath. It might have very little evidentiary value in court, but that doesn't mean people in this town won't regard it as true. Now, do you really want to prevent this very decent man from receiving an honor he so richly deserves?"

Wanda bolted out of her chair so quickly it fell backward. "Go straight to hell, Katherine. No one cares about anything you have to say, and they certainly don't care about some idiot that digs around in dumpsters. He wouldn't have even found it if my son had done a better job of hiding…"

Mayor Phillips was already pounding his gavel. All city council members were instructed to meet immediately in his inner office.

When the aldermen returned, they numbered seven. Wanda Sullivan-Langston had exited the building. The mayor's proclamation was approved, unanimously, and Sam stood before all as the mayor draped a beribboned medal around his neck. While the term standing ovation was not in Sam's vocabulary, he learned what it was to be honored and loved.

When they returned to Sam's house that evening, he smiled sheepishly at his transfigured image in the mirror. Admiring the medal hanging so majestically around his neck, he said aloud to no one in particular, "Know what? They think I'm somebody."

And that year, it was Sam P. Higgins who rode atop the finest fire truck in the Christmas parade, and the roaring crowd gave him a hero's welcome.

THE REVEALING

It was late summer of the following year. Katherine knew Lily Mae's days were numbered, and soon they would be reduced to a countdown of final hours. Lily Mae knew it, too. The cancer diagnosis felt like a death sentence when it was delivered nine months earlier. It was Lily Mae's decision to decline treatments, knowing her liver was old and tired. She was ready to go. She had lived an entire life anticipating her homegoing, and she knew it was time.

Father Drew brought by a still-warm loaf of banana bread and asked if he could sit with Lily Mae for a few minutes. Katherine knew he wanted to do more than just sit and the knowledge pleased her. She ushered him to Lily Mae's room and stood stoically by the door as he lowered himself into the armchair and reached out to hold her withered hands. Lily Mae opened her eyes and gave him a nod as he offered a prayer, "Bless the Lord, O my soul, and all that is within me bless His holy name." Katherine stepped out and quietly closed the door behind her.

Katherine saw wet streaks on his cheeks when he suddenly emerged from the bedroom. Frightened, she watched him rush to his car as if he'd just been called to an emergency. He turned just before climbing in the front seat of his sedan. With a sense of urgency, he said, "I won't be gone long. There are some," he faltered briefly before continuing, "*things* I need to gather."

This frantic behavior from Father Drew was unexpected, but she realized he must have surmised these were Lily Mae's last few hours on earth. Whatever he was sent after, he was obviously intent on carrying out his mission.

Katherine entered Lily Mae's room and sat quietly by her bedside watching as she slept, her breathing labored. Looking up from checking her pulse, Katherine was surprised to see Lily Mae gazing at her with that tender smile she had loved almost all her life.

In a whisper, Lily Mae asked, "Queenie, do you remember the first day I met you when you were nesting up in that shade tree, the day you and your mama moved above the diner?"

Katherine took Lily Mae's fragile, aged hand and gave it a slight squeeze to let her know she remembered it well.

"Queenie, do you remember asking me to promise to come back and see you the next day?"

"I do remember." Katherine smiled at the thought. "I'm surprised I let you go without following you home that day. I just remember always wanting to be by your side, no matter where you were."

"I told you that day I always kept my promises."

"Yes, and you've never disappointed me."

Lily Mae's tired old face winced. "Queenie, I'm asking you now to forgive me. You might think I did a terrible thing, something that might fill your heart with hate for me but before you hear it, you have to know I did it because I made a promise. But it was a promise that has done nothing but eat at me every day of my life since you've been in it."

Lily Mae stopped, drew a deep breath, and closed her eyes. Her frail body began to shake as if she had been exposed to a cold north wind. Katherine covered her tightly and checked the thermostat. As Lily Mae struggled with her breathing, Katherine sat steadfastly, holding Lily Mae's tired crooked fingers tightly in her own.

When her breathing seemed to stabilize, Katherine stepped into the kitchen to prepare a warm cup of broth in hopes she could entice Lily Mae to take a sip or two of nourishment. It was then she heard not one, but three cars pull into her circular drive. Looking out to see who might have arrived, she was surprised but delighted to see Thomas, Lily Mae's beloved nephew, climb out of one vehicle. Anyone who knew Lily Mae knew how proud she was of her nephew who served as an illustrious judge on the Federal Court bench. To many folks in Kingston, his claim to fame during his childhood was his brilliant mind. As an adult, his claim to fame was his record for the least number of overturns in a federal courtroom. Katherine knew, however, in Thomas' eyes, his claim to fame was the honor of being Lily Mae's nephew.

She was equally delighted when she saw Clarence emerge from the second car. Lily Mae's suggestion for Murphy to hire him after Beechwood's fire was one of her wisest decisions. Neither he nor Lily Mae had lost their desire or ability to outthink, outsmart, outtalk, or outwit each other. Mentally, they were equals. They shared a rare bond, a friendship, a powerful connection. Katherine was saddened to know his life was about to change as drastically as her own. Together they would have to figure out how to live life without their Lily Mae to guide them.

She wrinkled her brow, confused and surprised, when she saw who sat in the front seat of Clarence's car. Sheriff Washington, the county's youngest but widely respected sheriff, slowly emerged. He'd promised justice in his campaign, and he kept his word. She saw integrity in his eyes and his actions. The county had been held under the grips of a scoundrel of a sheriff for three decades, and the two before that were not much better. Sheriff Washington had never called on her before, and Katherine was certain he had never had any reason to call on Lily Mae. His arrival was bewildering.

William, Father Drew, and Clark emerged from the third car. It was evident Father Drew must have summoned this unusual congregation, realizing how close Lily Mae was to departing this life.

She watched as the six men shook hands and exchanged somber looks. They engaged in a quick, hushed, huddled conversation. Each nodded in agreement and walked single file to her back door, with Clarence leading the queue.

Now Katherine knew something was wrong from the look of dread on all six faces. Opening her door, she frantically searched each face for a clue to what could possibly bring such torment and pain to each of them.

Clarence was the first to speak. "Katherine, we're here to fulfill a promise we made to Lily Mae. We ask that you join us now in her room."

Katherine protested. "She's just had a terrible spell and has fallen back to sleep. Whatever this news is you have to tell me, I promise you, we can take care of it without disturbing her."

The men exchanged glances and then they all focused on Katherine. Thomas, the retired federal judge, emerged as the speaker of the group.

"Miss Katherine, your choice of words is commanding. I understand your reticence and it is not our intent to disturb her. We have gathered today at her insistence for the sole purpose of fulfilling a *promise*. One she made to Clarence exactly sixty-six years ago last month. She wants to be with you when it is explained, and it will take all of us to tell the story from beginning to end."

Katherine searched each of their faces, hoping for a clue to help her understand what they were thrusting upon her. Tears began to fill in her eyes as she recounted what Lily Mae had said only minutes before. "She was trying to tell me something about a promise she made a very long time ago. She said something about being afraid I wouldn't understand and then began to shake terribly. Violently. I was afraid I was losing her. I don't think she has the strength left in her to survive the weight of whatever this information is you've brought me. I'm begging you that we not do this in her presence."

Although she didn't understand what was happening to her and around her, Katherine suddenly felt the enormity of the situation and for one of the few times she could remember she was terribly afraid.

Father Drew rested his hands on her shoulders and said, "Katherine, earlier today I asked Lily Mae if she would like to receive the Lord's Supper, and she had one request. She doesn't think she's worthy of receiving her last communion until she's had an opportunity to make peace with you about a promise from years ago."

Pausing to give Katherine time to let his words sink in, he continued. "She acknowledged it's the one thing in her life she has not finished, and she feels God is expecting her to make it right before He calls her home. These gentlemen are here to help her do that, and I'm here to offer communion to all of us when the story's been told."

For the first time since entering her kitchen, the sheriff spoke. "It isn't by accident you have a judge, a member of the clergy, a lawman, an attorney, and one of her oldest friends gathered in your home to help her make this right. We wouldn't have participated in this if we didn't believe it was our duty to see that justice prevails."

Katherine leaned against the kitchen countertop to steady herself. Trying her best to comprehend all that had been laid at her feet, she slowly and deliberately chose her words. "There's nothing in this world you could ever tell me that would change the way I feel about Lily Mae." She paused, trying to control her trembling voice and hands because she needed to say the next part forcefully. "I will participate in this only because it is *her* wish."

Whatever this debacle entailed, it was powerful enough to cause both a dying woman and a healthy one to tremble. None of them knew it at the time, but the situation had the same impact on the sheriff, which he covered well by standing tall with both hands in his pockets.

As if they'd rehearsed it earlier from a script, all seven of them entered Lily Mae's bedroom and took their place. Katherine sat at Lily Mae's bedside and instinctively held her left hand. Father Drew stood at the foot of the bed. Clarence pulled the wingback chair to the other side of the bed and perched on the edge, giving Katherine reason to think he might bolt at any second. Thomas settled on the ottoman. The sheriff stood propped against the doorway, with his hat resting on the top of the chestnut dresser. William stood an arm's length from Katherine, knowing his role was to support her and Clark positioned himself in the far corner, using the top of the bureau to support the legal pad he would use to record an account of all they were about to hear. From the brief amount he was told beforehand in the car, nothing at Harvard Law had prepared him for what they were about to hear.

As if on cue, Lily Mae opened her eyes, saw the assemblage and began rearranging herself to a sitting position.

Clarence reached for her other hand.

Thomas cleared his throat.

Drew pulled two handkerchiefs from the inside pocket of his sports coat and silently offered a short prayer. "Lord, you know everyone's heart. Speak through us today."

The sheriff wiped the lenses of his thick black glasses and pulled out a pad and ballpoint pen.

William wrestled with the feeling of dread within him.

Clark wished Savannah were beside him to hear the news Katherine had waited almost her entire life to hear.

Lily Mae nodded at Clarence to begin. Looking into her eyes, he began unfolding what had been locked up for decades.

"I turned twelve years old on the thirteenth of May in 1941. It rained hard that entire day just like it had for four days before that. My papa made me a wooden tackle box and inside he put three lead sinkers, three fishing hooks, a store-bought cork bobber and a long line of string. That doesn't seem like much these days but back in those days most folks, no matter your color, were either already poor or they were getting close to it. Times were hard, and I was tickled to death to have my own tackle and a box to put it in. That meant I could fish on my own whenever I wanted and didn't have to borrow anybody's stuff. The only thing he asked of me was to be sure I told somebody before I headed out."

Clarence paused and then slowly nodded his head as if his brain was secretly sending his mouth courage to continue. "I woke up the next day before the sun rose and saw that it was still raining hard. I told Papa I was going fishing on the backside of the lake in spite of the weather. I remember him telling me not to expect much from the fish because of the rain, but he knew it was burning me up to have my very own tackle and not be able to use it."

"He reminded me as I walked out the door to be careful because the dirt roads were flooded, and the water was rising. That didn't scare me none because I was headed on foot through the back way to my lucky fishing spot. The one up under the pier. Most boys my age didn't have the gumption to climb through the tall reeds to get to it but if they had caught as many big catfish as me, they'd have done what I did."

Katherine sat only inches away from Clarence, mesmerized by his words. He had transported them back to a time when many folks sustained their families on what they raised, hunted or caught.

Without taking her eyes off Clarence, Lily Mae slid her hand out of his grasp and used both of her leathery hands to hold Katherine's dainty one. It was her attempt to try to pass strength and courage from her body into Katherine's because she knew Katherine's heart was about to break in two.

Clarence continued. "By the time I walked that distance from our place up to the road, the dawn was breaking through, but it was still raining mighty hard. I saw my father was right about the road flooding. But really, by that morning it was more of a wet, muddy strip of sludge than a flooded road. That road hadn't been paved yet so it was always a mud hole when it rained. This was the worst I'd ever seen it though. Wasn't long and I spotted Miss Effie coming down the road. She was trying her best to walk barefoot in all that mud, but she was slipping and sliding all over the place."

Katherine was confused. This was not a name she recognized. "Who? Do I know her? I don't have any idea who you are talking about."

Lily Mae's nephew, Thomas, clarified. "Effie was the daughter of James and Ernestine Barnes. She lived in *our* part of town. I'm sure you never met her." His jaw was tense, and his voice was commanding. Everyone in the room witnessed an inkling of what he sounded like in his federal courtroom. "Continue, Clarence."

Clarence obliged. "Effie had her shoes wrapped in an oilcloth bag and was holding it over her head. She must have had her work clothes in that bag too because she sure couldn't walk into work dripping all over somebody's beautiful wood floor. She was working over at the Morris place, that big house halfway between Kingston and Burke, and it was a good three-mile walk for her every morning."

"I yelled out, 'Hey, Miss Effie,' but I guess she didn't hear me because she didn't look towards me. I figured I'd wait till she caught up to where I was under the pier and then I'd greet her. She might not have heard me from the rain, but I think it was because of the truck pulling up behind her."

Clarence stopped and studied his calloused hands as if the script was etched somewhere on his skin and he had forgotten his next line. Without uttering a word, Thomas reached over and rested his hand on Clarence's back. He looked over the rim of his glasses perched on the end of his nose and nodded at Clarence with a look that indicated, *Proceed.*

Clarence took in a big breath. "Katherine, your daddy stopped to help Miss Effie that morning. He was going to help her get out of the rain and drive her over to the Morris place. It was on his way to where he was headed. I saw him get out, open the passenger door for her, and then get back into the truck. He put it in gear and started to drive on but his back tires were spinning and he started sliding across the mud."

When Clarence referenced May 24, 1941, Katherine knew this story was somehow going to be linked to her father. In the timeline of her life, it was not only the day her father disappeared; it was also the day her mother lost her will to live.

She turned to Lily Mae for help and saw only grief in those tired brown eyes. She then looked in the faces of all those gathered, and she saw looks of utter agony. It was clear to her there was an avalanche of inescapable pain headed directly towards her.

"You saw my father stop to help someone that morning?" Katherine muttered, but more to herself than to Clarence. She had to say the words aloud to make sure she was processing it correctly. The one mystery in her life was unfolding, and she knew this time it wasn't just another bad dream. Her mind was frantically trying to rebuke this evidence. "Are you sure it was him, Clarence? Did you even know my father? You were only twelve. You might have been mistaken."

Clarence studied her face, taking in her fear. "Your daddy used to pay me a few coins when he needed help unloading a big order of special lumber off the boxcar down at the train station. I knew him, Katherine. He was always good to me."

Lily Mae whispered weakly, "That was the kind of man your father was, Queenie. He was a good, good man. The kind mamas want their little boys to grow up to be like." She then reached up to wipe the tears from Katherine's eyes. Several others in the room took that as an opportunity to wipe their own.

"My father was on his way to work on a house in Burke that morning, but he never showed up. I don't ever remember hearing anything about a second person disappearing that same day." Katherine shot off questions like a marksman at a firing range. "Was she ever questioned about my father's disappearance? What did she say? Where is she now?"

The sheriff spoke his first words since Clarence had begun his monologue. "I think it's fair to say we now know Miss Effie was never seen again after that morning."

Katherine gasped and placed her hand over her heart. Whimpering, she uttered, "I just don't understand what you're trying to tell me."

"I started climbing out from under the pier to see if your daddy wanted me to push from the back of the truck so it wouldn't slide but just that quick, I saw another car headed his way from the other direction. At first I didn't recognize the car, but then it got closer and that's when I got scared. It was a big shiny black Oldsmobile with whitewall tires. I'd seen that car only one other time and I knew the person who owned it was trouble when he'd been drinking."

Clarence paused and addressed both Thomas and the sheriff. "I'm not going to tell the story of what I saw that man do down in our neck of the woods at the Fisher's place. That happened at least a year before our story here." In unison, Thomas and the sheriff nodded in agreement. Clarence then looked at Lily Mae to receive the ultimate approval. She too nodded, so Clarence began again, this time looking at the windowsill as he spoke. His hushed voice continued, reliving the secret.

"It was old Tate Sullivan and his drinking buddy, Walter Campbell. Sullivan was driving and he pulled his car across the road so your daddy couldn't pass. I knew right off when they climbed out of that car they were drunker than drunk and they looked mean. Looked like they'd been hunting trouble all night."

"Tate Sullivan? Was that Wanda Sullivan's father?"

"Yes, Queenie. That's him."

"He had something to do with my father's disappearance? Wasn't he somehow related to Sheriff Sullivan?"

"Tate was Sullivan's brother," affirmed the young sheriff. I don't know if Don was crooked when he took office in 1920 but if he wasn't, old man Tate Sullivan and his cronies didn't take long to convince him he needed to look the other way while they took control of his county."

Katherine was flooded with memories of the sheriff's visits to her mother after her father disappeared. "I remember his face and voice and the memory of him conjures a strange odor, a stench of something bad. What was that? Do I remember a smell about him?"

"Queenie, evil has a bad smell to it. It was his soul you smelled. An evil soul."

"Do you think all these years Wanda has always known her father might have been connected to my father's disappearance?"

"She must have known it all these years. She's always had a lot of hate towards you stored up in her. You had something her family never had. It was your strength she hated the most. The weak covet strength, and if they can't have it for themselves, they set out to destroy it in others. That's a lot of ugliness to grasp."

During the talk of the lineage of Tate Sullivan, Father Drew exited and returned with a glass of water which he handed to Clarence, who took several large swallows and mopped his brow with his handkerchief. Sweat was streaming down both temples as he turned his head to look Katherine directly in the eye.

"You're probably going ask me why I didn't climb out from under that pier and do something. That's the demon that's haunted me every day of my life since May 24, 1941. I've got nothing to say for an answer other than I was frozen like a dead bird in winter. I was yellow. I just hid and watched it all happen in front of me. It's the one thing in my life I'm most ashamed of and Satan won't let me forget it."

And it was then that Katherine realized those streams of sweat had turned into streams of tears. She got up from Lily Mae's bedside and sat on the floor at Clarence's feet, holding one of his big calloused hands with her left hand and one of Lily Mae's with her right. When the storytelling began, she had no way of predicting it would turn into a confession from Clarence.

With a voice so choked she could barely say the words loud enough for anyone to hear, Katherine said, "I know this is hard, but I need to know what you know. Please. Please." Her eyes were begging while her heart was breaking.

Clarence struggled, trying to know how to say the next part, but there was no going back now. "The two drunks started yelling at your daddy and then old man Sullivan pulled out a gun and aimed it towards the windshield right for Miss Effie's head. He told his drunk buddy, Walter Campbell, to get Miss Effie out of your daddy's truck and that's what he did. She was kicking and screaming and put up a good fight as he was pulling her out. I figured old drunk Campbell didn't expect her to be so strong because she got in a couple of good licks before he knocked her to the ground. I couldn't see her once she fell because I had my head down low, but I could still see your daddy. He was yelling at both of them and trying to get to Miss Effie and saying they had no right to do that to a woman. Then they turned on him and asked him what he had been doing with her all night long. They said some ugly things, but I wouldn't feel comfortable saying that to you, Katherine." He then looked at Lily Mae for a nod of assurance which she gave him.

"It made them mad that your daddy was trying to protect her, so Sullivan knocked your daddy to the ground and both of the drunks started kicking him hard and he was scrambling trying to get out of their reach. If it wasn't just one big mud pit, I think he could have, but he couldn't get his footing."

"In all the commotion I guess one of the drunks fell over Miss Effie and it was then they realized she wasn't moving. She must have died as soon as her head hit, I suspect. It was hard to tell one drunken voice from another, but I could sure pick out your daddy's voice, it had a sense of righteousness about it. The other two voices just sounded drunk and angry, full of meanness aimed for destruction. "

He paused and inhaled a gulp of air and held it tight within his lungs. Then he slowly exhaled, parting his lips like he was blowing out candles, trying to gather the energy or the nerve within himself to continue.

Lily Mae said in the strongest voice she had left, "I'm mighty proud of what you're doing right here and now, and I know you're doing it for me. Takes a big man to go back and tell this ugly story. You're making it sound like it happened last week. Tells me you've wrestled with it even more than you ever let on. I wish we'd done what we're doing now the very day this good sheriff was sworn in."

"I've been scared my whole life about the telling of this story. Used to be afraid for what might happen to me and my people. Then I moved all my worry over to what this story might do to Katherine. If a person has wondered most of her life what happened to her daddy, I know it would be hard to find out almost seven decades later. Especially finding out this kind of brutal truth."

"Guess they all realized Miss Effie must have hit her head on a rock when she was knocked to the ground, so Campbell checked to see if she was still breathing. When he turned and looked at Sullivan and shook his head, I guess we all knew she was gone. You're daddy started screaming at them and he said he was going to go back into town and find the sheriff and tell it all, from beginning to end, and they'd have to pay for their sins.

"Those two drunks just laughed in your daddy's face. They laughed so hard Sullivan had to lean against his car to keep from falling down. Old Campbell did swagger and fall, laughing so hard. But, by this time your daddy had gotten back on his feet and his voice thundered like a cannon ball boom when he yelled, 'How dare you laugh at what you've done. You've killed a good, innocent woman, and I'm going to make sure you pay for it.'

"Sullivan stopped laughing and switched to anger as quick as you flip a light switch and he started screaming mean, saying things like, 'Why do you care about a colored woman? What did she mean to you? Just wait till I get back and tell my brother, and you know he's the sheriff. I'll just have to tell him what Campbell and I saw when we drove up on you two and found you with her in your back seat. And don't think we won't tell the entire town of Kingston how we saw you drag her out of the car and beat her up and knock her head on that rock. We'll tell it just like it happened.'"

Clarence stopped to suck in more air. The room was silent. The words were excruciating to hear.

"It was then that Campbell added, 'I saw it happen just like you said, Boss, and I'll tell it a hundred times if I have to. I'll put my hand on a Bible and swear it.'

"My heartbeat sounded like a drum pounding in my head and my gulp felt like it had its own echo. I was afraid they'd hear me, and I knew if they did, they'd think nothing of killing another one of us."

Everyone shuddered at his implication.

"Your daddy pushed past Campbell and scooped up Miss Effie in his arms and then he gently laid her down in the front seat. I couldn't see that part very well, but I think he was probably straightening her dress, so she'd look decent when he reached the sheriff's office in town. That's the kind of respectable man your daddy was."

He gave Katherine a moment to let it all sink in because the hardest news was yet to be told. Each time Katherine dabbed her own tears she did the same to Lily Mae's.

This time it was Lily Mae who spoke in a hushed voice, one that was quickly losing its strength. "Queenie, you're looking at me with the same pain in your eyes you had the first day I met you when you were nestled way up in that tree. I wanted to take your pain away then just like now, but you need to know what I've known all these years." She paused and added, "I'm proud of my girl."

Those gentle words were what Katherine needed. She then looked at Clarence and nodded to indicate she was ready for more of the onslaught.

"Those two drunks," Clarence continued, "watched your daddy close the passenger side door and walk toward his side. When he got face-to-face with them he yelled, 'I won't stop with the sheriff. I'll go straight to the Attorney General and tell him personally and if for some reason you have him in your back pocket, too, I'll not stop until I've met with the governor!'

"I'm here to say by the time he led up to the words about going to the governor, he was bellowing it with such force, I'd have thought the folks clear across town could 'a heard him. He was angry, and more than that he was strong and determined. I'd never seen a man look like that before. He was going to make sure the men who killed Miss Effie would pay and not a person in this world was going to stop him. I could tell that's what he intended.

"I watched him as he stormed past the two drunks and got in his car and started the engine. I thought to myself, *He's really going to do it. He's going to turn those wicked devils into the law.* In all my long life, I can honestly say even to this day I've never seen any man more committed than him. But just as he began to shift the car into gear, Sullivan walked right up to your daddy's side of the steering wheel, raised his gun, and pulled the trigger. Your daddy slumped over the steering wheel and I knew instantly he was dead. Wasn't nobody going to know what really happened now except three humans and one of them was a yellow chicken hiding in the marshes."

"And the evil shall be reckoned with," said Father Drew in a gentle, hushed murmur, and it was all they needed to hear.

Katherine, sitting on the floor between Clarence and Lily Mae, rested her head against the side of the mattress and sobbed. There was nothing anyone could do but grieve with her.

When the sobs subsided, Katherine sat very still with her eyes closed for several minutes. Then she looked at Clarence, not sure if she was strong enough to hear more but certain he had more to tell.

He falteringly began again, although he knew these were brutal assaults he was delivering. "Well, the two drunks looked at each other and they both seemed pretty pleased with themselves. It seemed as if the rainclouds had watched the tragedy and must have decided it was time for a downpour because almost instantly the bottom fell right out of the sky.

"Once it started raining hard, I couldn't hear much but I watched it happen. Kind of like watching a silent movie, you know what they're thinking while they act it out. I saw Sullivan say something to Campbell and he just shook his head and shrugged, seemed like he was saying he didn't know. Then Sullivan started waving his arms around and pointing to the truck and shoving Campbell to the back of it. All of a sudden I realized they were planning to push your daddy's truck right into the lake and that's exactly what they did. Campbell pushed from the back and Sullivan straddled the running board as he steered, and they watched that car slowly twist and turn in the water and eventually go under completely. After it disappeared, they started yelling. I was hoping they might kill each other, but I guess they were just mean and evil enough they only used their bullets on good, decent folks."

Those in the room saw Sheriff Washington's head nod, but his jaw was set such that you'd need a crowbar to pry it open. For a lawman with integrity, it was a difficult story to hear.

"They sat in their car for what seemed like most of a full morning, but I never climbed out of that water. I knew it would be the end of me if they spotted me, so I held onto the planks of the pier for hours. I kept watching the spot where your daddy's truck went in because I thought it might float back up to the top, but it never did. After a while the water started to rise quickly, and I was scared the swift water was going to force me to climb out from under the pier. Those evil men were still sitting there in their car like they were waiting to find somebody else to kill.

"Back in that day, lots of folks in our part of town had respect for the lake for fishing but weren't brave enough to get in it because every two or three years it seemed like one of us would drown and that only magnified the fear of water for our people. My grandpa's littlest sister died that way, so he made sure every one of his children and his grandkids learned how to swim. I guess he saved my life because if I had been somebody who was afraid of the water, I wouldn't have survived that day. The water took on a mind of its own. Seemed like it was wild and angry. I always thought the lake knew it had just been turned into a graveyard, and it was thrashing and swirling, looking like water dragons were turning circles underneath."

Katherine began piecing together her memories of those days in 1941 with the facts she was learning for the first time. "I remember the sheriff coming by the house each day for a while to tell Mama they didn't have any leads, but they were still looking. One of those times my mama asked if they could get more lawmen to investigate, and the sheriff got loud and angry with her, so she never asked again. I guess he bullied her to make sure she stopped thinking like that. Mama never was very strong. She loved daddy so much and she knew he was dead, even if they never showed her a body, because there wasn't anything, other than death, that would keep those two apart."

Looking at the sheriff, she asked, "Is there still a report or anything that deals with my father's disappearance?"

"There actually is, but I was hoping you wouldn't ask. When these men came to me earlier today with this information, I did a quick check in our archival room and found a couple of entries about the investigation of your father's disappearance. On the forms they used in those days there was a small section that provided space for the sheriff to indicate any undocumented theories." The sheriff stopped suddenly.

"And?" Katherine prompted him.

Sheriff Washington hesitated then continued with a pained look. "Sheriff Sullivan wanted people to think that your father had run off with a woman and that they'd probably settled in a different part of the country."

"He had the nerve to write something completely fictitious knowing full well he'd been murdered?" Father Drew asked, just as incredulous as the others.

Wincing, the sheriff replied, "Well, if anyone other than the county sheriff's office had bothered to investigate, they would have immediately recognized the case was officially closed on May 25, 1941."

In unison, the minister, the judge, the witness, the daughter, and the woman who had been the glue that held them all together responded, "Only one day later?"

"I'm not proud to be the one to deliver that part of the story, but you need to know I suspect the sheriff, his deputy, and probably the Justice of the Peace were all a part of this horrendous lie." Then the sheriff waited a couple of seconds before adding, although it wasn't necessary, "From this point forward I can assure you that you will receive nothing but the truth from the Sheriff's office. I'm just so very sorry it wasn't always that way."

"I still don't remember anyone saying that someone else disappeared at the same time. What kind of story did Miss Effie's family receive?"

Thomas explained, "The sheriff's office never pursued an investigation. They ignored the family completely until a couple of weeks later when an oilcloth bag washed up on the shore, and her family recognized it as one that contained her clothes and shoes. From that point on, her death was listed as an accidental drowning,"

"Do they now know what actually happened?" Katherine asked. She suddenly felt the urgency to contact the family to let them finally know the truth.

Lily Mae gathered her strength. "Queenie, they knew from the very beginning. Her mamma and daddy almost never got over it, but you were the one thing that helped them want to live."

"Me? Do I know Miss Effie's family?" Katherine frantically searched the faces of Clarence, Lily Mae, and Thomas.

"Well, you don't know them by name, but you know them by their handiwork," replied Clarence.

Katherine rubbed her temples. "I'm feeling sick. I just don't understand any of this. It's too much all at once."

Father Drew suggested, "Let's have a moment of silence and let Lily Mae have a little nourishment." He carefully lifted the mug of broth to Lily Mae's thin lips and encouraged her to take a sip. She complied, but she never took her worried eyes off Katherine. She took a few sips, more to please Katherine than to sustain her life.

"You okay, Queenie?"

"I'm okay," was about all Katherine could muster.

Clarence began again. "Do you remember meeting me for the first time at Lily Mae's house? I was twelve and you were seven."

"I remember. I didn't think you liked me being at Lily Mae's house because you wouldn't talk to me. I thought you acted like I had no business being there. She scolded you and told you to make me feel welcome, but you'd just stare at me time and time again."

"That's because you made me feel guilty my father was alive and yours was dead. I knew you couldn't even bury yours because you were still hoping he'd one day walk through your door. I was covered up with both anger and sorrow and I didn't know what to do about it.

"The first time my folks saw the way I was looking at you, they got me right out of there and took me home. They knew what was eating me up inside. That night Papa told me the good Lord let all that evil happen for a reason and it wasn't up to us to make sense of it. He told me to be wise and listen because the Lord had something to reveal. Papa didn't know what it was, but he said when times are the worst the Lord always tells us something we couldn't have thought of on our own.

"So, I started listening good every day. About three weeks after you started coming home with Lily Mae, I heard you tell how your daddy used to tell you stories about fairies and pixies. I told that to Mamma and Papa that night at supper about you not being very smart because you thought fairies and pixies were real. They gave each other a funny look and as soon as we finished eating, we walked down to Effie's house and told her parents what I'd said. Early the next morning, Effie's pa brought me a little strip of blue ribbon and asked me to wait till after dark and then sneak over and put it by the back door at the diner where you lived but to be careful not to let anyone see me."

Amazed, Katherine's bottom lip quivered. "My very first pixie gift was a little blue ribbon tied to the screen door of the diner."

Without saying another word, she went to her closet and brought out a beautiful walnut hinged box. "One of the first gifts I ever received from Murphy was this beautiful box. He stayed up half the night making it for me after I told him about my pixie gifts. He was intrigued that I had kept them all and he asked to see them. I used to keep them in a couple of saltine cracker tins, so I pulled them out one by one. He marveled at each one and held them in his hands as if they were delicate artifacts from an archeological dig. He brought me this box the next morning."

Thomas, who wasn't even alive at the time of the pixie gifts, knew all about them. Holding his head high, he explained,

"Katherine, you had a great many folks who were looking out for you without you ever knowing it. They felt it was up to them, their duty and their honor, to bring some joy to your young life. They knew how drastically it had changed in one short day. The gifts were just little things meant to help you stay a child a little longer. It was a way to provide some dignity to a tragic death. Our people felt responsible."

Katherine began to unwrap the gifts and laid them at the foot of Lily Mae's bed. For the first time in her life, she learned the names of those who had given her these tiny gifts at a time when she had very little.

Lily Mae recited the origin of each one as Katherine held it in the palm of her hand, and as she told it, Clarence nodded in affirmation.

"Effie's mama managed to find that blue hair ribbon after I told her your eyes were the kind of blue the Lord intended his white clouds to float in. Clarence's father carved the rabbit for you. Thomas' daddy found that little brown rock shaped like a heart down by the creek bed. Rev. Dade's wife contributed your tiny doll and every woman in the church made something for her to wear. Didn't take but a swatch of fabric because she's so small but we had to take care that none of the cloth we used was from anything you'd see any of us wear."

Clarence knew she'd ask so he told it before she had the opportunity. "It was my daddy who delivered the rabbit muff to your classroom that early morning. Lily Mae made sure every one of us knew what happened to the old one. I've never seen her so mad, not before and not since. Miss Effie's folks stayed up all night making you a new one."

She lifted the soft fur to her cheek, remembering how it felt to know the pixies were taking care of her so long ago. "What about this?" Katherine held up a small blue velvet box. "This wasn't homemade. Who had money to buy me something?"

When no one volunteered the answer, Katherine addressed Lily Mae. "Just tell me."

"Queenie, Doc was part of the pixie gifts, and he gave you that."

"Doc? He knew too? That was the last pixie gift I received. It was just before Mama and I moved from above the diner to the apartment Doc created for us above his clinic."

Silence filled the room, and everyone knew what was coming next. This was the crescendo. This would be the moment they gathered to witness. This was the invisible binding that tied them all together and it came in the form of a promise made to a little lost girl so long ago.

She turned and looked at Lily Mae. Her Lily Mae. The woman who just happened to pause under a large shade tree after a long day's work many years ago. Who just happened to look up and see a little girl who was hiding. Hiding from the awful truth that something had somehow destroyed everything good and reliable in her young life. Her eyes were brimming. Her quivering lips tried their best to form a smile.

"You knew all of this the day I met you? It wasn't a coincidence you stopped under that tree and saw me sitting in it?"

Lily Mae couldn't speak. She was growing weaker by the minute, but she had willed herself to live long enough to see this through. She gently squeezed Katherine's hand.

"I prayed you to me, Queenie, and God answered that."

"You've known this all these years?" Katherine was amazed at the very thought, but none of it made sense to her. "And you never, ever gave me the slightest clue that you knew? Why? Why, Lily Mae?"

Clarence spoke for her, but Lily Mae never took her eyes off Katherine. "Lily Mae did that for me, Katherine. It's something she did for me the morning after your daddy died. When I got home that day, my mama and papa fell to their knees and cried because they and lots of other folks had been searching for me for hours. They thought I'd drowned in the raging water. When I walked in the house they said I had a look in my eyes that scared them all. They didn't know what had happened, but I just stood there and stared as if my brain had left my head. I'd gone mute. Mama filled the tub with the hottest water she could boil and let me just soak. They had to take the soap away from me because I wouldn't stop scrubbing my skin. When Papa got me out and put me in warm clothes, he said I shook so hard my teeth were knocking against each other. Said it looked like my soul had left my body. I never closed my eyes that night. I just sat up in bed and rocked and cried. Folks gathered around me and prayed through the night. Said the devil had me and they were going to pray him out of me. Before daylight the next morning, Lily Mae came walking through our door and she was carrying a candle. Something about the way she stood in that opened door frame with the light against the darkness outside made me turn my head and when she saw me she yelled out in anger, 'Satan, I rebuke you!' and then she started singing to Jesus. Asking Him to bring back my soul. My whole body went warm the instant she started singing. I'd been so cold, so cold my body was tense and sore from shivering and shaking, but all of a sudden I went warm like toasting-myself-by-the-fire warm. More than that, I felt a sudden calm spread over me, and I started humming with Lily Mae. Mama said they knew then they had me back. The room grew hushed and all those folks who'd gathered through the night started filing out the door one by one knowing we needed to spend some time without a crowd. By the time Lily Mae finished her singing the only folks in the room were me and her and my mama and papa. I went and got Papa's Bible off the mantel, and then I made each one of them swear with their hand on the good book they'd never tell any white folks what I was about to tell them. And they did. First Mama, then Papa, and then Lily Mae."

Clarence stopped and drew in a deep breath, filling his lungs with the power to continue. "Then, clear as if I had told it a hundred times, I told them what happened. Every detail. Mama just sat there and cried as I told it and Papa kept rubbing those big farmer's hands of his against the sides of his thighs. Like he was trying to hold his legs still, trying to prevent them from getting up and running. Not Lily Mae though. She just kept looking me straight in the eye like she was sending some mighty strength out of her body into mine and she was nodding her head as the words were spilling out of me. Like she knew what the next word would be before I ever said it."

He stopped to search Katherine's face and then Lily Mae's. He knew then he had better hurry.

"It was because of that promise she made to me and God that day that Lily Mae never told you any of this, Katherine. You have any idea what would have happened to me or my people if we'd walked into the sheriff's office and told that story? The whole group of us could've gone missing. Those folks in charge of the law back then didn't know the meaning of justice. They just knew the kind of law that let them get their way with folks."

The room was quiet for a long time. Emotionally, they'd climbed to the top of Mt. Everest and back down again. All eyes were now fixed on Lily Mae. Her breathing was labored, and her eyes were closed.

Katherine had one final question but decided she would ask later, after Lily Mae's passing. But the dying woman had read her mind, and she asked as her eyes remained closed, "Are you wondering how Doc found out, Queenie?"

"Yes, but you don't have to tell me now if you're too tired. We can talk about it. Later."

The impossibility of *later* hovered over the room and permeated the air they all breathed.

"Now," Lily Mae commanded and still not opening her eyes pointed her finger in the direction of Thomas. There he was, a distinguished federal judge, being ordered to speak by a woman who still wielded immense power over him.

"My world revolves around the truth and what can be proven to be truth from circumstantial evidence. What I am about to tell you would be ruled as inadmissible in my courtroom. It is all circumstantial." He looked at Katherine to make sure she understood, and she nodded for him to explain more.

"None of us ever really knew how Doc came into the story. We know none of the four who swore on the Bible ever broke that promise."

"Until now," Lily Mae whispered.

"Yes, until now," Thomas continued. "We suspect he overheard a conversation somehow. Our people knew how dangerous it would be if word got out that we were accusing the sheriff of a cover-up. Folks knew not to talk about it outside the boundaries of our part of town. Doc was the first doctor who felt comfortable to walk the streets in our part when someone was ill enough to need a doctor's care. That's why he was revered and respected by so many of us. He came into our homes and doctored us just as he did anyone else in this town. We think he overheard some folks talking about it while he was doctoring one of the black families, but he never let on and didn't pry for more details."

"So how did you know he knew?" Katherine asked.

"Well, according to Lily Mae, he told her one day he had been to the diner to check on your mother and you showed him a little shrine you'd set up on the windowsill near your bed. He asked you where the gifts came from, and you told him pixies brought them to you and showed him the three different places out back where you found them. He remembered you had them lined up on the windowsill in the order in which they were given to you. Lily Mae was the one who came home one evening and told us you had just shown her your newest pixie gift, and she was positive it had not come from any of our people. Said it was a gold locket in a..."

"...a blue velvet box with a gold ribbon tied around it," Katherine completed the sentence for Thomas. She opened it to reveal a gold locket that had long since lost its patina.

"So how did you know it was from Doc?" Katherine wondered aloud. The clues still did not seem to fit together in a neat array.

Lily Mae spoke softly. "For the longest time I suspected it was from him. I thought it was his way of letting us know he also felt a responsibility for fixing a terrible wrong. The closest he ever got to confessing was years later when he explained that lockets were a beautiful way to hold the face of the one you love the most. To remind your heart in case it ever forgot."

Slowly, Katherine opened her locket to reveal a faded photograph. She clutched it to her heart and began to cry.

Clarence reached out to hold the locket and she gently placed it in his big, calloused hands. Silently, he studied the face looking back at him. "The last time I saw this face, he was showing me what bravery looked like. Bravery on the battlefield, when you think about it. He knew he was an unarmed man fighting the enemy. I've spent my life remembering the face of this courageous man, and now I have the honor of seeing him one more time. I've tried to live up to his code of honor, Katherine. Lily Mae told me a long, long time ago she felt God put me there for a reason and maybe that reason was for me to see what a man of honor does in the face of evil."

Then, just as Katherine had done, Clarence clutched the locket to his chest. His closed eyes could not hold back the river of his tears. Finally telling the story released him from the ugly memories that bound him so tightly for so long.

Father Drew placed his hand on Clarence's shoulder. "And you have lived your life with honor too, my friend. You witnessed courage and evil at the same moment, and you chose to take the high ground. God's grace reaches us through the thorns."

Lily Mae's breathing had become more faint. Katherine took her pulse and silently shook her head to let the others know Lily Mae wouldn't be with them much longer.

While Father Drew began preparing communion, Katherine leaned over and whispered into Lily Mae's ear, "I love you more now than I ever have, and I understand why you never told me. Now I want you to do one more thing for me. Free yourself from any pain or guilt you've carried all these years. I want you to take your last breath with peace in your heart."

Lily Mae squeezed Katherine's hand to indicate she'd heard both her words and her command. She was able to let the wine of communion touch her lips and the wafer dissolve on her tongue, but she never opened her eyes again.

There was still one more surprise before she drew her last breath. Unprompted, Sheriff Washington began singing the first stanza of "Amazing Grace" with the most beautiful tenor voice any of them had ever heard. He sang all four verses and then hummed the tune, and it was during the final stanza that Lily Mae took her last breath as she whispered "I'm not scared of dying now. Take me home."

That group of people, so connected through the truth they all now knew, witnessed a beautiful passing. Thomas verbalized it. "We saw the peace of God spread through Lily Mae's body, and then she ceased breathing. The angels have welcomed her home now. Our beloved is now standing before the face of God."

Five days later, Katherine walked down the aisle with Clarence holding her arm at Bethel A.M.E. church for her beloved Lily Mae's funeral. Wearing her navy suit with a double strand of pearls and a golden locket that had long since lost its patina, she carried Lily Mae's tattered, old Bible in one hand and a crisp hankie in the other. They sat in the second pew, just as she had all those countless Sundays long ago when she attended with Lily Mae.

Walking down the aisle behind the casket, she and Clarence both overheard someone say, "There she is. That's Lily's girl." They smiled to each other, knowing that a person could never receive a finer compliment.

The drive from the church to the cemetery was only a seven-mile stretch, but it took well over an hour because both sides of the street were lined with friends and strangers. In the five days since Lily Mae's passing, the story of Katherine's father and Miss Effie's fate was revealed and spread through Kingston quicker than floodwaters. The town was wise enough to feel shame over what happened all those decades ago to two innocent people, simply trying to get to work, to provide food and shelter for their families. Two people who fought with all they had to defend the golden rule.

Do Unto Others

There were signs everywhere of nature sweeping away the remnants of the long, cold winter months. They were in their usual positions, Sam riding shotgun and Katherine alone in the backseat, as they drove through the countryside. William had been working on a plan that he hoped would relieve some of the sadness that seemed to have settled permanently on Katherine's shoulders since Lily Mae's death.

"Three weeks from Monday I have a surprise for Royce Thessing, and I would like very much for both of you to be there." Their driver gave no more explanation, but there was an obvious twinkle in his eye.

"You mean Royce Thessing, the old gristle at Shady Valley Assisted Living, our friend who used to be friendless?"

"That's right. Used to be."

"Son, I don't know what you've planned, but it can't be anything finer than the gift you've already given him. He's not at all the same man I introduced you to two years ago. His crustiness has disappeared. He's had a metamorphosis."

"Remember these words in three weeks…it has been my honor to get to know him, with emphasis on honor."

The only other clue Katherine had concerning the surprise for Royce was William's request for her recommendations for the purchase of two particular items.

"No question, Thornton & Hawthorne Menswear on the square for the suit. Dave DuVall will do you right, and three weeks will provide plenty of time for alterations. I'd definitely recommend the Flower Box for the flowers, also on the square. They do good work, and they appreciate their customers. Tell Todd I sent you."

Katherine had never seen her two men look as dapper as they did on that eventful Monday. William's charcoal suit made his deep green eyes dazzle with intensity. Sam looked dashing in his new blue shirt and blazing red tie. No doubt, she had handsome men.

She settled in the backseat, pleased to be in their company. Sam proudly held up a corsage box. "Not telling who it's for but I know this, it ain't for nobody in *this* car."

Their laughter had energy to it, the kind reserved for the most special of life's moments.

There was a buzz about the place when they entered Shady Valley. Residents had already begun gathering in the event room, scrambling to get their worn-out bodies or walkers or wheelchairs closest to the front row. Royce Thessing was among them, sitting on an end aisle about midway up, in his dingy white polo shirt, still showing remnants of breakfast.

A newspaper reporter for the *Kingston Daily* began working the crowd, and a cameraman and news anchor for KWRK Channel 7 set up in the back of the room.

Katherine and Sam watched as William placed the corsage on Annabelle's wrist. The librarian was clearly moved. He then presented Katherine with a starched handkerchief. "You can thank me later."

Helping Royce into a dark blue gabardine sports coat, he asked him to join them on the front row. No one was more surprised than Royce.

Many old withered soldiers saluted as the Kingston High School Junior R.O.T.C. Color Guard presented the flag, and the entire room joined together to recite the Pledge of Allegiance and sing the Star-Spangled Banner. America's greatest generation sang her greatest anthem. Their love for America was as abundant as clover in spring. It blanketed the entire room.

William addressed the crowd. "Before we begin, I would like to thank someone who worked very hard to make this possible. Kingston's reference librarian, Annabelle Curry, has spent hours, days, weeks, and months researching and sorting data and putting the pieces together. Thank you, Ms. Curry."

Katherine saw something in his eyes, and she knew Lily Mae would be squeezing her hand if she were with her now. William had discovered his purpose.

"Unlike many of you, I have never served on a battlefield to defend our country's many freedoms bestowed on us by our forefathers. I would like to think I am of the caliber of those who served, but I will never know. One thing I do know for sure is many who served across the globe during World War II did heroic deeds on the battlefields but then came home to their wives and families and for many, those acts appeared to go unnoticed. We've gathered today to recognize the heroic action by one of our own that took place seventy years ago this week. It gives me great honor to present to you Brigadier General Giles Croxton of the United States Air Force."

The air in the room was electric. People leaned forward, eager to hear the words of the visiting general, dressed in full regalia. The reporter's camera was set on high-speed advance, shooting eight frames a second. Katherine sat expectantly, eager to hear the announcement.

"Ladies and gentlemen, it is an honor to be here with you today. In 1941, America joined with the Allied Forces to fight inhumanity in its ugliest form. The call went out, and America sent her best and her bravest. Some of our heroes never came home. Others returned but never received recognition for what they did in the air or on the field. Instead, they came back ready to get on with their lives and families, eager to put the past behind them."

The general paused, letting his words sink in. "I'd like to bring one of your own to the front, because unbeknownst to him, we are going to right a wrong today."

William stood and extended his hand to his friend, the one about to be honored, Royce Thessing, the crusty old bird who was now limp with emotion, trembling before the crowd.

"Royce Thessing, when you and your crew flew a bombing mission out of England for the United States Army Air Corps on February 13, 1943, your B-24 was hit by a German plane. A Danish plane approached, tipped its wing, and signaled "follow me." You skillfully landed your plane safely although two of your crew members, your navigator and your tail gunner, were injured. You carried your tail gunner on your back for about a mile, following a member of the Danish Underground Resistance who led you to safety. You then returned to your plane and did the same for your navigator. It is doubtful either of these two crew members would have survived if you had not acted with bravery to risk your life in order to save theirs. Meanwhile, on the homefront, the families were notified that your entire crew was missing in action. You and your men remained with the Danish Underground Resistance for three weeks until they could successfully return you to your base in England. You went on to fly twenty-two more successful missions throughout the war, but you were never recognized for saving the lives of two of your crew members."

Another pause. The audience was captivated. There had been a hero in their midst who had come across as a crusty old curmudgeon.

"These facts have been brought to our attention by two citizens who felt compelled to research and provide the enormously complex documentation to the Air Force Board for Correction of Military Records. The paperwork required to prove the forgotten bravery of a young soldier is equivalent to a small mountain."

Still another pause as the old soldier looked into the faces of the man and woman who had done all of this for him.

"Captain Royce Thessing, it is my honor to present to you the following medals you should have received seventy years ago for your heroic acts. I bestow on you the Victory Medal for your service in World War II, the Distinguished Flying Cross for your heroism and extraordinary achievement while flying, and the Good Conduct Medal for your exemplary behavior, efficiency, and fidelity in the United States Army Air Corps."

The press had a field day as the general pinned the medals on the old soldier's borrowed gabardine jacket.

Many remarkable things were said that day and well into the evening. Katherine was proud for Royce Thessing but even prouder for William, and she told him that privately.

"What you did today was evidence that you know there is a purpose for your life. Others could have done what you and Annabelle did, but no one ever attempted it."

"I couldn't have done it without Annabelle, that's for sure."

The tiny creases that had accumulated around Katherine's eyes over the years seemed to disappear as she smiled and explained, "There was a lot of love today. Love for your country, love for another human being, love for an old, tired, and cranky heart. It's the kind of thing you might expect a family member to attempt for one of their own, but you two took it on like you were his family. You'll do many other fine things in this world, but I suspect nothing finer."

"As a boy I thought I knew what families were. I thought it was a group of people who all shared the same name and usually looked alike in one way or another. That's what I longed for. I didn't know a person could make their own, if they were willing to love that hard." He stopped for a moment, wanting to say more. "The people who gather for Sunday night dinner around your table are the best example of family to me. Not one single person shares ancestry, or DNA, or skin tone, or surnames but look what they do share. It's powerful. You taught me to open my eyes and search. I'm the blind man who can now see."

KATHERINE

I t was a Monday. William thought he'd arrive just a few minutes early, eager to share the news. He'd barely slept in anticipation of telling Katherine. He called to give her a heads up that he had something special to tell her, but there was no answer.

It wasn't until he stepped out of his car that he was immediately overcome with a sense of dread and felt gooseflesh spread over his body. The newspaper still sat on the sidewalk, bundled with a rubber band, untouched. Katherine had not yet come outside.

He rattled the doorknob and began frantically combing through his keys, yelling her name as he unlocked the door, fighting a growing panic.

He raced to the kitchen, praying he would find her sitting there with a cup of something. He then ran to the bedroom, already prepared to knock down the door if he had to. But he didn't.

She was still lying in bed, her eyes closed, her head centered on the pillow as if someone had placed her there, her arms outstretched on each side in perfect symmetry. When he saw the look of complete serenity on her face he knew. Katherine was no longer with them. He was convinced she was reaching up to someone or something when she took her final breath. When he touched her face with the back of his hand, she was cold. Gone. And he wept.

His first phone call was to Father Drew, who agreed to break the news to Sam and bring him to the house so he could see for himself. His next call was to the sheriff's office, and he requested that he be put directly through to Sheriff Washington. There were many others to contact, but he just didn't have the strength. He would wait for his reinforcements to arrive.

He sat on her bedside, took her cold hand in his, and he thanked her for loving him and teaching him how to live a worthy life. He thanked her for other things too. Countless things. And he was grateful to be the one who found her.

Just as he saw Father Drew's car speeding down the winding drive he told her the news he had intended to share with her when he first arrived. "I finally got the nerve to ask. Annabelle is going to be my bride."

And then he opened the door so that Drew and Sam could join him in his grief.

READING OF THE WILL

N one of them had any idea how their lives would be connected by the reading of the will. Having been summoned by her attorney, the retired Honorable Judge Thomas Warren, they gathered to hear what Katherine had bequeathed to each of them.

Each one straightened a bit as the judge entered the room, carrying a calendar atop a cumbersome stack of files. He paused in front of each of them, regarding them directly before extending a warm, strong handshake. He knew. He knew the depth of their pain and sorrow. He feared his own grief from losing her would reside permanently in a portion of his heart, but today he would fulfill one of the most important tasks of her life, and he was damn proud to be her messenger.

Arranging the folders at the end of the long table, he gave a nod of dismissal to the two young clerks. One exited through the north door and closed it securely while the other exited through the south door, leaving it slightly ajar. Not wide enough for one to enter or exit, but plenty wide enough for someone to sit clandestinely in the adjacent room and absorb all the words soon to be spoken.

"Within minutes, your lives are going to change, and I want us all to remember this time, this place, this collective group." Holding the calendar in midair for all to see, he used a felt tip pen to draw a thick red circle around the date, making sure they understood the enormity of the moment.

"Katherine very recently received word from her cardiologist that her heart was failing. He suggested she get her affairs in order which prompted the two of us to spend considerable time together the last few months. It may ease your grief to know that she hoped to go peacefully in her sleep, and as you well know, that's exactly what happened. And if that was what she wanted, isn't that what we would have wished for her?"

The gathered faces nodded. They wanted what she wanted. Nothing less, nothing more.

"There are two churches in town that have listed Katherine on their membership rolls since she was just a young girl. Both of those, Bethel A.M.E. and St. Thomas Episcopal, are now recipients of the largest donations either of these two churches have ever received. This was what she and Murphy planned all along, no matter who went first.

As for these letters, Katherine specifically requested that you read them aloud, one by one. What you're going to find is each of these four letters is the sum part of a whole." And although it was something they already knew, he reminded them as he distributed the envelopes, "Katherine loved you very much, no doubt. She kept each of you in her heart as if you were her own."

Holding their envelopes gave each a sense that she was with them still. One raised the envelope to his nose to see if it smelled of her; one held it cockeyed to the light to see if she could decipher the contents; one held it in his lap and traced her handwriting with his finger; and one clutched it to his heart and closed his eyes.

Never taking his eyes off the assembled, he magnified his voice and dropped a bombshell, "And if all goes as planned, we'll be joined by one other."

He then took a long sip of his iced tea and said, "We now know the full story of Katherine's life, and as we proceed we will begin to learn how her gifts will become a part of you. I have been instructed to read Sam's letter aloud after he opens it, so I think it's time for us to begin." Realizing he might be rushing the man, which Katherine would have adamantly opposed, he corrected himself and said, "That is," nodding sincerely as he continued, "whenever *you're* ready, Sam."

And it was then that Sam clumsily and wordlessly ripped open his sealed envelope and handed it over to be read aloud.

From the desk of
Katherine McGregor

My Dearest Sam,

I want to thank you for being such a good friend to me. You always took better care of me than I did myself and because of that I always felt very safe and very loved. You were the first to call to give me a weather alert if we were under a storm watch, you always insisted on carrying my packages or stacks of library books, you always made sure I wasn't too warm or too cold, and you were always willing to share anything you had with me, except the front seat, of course.

They say if you want to really know the goodness of a person you should see what they do when they think no one is looking. You certainly proved your goodness to our town, and you made Kingston proud. As the Citizen of the Year, you have a Medal of Honor to prove it.

I would like to leave you something so that you may continue taking care of those around you. There is a small storefront downtown right next door to our police department. The Kingston Police Department Bicycle Maintenance Department is looking for someone who could be his own boss and work to make sure the bicycles are always in good working order. If you are interested, your job would be to air the tires, grease the gears, tighten the handlebars, adjust the seats, and anything else you feel is important. You would be doing for the policemen's bicycles all the things you know so well about maintaining your own bicycle. As your mother always taught you, take good care of your things.

By doing so, you would be providing a valuable service to our policemen. They all think as highly of you as I do. It brought me great pride to watch you develop friendships with so many of Kingston's police officers. They admire you for your loyalty. You would wear a badge as an honorary policeman, made especially for you to honor your service and good deeds.

William will be in charge of ordering all your tools, equipment and furniture. He will check on you each week to make sure you have everything you need and will deliver your paycheck. You will be your own boss. No one will work with you. I think you would prefer it that way. I hope you will take care of the police department's bicycles the same wonderful way you took care of me.

I don't want you to feel alone now that I'm gone. William will be with you as he has been the past few years. You can depend on him, just as he can depend on you.

I received many gifts in my life and I had many friends, but I never had a finer gift than the gift of friendship you gave me.

All my love,
Katherine

From the desk of
Katherine McGregor

My Dearest William,

Of all the people gathered around this table, I have known you the shortest amount of time. If I could change that, I would have met you when you were nine so you could have grown up on our land, under a canopy of trees.

Instead, you were thirty-eight when your feet touched this land for the first time. You were instantly drawn to the trees standing so tall, watching over you as you explored and discovered and grew and began to take root. I loved knowing how much you enjoyed your solitary walks in our woods. I always felt my Murphy was somehow there with you, guiding you as you discovered the beauty of life, helping you shed the armor that protected your heart. You wore that armor for most of your life, and I had the honor of watching it slowly disintegrate.

You told me once it was our Sunday night dinners that helped you realize what family really meant. You discovered it had nothing really to do with DNA or surnames. It all had to do with loving those around you.

I want you to look at those gathered around you now—the people in this world I love the very most. You are sitting at the table for a reason.

Your mother's heart would be filled to the brim if she had known you as a man. Mine was full enough for both of us. I've never known a finer man than you.

I want to charge you with some things to guide you in the days ahead:

Go forth and love.
Love everything you do.

Love the opportunities God puts before you.
Love the days ahead and leave the past behind.
Love the woman God intends for you to marry. Go ahead and ask her.
Find more Royce Thessings in this world and soften their final days with love.
You have discovered your purpose in life. Continue to act on it.

Families often inherit things from their ancestors. It's a remarkable feeling to own something that belonged to someone before you. I want you to know that feeling.

The north quadrant is the oldest piece of McGregor land. It was first owned by Donovan Colin McGregor, my Murphy's great, great, great, great, great, great grandfather. He began acquiring it in 1740. I have no doubt, every McGregor who lived on it or owned it would agree you are worthy of it. It is yours now. You may keep it and live on it. You may decide to sell it. If you do, Thomas has a list of interested buyers. Listen to your heart. You will know what to do.

Always remember this . . . you came into my life as the driver who delivered ten large crates of carved figures. The rest of it is a love story only God could have authored. And I was the lucky one.

I love you as if you were my own,
Katherine

From the desk of
Katherine McGregor

Dear Hollis,

Murphy and I watched you find life again, among the trees. The land taught you how to cultivate and regenerate because it knew you needed to be reminded. It is no surprise that you now own the west quadrant of the McGregor empire. When I first presented the idea to you a few years ago, you were humbled. That's exactly how Murphy and I felt when you decided to take the job and work on our land. We knew good things were in store for all of us.

My gift for you, dearest Hollis, is freedom. Freedom to do whatever you please. And I hope it will involve the talent you have deep within you. Bring those sketch books to life. Stop taking care of the land, and let it take care of you. Walk your acreage and select the perfect tree and give life to one of your sketches. Get lost in it. Mull it over and let the artistic energy within you spring forth.

Listen to the crunch of leaves underfoot, the Coopers hawks swooping past, the rush of the stream after a melted snow, the messages whispered in the trees as the wind blows through them. And then listen again. The land will tell you what to do.

I have one request, an endeavor you will be able to do well, no doubt. I ask that you find a way to record the stories of all the McGregors who lived here before us. You and I both know the tales by heart. I always wished Murphy and Savannah had penned them, but they did not. If you get some sort of a writer's block, spend the night under the stars. The McGregors will whisper their stories to you as you sleep. Begin with the wild Irish tales of Donovan McGregor and detail them all, ending with the greatest McGregor, our Murphy. They deserve to be remembered by those who come after us.

Freedom, Hollis, is a remarkable thing. Men fight wars for it. You fought a war and came out on the other side a strong, remarkably talented man. Freedom has arrived. Ring the bells and go forth, proclaiming your life exactly as you want to live it, surrounded by trees to protect you and all those you love.

With all my heart,
Katherine

From the desk of
Katherine McGregor

My Dearest Savannah,

What a treasure you have been to us. I remember laying eyes on you for the first time. It's funny how our hearts have a way of allowing us to remember so vividly those joys in life which take our breath away. From the time you stepped foot on our land, the trees were greener, and the air was fresher. Murphy and I bathed in your love like birds in a fountain.

We were not surprised when you became a journalist. It was within you all along, as if you were born to be one. Did you know I saved every note, letter and email you ever sent us? You will find them in my things, tied up neatly in several stacks with blue ribbons. Save them. They are treasures to be passed from generation to generation.

Even as a very young girl, the mystery of my father's disappearance seemed to haunt you, making you determined to be the one to unravel the mystery. I can still hear your young voice saying, "I'm going to find out what happened to him and give it to you as a gift, from me to you."

I had to wait a very long time to finally learn the truth about my father's death. As she was leaving this life, Lily Mae told me she wished she had spoken the truth years earlier because the secret of it had eaten at her every day since the day she met me. That was a very long time. Did she think I wouldn't be able to forgive her for not telling me years ago? If that was the reason, she didn't understand the depth of my love for her.

Was she afraid I'd turn away from her and somehow shift the blame of a terrible event to her? How could I have done that? She was only the messenger. My father's death had nothing to do with her, but she allowed that worry to fester, not realizing there wasn't a thing in this world she could have told me that would have lessened my love for her. Forgiving someone is part of loving someone.

My last gift for you, my Savannah, is liberation. You have a secret you've held tight within you for many years now. It must have taken great strength all these years to keep it buried so deep within you. The kind of strength that comes when you love someone fiercely with all your being. I know your secret and now is the time to release it. Set it free, my dear sweet girl, so you can begin to live your life again, the way God intended.

I recently spent some time doing my own research. With William and Annabelle's guidance, I discovered why you broke away and fled to the other side of the world. As hard as it is for you to read these next words aloud, I ask that you do not put this letter aside, because my gift, my very last gift to you, is in the revealing.

I now know that through your research you made the painful discovery that your mother's accident was not due to an icy bridge and that it was not a single car accident. You learned that your mother's alcohol level was over the legal limit. Your father kept the details from you because of his fierce love, not just for you, but also for your mother. We sometimes protect those we love the most from ugly truths we fear will destroy them.

Try to imagine that kind of love. It can't be difficult for you because you have that same kind of love within you. You discovered a secret so ugly that you thought it would ruin a love that was gentle and healthy and whole. But that kind of love cannot be destroyed. You just weren't brave enough to test it.

There was no icy bridge the night your mother died but there was a second car—details you found reading the files at *The Boston Globe*. I can only imagine how your journalist's mind raced as you read the name of the driver of the second car, Margo Adkisson, and you began putting the pieces together. You discovered that Margo Adkisson was three hundred miles from home when the accident occurred. And when you saw that she was from Camden you knew you had to learn more about her. And then the journalist in you searched the microfilm for anything else you could find, and her obituary confirmed what you desperately feared. She died nine days after the accident. It listed the names of the children who survived her. She had kept her maiden name when she married, just as your mother did. You knew then you and Clark had lost your mothers in the same accident. And the fact that he did not know tore your heart in two.

I can only imagine how your world trembled at that moment. You thought Clark could never love the daughter of the woman who stole his mother. You thought he would see you as an extension of the ugliness. You thought he would never forgive you.

Lily Mae once told you something so powerful you wrote it in your journal and said you would remember it forever. You wrote, "We aren't responsible for the sins of others, only our own."

My gift to you is sitting in the adjacent room, and I hope it is a gift you are willing to accept. Clark has never stopped loving you. He now knows all that you know, and it will be your decision to take the next step.

You can either stand up right now, walk out the door and return to South Africa with the knowledge that your secret is no longer buried, or you can stand up, walk into the adjacent room and allow the man who has loved you all these years to hold you once again.

The secret to life is love and forgiveness. It's as simple as that. Forgive your mother's mistake, and stop owning it.

Love the man who married your mother, and love the man who has waited all these years to marry you.

This I know—love and forgive, forgive and love.

What do you know?

All my love,
Katherine

Postlude

Five years later

Wanda Sullivan-Langston no longer remembers the pain she inflicted on others. She has advanced dementia and lives in Shady Valley Assisted Living. Following her example, her children are bitter and corrosive and feel no guilt that they have abandoned her. There will be no one to mourn her when her days have ended.

Sam wears his badge and sits beside Santa every year in the Kingston Christmas parade as the Kingston Police Department Bicycle Mechanic. The town has never forgotten his loyalty.

William and Annabelle's summer camp for foster children will open this summer. It was and always will be sustained from the thinning and harvesting of a small area of beechwood trees on the north quadrant. The camp is called "Hallowed Ground." William sometimes hears Murphy's voice and sees Katherine's face as the sun is breaking through the trees during his early morning walks.

The forest on the south quadrant of Beechwood forms a canopy to shield and nurture the curiosity of Katherine Margo Abigail Courtway where she lives with her parents, Savannah and Clark. *"Living Among the Trees, a Chronicle of the Ancestral Stories of the McGregor Clan"* by Savannah Courtway and Hollis Walker has just been published. It's predicted to be a non-fiction bestseller before the year's end.

Hollis owns the west quadrant. He sometimes hears those who came before him whisper through the trees. He pauses and takes it all in, cherishing his freedom. His sketchbooks are brimming, and his works of art are in demand from galleries around the country.

After seven generations of McGregors, the National Forestry Commission finally owns the east quadrant.

ABOUT THE AUTHOR

Pattie Howse-Duncan lives in Arkansas with her husband. She spends her time enjoying family, creating, entertaining, reading and traveling. This is her first novel. She can be reached via Facebook.

Made in the USA
Coppell, TX
27 January 2020